The It Girl

The double doors flew open and a group of people entered the lobby. I spotted a young girl in the middle of the group. She was wearing a baseball cap, large sunglasses with black-and-white-striped frames, and an oversized red-and-black-checkered jacket that looked like it was stolen off the back of a six-foot-eight-inch lumberjack.

I had to look closely. Was that? No way! It couldn't be. But it was! It was *her*! Sabrina Snow! The girl of the moment! The actress every boy in my school had a crush on. And she was standing right in front of me!

I had studied countless pictures of her in magazines strutting around in Michael Stars tank tops with her red-haired cockapoo puppy. And of course, I had examined the infamous picture of her flicking off the camera while dancing in a sequin-studded bikini at the after-party for the Rock the House Awards, New York City's notorious party where every top rock star and movie icon gathered to honor the year's best accomplishments in cinema and rock and roll.

I stood up from the couch and wanted to run over and introduce myself, but then I stopped. I needed to make the right first impression.

OTHER SPEAK BOOKS

Girl of the Moment

LIZABETH ZINDEL

speak

An Imprint of Penguin Group (USA) Inc.

For Mom and Dad

SPEAK
Published by the Penguin Group
Penguin Group (USA) Inc., 345 Hudson Street, New York, New York 10014, U.S.A.
Penguin Group (Canada), 90 Eglinton Avenue East, Suite 700, Toronto, Ontario, Canada M4P 2Y3
(a division of Pearson Penguin Canada Inc.)
Penguin Books Ltd, 80 Strand, London WC2R 0RL, England
Penguin Ireland, 25 St Stephen's Green, Dublin 2, Ireland (a division of Penguin Books Ltd)
Penguin Group (Australia), 250 Camberwell Road, Camberwell, Victoria 3124, Australia
(a division of Pearson Australia Group Pty Ltd)
Penguin Books India Pvt Ltd, 11 Community Centre, Panchsheel Park, New Delhi - 110 017, India
Penguin Group (NZ), 67 Apollo Drive, Rosedale, North Shore 0632, New Zealand
(a division of Pearson New Zealand Ltd)
Penguin Books (South Africa) (Pty) Ltd, 24 Sturdee Avenue, Rosebank, Johannesburg 2196, South Africa

Registered Offices: Penguin Books Ltd, 80 Strand, London WC2R 0RL, England

First published in the United States of America by Viking,
a member of Penguin Group (USA) Inc., 2007
Published by Speak, an imprint of Penguin Group (USA) Inc., 2008

1 3 5 7 9 10 8 6 4 2

Copyright © Lizabeth Zindel, 2007

THE LIBRARY OF CONGRESS HAS CATALOGED THE VIKING EDITION AS FOLLOWS:
Zindel, Lizabeth
Girl of the moment / by Lizabeth Zindel—1st ed.
p. cm.
Summary: Fifteen-year-old Lily has a lot to learn when she spends the summer working
as the intern of a spoiled and powerful Hollywood starlet.
ISBN-13: 978-0-670-06210-2 (hardcover)
[1. Internship programs—Fiction. 2. Actors and actresses—Fiction.
3. Interpersonal relations—Fiction. 4. Conduct of life—Fiction. 5. New York (N.Y.)—Fiction.]
I. Title. PZ7.Z646Gi 2007 [Fic]—dc22 2006011465

Speak ISBN 978-0-14-241104-9
Printed in the United States of America

Prologue

THIS BOOK IS MY confession of the summer I chose to break all the rules and go after my dreams. Even when it led me inside the backstabbing world of teenage celebrity. I may get in trouble for everything I'm about to tell you, but I can't keep it a secret any longer. If I mysteriously disappear off the face of the earth, please send the cops first to _____ _____ 's* loft (she just bought one in the Meatpacking District). And if she's innocent, track down her hairy manager named Bert.

I've never told anyone this before. You are one of the first people to read these words.

It's amazing how two months can change your life forever.

★ I am only sixteen years old and I do not want to go to jail—today, or ever. Therefore, because I signed a confidentiality agreement, I had to change the name of the actual starlet I worked for, or else I could be slapped with a huge lawsuit for exposing the truth about what really happened. Henceforth, I shall call her Sabrina Snow.

IT WAS THE SUMMER after eleventh grade, and for the first time I was staying behind in New York City while my best friend, Evie, ran off to soccer camp without me. We had gone to Ace Soccer Academy together for the last three summers. It was held on a college campus in Hartford, Connecticut. As soon as Evie and I arrived at the dorms, we would always: 1. Lie out by the waterfront and get our legs tan ASAP so we didn't look like albinos in our Puma shorts; 2. Chow down on grilled-cheese sandwiches from the cafeteria because the cook, Old Man Randy, made the yummiest ones ever; and 3. Strategize how to sneak out of our dorms to party late-night with the cute boys on Bryant Hill, including adorable Maximilian.

Max's features weren't quintessentially good looking or perfect, but there was something extremely attractive about him. Like the way his black hair fell along the sides of his face, or the way he stomped around campus after he changed out of his goalie uniform into beat-up jeans, steel-toe shoes, and a worn-in T-shirt with holes. His dad was a respected architect, and I remember how, once in a while, I would see Max sketching building designs of his own.

Max had admitted to me on the final day of soccer camp

last year that he had a crush on me. I was sitting next to him on the steps outside the Butterfield Dorm, hoping that he would finally turn to me and we would have our first kiss before he went home to Scarsdale, a forty-minute train ride outside the city.

"Tell me something you've never told anyone before," I said. We were in the middle of playing a game of Truth.

He thought for a moment and then said, "I can't sleep at night unless my hands are covered under pillows or below the blanket. I'm a freak about my hands because I'm a goalie. I never want them exposed or vulnerable. Last year at school, I was terrified in wood-shop class. I made my mom write a letter saying I wasn't allowed to operate the band saw."

"You're crazy," I said, laughing, but I understood how he felt. I could imagine how devastating it would be if his hands got cut in a freak accident and he couldn't play goalie anymore.

"What can I say? I cherish my mitts," he said, smiling. "Now you go. Tell me something crazy that no one else knows."

I wanted to blurt out how much I adored him. That I dreamed of walking with him through a soccer field at sunset and making out with him in between the goalposts.

I had almost got up the guts to tell Max how I felt when I spotted my parents' car heading through the campus gates.

"Oh, no," I said.

"You better answer quick," Max said.

I looked over at my parents' Explorer driving around the welcome circle. Then I looked at Max's brown eyes. "Sometimes when I brush my teeth, I leave big globs of toothpaste stuck to the bottom of the sink and it looks really nasty."

"Cop-out! Everyone does that! I'll let you off the hook this once," he laughed. Then my favorite part happened. He leaned into me. I felt his warm breath on my earlobe. "You know, for the longest time, I've had this *thing* for you. Let's pick up right here next summer."

And Gloryhallemama! Next summer was finally here!

The only problem was that I wasn't going back to Ace Soccer Academy. I had pined over Max all year long. I jumped up and down on my bed while blasting Love Lines at Nine on the radio and sketched a picture of what I thought Max would look like naked and carried it around in my favorite purse. I even wrote poems dedicated to him.

> *I hope you're not intimidated by my sixteen-year-old sass,*
> *'Cause I love you! Max, you're my poetic badass!*
> *I want to give you sweet kisses all day long,*
> *Until the sound of our lips becomes the drumbeat to a song.*

★ ★ ★

Still, after all this rhyming and pining for Max, we wouldn't be together this summer. You see, after my parents and I met with my school's college counselor, I was advised that it was best to spend my last summer of high school doing a serious internship. An internship would look great to college-admissions committees and give me the edge I needed to get into my dream school, Brown University (the alma mater of my mom and her dad, Grandpa Fred, who recently passed away).

Grandpa Fred always wanted me to go to Brown. He came over from Poland when he was five years old. His parents didn't have much money, but he worked his butt off so he could get into a great college. He was the first one in his family to attend university and saw the opportunity as a turning point in his existence. My mom followed in his footsteps and went to Brown, as well, and now it was my turn to continue the family legacy. It was the least I could do to make my ancestry proud. Especially now that Grandpa Fred was no longer with us.

After making tons of phone calls, I scored an internship at New York's Museum of Modern Art helping a woman who was in charge of coordinating an exhibit showcasing hundreds of sculptures celebrating the four seasons. My summer seemed locked and loaded. Until I got the dreaded phone call.

It was the day before the last day of school. Marilyn McFoster, the woman who hired me at the Museum of Modern Art, placed a call to my cell.

"Bad news. We can't offer you an internship anymore. The museum lost the funding it needed for the exhibit. Try back next year," Marilyn said.

"Isn't there another department that you can fit me into?" I pleaded.

"All the other departments have more interns than we know what to do with. There is no room for an extra one. Sorry."

It didn't matter how hard I begged, Marilyn McFoster was inflexible. It was easy for her to say there was no longer an opening for me.

You can imagine how crushed I was during Arch Day, the last day of school when all the high-school kids gathered in the auditorium and walked, one at a time, through a white archway set up on the stage. Passing through the arch symbolized graduating on to the next grade and, more immediately, the beginning of summer. But now that I had been ditched by the MoMA, I wasn't sure what I had to celebrate.

I sat in the auditorium next to Evie. We watched as the sophomore class walked through the archway.

"Don't worry, Lily. Everything will be all right," Evie said. "I told my mom that you lost your internship. She said you could come work for her at the salon. She always needs a helping hand."

"Thanks." I forced a smile. It was sweet of her to offer. But working for Evie's mom at Diva Hair Salon didn't seem like the perfect fit. Although I loved getting my hair done, learning about how to cut and color wasn't something I was remotely interested in. Besides, I imagined it wouldn't have the same ring on my college résumé as working for a prestigious museum in Manhattan.

"I wish I could climb into your duffel bag and run away with you to soccer camp," I said.

"Tell me about it," Evie said. "You're my partner in crime. It's gonna be tough being there without you this summer."

"Maybe I made a bad decision," I said.

"You're under tons of pressure," Evie said. "Most of the kids in our grade's parents can buy their way into the Ivy Leagues. I mean, we actually have to worry about our transcripts. I'm psyched I have my scholarship, but it's hard being around so many ultra-rich kids, you know?"

"Tell me about it," I said. "I wouldn't be here if my grandpa hadn't offered to pay my way through high school."

The principal walked to the center of the stage and clasped her hands. "I would now like to invite the junior class to come up on the stage and walk through the arch. Today, you officially become seniors."

My class burst into cheers. "Woooo-hooooo!"

"Man, I can't believe this day has come," Evie said.

"Me neither. One more year and we're off to college."

"We have to cherish every moment, promise?"

"Swear," I said.

Evie and I walked down the aisle to the stage with the rest of our classmates. The kids and teachers applauded as my grade symbolically graduated on to senior year. As I walked through the arch, I looked at the kids from my school, laughing and hollering with excitement. The summer was finally here. But tomorrow I would have to start searching for an internship all over again. And most probably, everything good was taken.

The week after school let out was very hard for me. I stopped by the high-school administration office before they closed for the summer. They gave me a list of internship possibilities and I went down the list calling all of them—the Lincoln Center Library, Brooklyn Botanical Gardens, Bronx Zoo, Mahoney's Real Estate Firm, and the Hudson Hotel. I also called a few architecture firms and marketing companies. No one was interested or offered me a position.

Then on June 25, Evie left for soccer camp. A chartered bus was scheduled to pick up the Manhattan campers attending Ace Soccer Academy on the corner of 87th Street and Lexington Avenue. I promised her I would see her off at the bus stop.

I found Evie standing by her suitcase with her overstuffed cheetah-print purse thrown over one shoulder. "What am I going to do without my BFF?" Evie said when she saw me.

"You won't be alone," I said. "Liv and Sally will be there."

"But you're my best friend in the entire world."

"Max will be there, too—"

"You have dibs on Max. You were supposed to make out with him on Bryant Hill, remember?"

"Trust me. I remember. I'm going to be so horny this summer."

"You did not just say that!"

"I did," I said.

"That is so disgusting!" Evie screamed.

"But it made you smile." I looked down the street. A bunch more kids were standing at the pickup stop now.

Evie looked down. A sad look glazed over her eyes. "Don't you realize this is the last summer before we graduate, man? It's like that song—'These are the times to remember . . .'"

"'Because they will not last forever.' I know! I know!" I couldn't believe I wasn't going with her. I had already dreamed up so many unforgettable adventures.

The chartered bus pulled up to the stop and we both turned our heads.

"I gotta go," Evie said.

I pulled a piece of paper out of my pocket. "Here," I said. "I made you a bus note."

"Cool beans! Slip it in my bag," she said.

I unzipped her cheetah-print bag and stuck the note carefully inside. "Fifty questions," I bragged.

"Wow, impressive." Last year, Evie and I had started making quizzes in history class. They consisted of multiple-choice questions, illustrations, and Truth questions.

"All right. This is good-bye," Evie said. "Have a good summer. Call me if you need anything."

"You, too," I said. "Keep me posted me on all the dirt."

"I promise." Evie gave me a hug. "Thanks for the quiz, man." Then she ran onto the bus, disappearing behind the tinted windows.

As I walked away, I started to wonder how I was going to survive. All my friends from school were leaving. Molly was heading to Florence, Italy, for an art program. Wendy was going to ballet camp. Bridgette was off volunteering teaching English at a school in Guatemala. I would be friendless in the city. It was truly terrifying.

Maybe Evie was right—this *was* the time to remember. For my last summer before graduating high school, I should be living it up, having as much fun as possible with my friends. What was my problem? Maybe I made a terrible mistake worrying so much about my college applications. Now I had messed up my entire summer. I had turned my summer on its ass.

I SPENT THE NEXT few days faxing my résumé to different companies, the Italian Consulate, the New York Philharmonic, and the Public Theatre, but still there were no bites. All the internship positions were already filled up.

I looked at the internship-completion form hanging above my desk. The college advisor at my school had given it to me. I was told to get this form signed as soon as I finished my internship because it would serve as an official document that I could submit to colleges.

INTERNSHIP COMPLETION FORM

This form is to be filled out by the Internship Advisor.

  This letter certifies that <u>Lily Miles</u> completed her internship working for _____ on the following dates: _____. Please write a brief evaluation on the page below.

I shivered looking at all the blank space. Mr. Gregor, my art teacher in tenth grade, taught the class that your life is like a canvas, and when you die, you have to sign the bottom corner. "Will you be happy with what the painting looks like?" Mr. Gregor asked us. Today, I feared my canvas would be an image of nothingness.

My favorite doorman, Damien, even started to worry about me. He called at me from behind his desk.

"Lily, aren't you leaving the city soon?"

"Not this year," I said, looking down at my platform flip-flops.

"I thought you were going back to soccer camp. You told me it's your—"

"Favorite place in the whole friggin' wide world. . . . I know."

"Well, my son, Junior, will be in town. Maybe you guys can hang out."

I tried my best to force a smile. Damien was always trying to get me to hang out with Junior. And I constantly had to come up with some fancy excuse. Junior was nice enough, but he had bad breath. I felt bad saying things like that, but it was true. He ate a lot of sour-cream-and-onion potato chips and then never brushed his teeth.

"Yeah, that sounds great! I'd love to hang out with Junior, but . . ."

But there was no but! I had no excuse! I had no plans! My summer was suddenly an open slate of availability. Do you want to hang out tomorrow? I'm free! How about next Wednesday? Oh, guess what? I'm free! Or how about some-time in mid-July? Let me think. . . . Uh, yeah, I'm FREE! FREE! FREE! Not one exciting plan.

"For sure! Absolutely! I'll give him a call next week. We'll catch a movie!" Damien slapped me a high five. "Great, I'll tell him you're around."

As I walked to the elevator, the cute guy from the seventh floor walked past me with his dad and a huge duffel bag. *An-*

other lucky teenage Homo sapien off on an adventure, I thought.

Suddenly I felt my phone vibrating in my back pocket. I looked at the caller ID. It was Evie. She had been gone for two long days now and I was dying to hear the first bit of soccer-camp gossip.

"Hello?" I said, answering it.

"L-Mama!"

"E-Girl!" I screamed into the phone.

"I promised I'd call. Remember I'm not allowed to take my cell outside of the dorm room. So I can only call you in between activities."

"The counselors are so strict about that. It's ridiculous. Don't they know the phone is our lifeline?"

"Tell me about it," Evie said.

"So are you having fun? Tell me everything."

"I'm on the same hall as Liv and Sally. Just like last year. We went swimming at the waterfront this afternoon and I already ate three grilled-cheese sandwiches from the cafeteria."

My heart sunk into my stomach. "That is the coolest," I said.

"Oh, and guess who I just saw? Max! He looks adorable. He has the cutest skater haircut."

"He must look soooo yummy," I said.

"And guess what?" Evie squealed. "He asked me about you. And when I told you you weren't coming, I swear I saw the disappointment in his eyes."

"Yeah, right," I said. It sounded too good to be true.

"Cross my heart. Oh, can you hear that?"

I heard the muffled sound of a gong ringing. "Is that the chime?"

"Yeah, remember Mr. Pit Stains, the counselor with the sweat rings? He's banging the chime! Gotta run to practice. I'll call you later. Give you updates."

"You better," I said.

I hung up the phone and went up to my room and shut the door. I felt awful. If I had gone back to soccer camp this summer, I bet Max and I would have fallen madly in love. My first real, true love affair. What I had admired so much about Max was that he was very popular, but he still liked to take walks by himself in the woods. He skateboarded and made the occasional tie-dye—he was this mixture of wonderful surprises. Boyish, with a mysterious, soulful side.

There were so many fabulous people at camp. If I was there right now, I know Evie and I would get all our friends to sneak out of the bunks tonight and we would all climb to the top of Bryant Hill and party together under the stars. Max's best friend, Luke, would snatch bags of doughnuts from the dining hall like he always did, and we would munch on them and play the game "I never . . ." and dance to Courtney's mini-stereo.

All this fun to be had, and here I was alone like an old maid. I would probably never have a real make-out session with a guy—not this summer! And maybe not in my entire life!

A real make-out session means Frenching a boy that I adore from the bottom of my heart. French-kissing a boy that I have a trivial crush on or am not deeply enamored of is not a real kiss. It is a play kiss. And just because you are probably wondering, I have had play kisses with five different boys up to this point in my life. Don't judge.

That night was terrible. I felt completely alone. My dad

was at his monthly poker game with his buddies from grad school, and my mom went out for Italian food with her best friend, Diane. My mom was obsessed with cuisine. Whenever we went out to dinner, she would take a bite of what she ordered, chew it slowly in her mouth, and try to guess all the ingredients inside the dish. Like right now she was probably sitting at the restaurant in front of a bowl of tortellini Alfredo and saying, "I taste mushrooms, heavy cream, pepper, Parmesan, and a hint of truffle oil." Then she would call the waiter over and make him confirm her predictions with the chef. That part would always embarrass me.

My mom never went to formal culinary school, but she learned to cook from her dad, who found that it was the one way he could relax from his job in accounting. She said many of her favorite childhood memories took place in the kitchen with him when they would close the door, not let anyone in, and cook and taste the food.

My mom even invented her own recipes, like the "Quiche of Four Cheeses," and my favorite dessert, the "What-the-Hell-Are-in-These-Bars?" in which she would take the batter for blondies and add every sweet morsel she could find in our kitchen cabinets. Often that would include coconut shavings, chocolate chips, butterscotch squares, and chunks of toffee.

I wished she were home right now cooking up one of her tasty little treats. Or my dad and I were watching a new release of an action movie. I lay in bed and looked up at the glow-in-the-dark stars on my ceiling. As I stared at the Big Dipper, I realized even though I was sixteen years old, I was home in bed at nine P.M. just like a senior citizen, while my parents were out in the world, living it up. It was like this summer, the 'rents had more of a life than I did.

*   *   *

The next morning, my dad called for a father/daughter conference to help me strategize how to find a new internship. He said he felt bad because he could tell I had been down in the dumps. My mom was still asleep in the other room. She didn't have a job right now. After graduating from Brown, she worked at an advertising agency for seven years until she gave it up to focus on being a mom and raising me.

My dad and I took our seats at the dining-room table.

"I did some research, Lily. Talked to a few people," he said. "And I am going to present you with three possibilities."

"Thanks, Pops," I said. But I knew it would be hard to top the coolness factor of working at the Museum of Modern Art.

"Option number one," my dad said. "I spoke to Uncle Ted. He could use some help Xeroxing at his life-insurance firm."

"Sounds breathlessly exciting," I said.

"Two," my dad continued, rolling over my attitude. "We could always use an extra intern in the philosophy department at Columbia. I'll be up there quite a bit teaching summer courses. You could work in my office and help with research in the library."

"But, Dad, working in your department all summer is not what I had in mind. Besides, it will look like total favoritism to college-admission boards."

"I was just giving you a nice offer," my dad said, giving me a disapproving look. "And your last option," he said. "I ran into my friend at the poker game last night. He's in from L.A.

for business. And he mentioned something about an internship working for one of his clients."

"What kind of client?" I asked.

"He works as a talent agent and this client is some actress type."

"Come again," I said. "What did you just say?"

"There's an internship available working for an actress. She's been in movies, but I've never heard of them," my dad said.

I froze. "Are you kidding? You're teasing me, right?"

"I'm completely and absolutely serious. Here," my dad said. He pulled a business card out of his pocket and gave it to me. The card read:

EDDIE FIELDS
WORLD TALENT AGENCY
5433 WILSHIRE BOULEVARD
BEVERLY HILLS, CA 90210

"Eddie Fields?" I asked. "Who is that?"

"My old buddy Eddie from grad school. I beat him in the poker game last night. And he agreed to call in a favor."

"Crazy Eddie? The wild Hollywood agent you've told me about?"

"Yes, the guy who went on from getting a doctorate in philosophy to representing celebrities. Anyway, he mentioned his client is your age. She's a young actress moving to New York from L.A. and she needs an intern. She already has a bunch of people working for her. But she wants someone her own age who she can relate to."

"How old is she?" I asked.

"Sixteen."

"Perfect," I said. "What's her name?"

"Oh, I forget. I'm so out of touch with who's famous now-adays. But he said she's a rising star. Been on the covers of those magazines you read," he said.

"*Vogue* and *Party Weekly*!" I clapped my hands with excitement. "Oh my God! Who could it be?"

"She's staying at the Mercer Hotel under a fake name. A pseudonym. I wrote it down on this Post-it."

I grabbed the paper from my dad. "Victoria Champagne! That's the best fake name ever! I'm dying to know who it is!"

"I'll call Eddie and get you an interview, but only on one condition. . . ."

"What?" I asked.

"Crazy Eddie is doing me a favor. And sometimes you don't follow through on things."

"That's not true. Like when?"

"Like the time I asked the Weinfelds for tickets to that concert at Madison Square Garden. You decided last minute to spend the weekend in Bridgehampton with Evie and her family."

"Oh, I forgot about that."

"And the time I convinced my editor friend at *The New Yorker* to personally read that short story you were writing—and never finished writing."

"I know. I'm sorry."

"You are getting older and you have to learn to follow through with your commitments."

"I will. I promise! This sounds like the chance of a life-time. I could never let it pass me by!"

"So it's a deal?"

"Deal!" I said, jumping in the air.

"If you let me down . . ." he said.

"I won't. I swear," I said. "You're the best dad in the universe."

My father grabbed the cordless phone. I sat there on the edge of my seat as he hit speakerphone and dialed Crazy Eddie's cell-phone number. The phone rang and rang. Then, suddenly, Eddie picked up.

"Talk to me," Eddie said.

"Eddie, it's Neil," my dad said.

"Neil! What's going on, bro?"

"I spoke to my daughter, Lily. She would love to inter-view. When works best for you guys?"

"How quickly can she get down to the Mercer Hotel?" Eddie asked.

I looked at my dad and flashed ten fingers in the air—two times.

"Twenty minutes," my dad said.

I nodded at him and started jumping up and down on the brown leather couch.

"Great. I'll call down to the Mercer and let them know she's coming," Eddie said, hanging up.

"Oh my God! What do I say? What do I wear? I have to wear black pants and one of those button-down shirts all those business types wear on the subway. And my lucky lip gloss. I have to act cool. Like I see famous people every day and she's just any other girl."

Just then my mom came into the living room dressed in her purple nightgown. "What's all the screaming about?" she asked.

"I've got an interview!" I told her. "With a famous actress!"

My mom raised her eyebrows at me. "Oh, my," she said. "Fantastic. That's great news, Lily. I knew something wonderful would come your way."

"Lily, you better get ready!" my dad said, suddenly moving into fast-forward mode. "You can't be late!" He turned to my mom. "I'll drive her down there and wait in the car," he said.

I gave my dad a kiss on the cheek. "Thank you! Thank you!" I said. "Maybe this summer will be amazing after all."

Chapter 3

MY DAD DROVE ME down to the Mercer Hotel in Soho. He pulled the Explorer over by a fire hydrant on Prince Street.

"Are you nervous?" my dad asked.

"Me? No, not all." I cracked a smile. "Are you kidding? I'm completely nervous."

"Just remember with interviews—drop a few compliments, don't fidget, and never apologize."

"Why shouldn't I apologize?" I asked.

"It makes you look weak," my dad said.

"I'll try and remember that," I said, opening the door and getting out of the car.

"Call me when you're done. I'm going to park and then browse used books at the Strand."

I slammed the door shut and turned around, bumping into a man selling knockoff designer handbags. "Oops, sorry," I said, straightening my button-down shirt and putting on some of my good-luck lip gloss that tasted like vanilla.

As I walked toward the hotel entrance, I took a deep breath. Then I opened the door and walked inside the lobby. Guests lounged on white and red couches under the light of enormous chandeliers. I walked past a row of dark wood bookcases and a table with the largest flower arrangement I had ever seen. It was overflowing with white lilies and bright pink roses that filled the lobby with their intoxicating scent.

I went over to the concierge. Two women in crisp black suits were working at the front desk, which was backed by a brick wall of hanging ivy. I walked up to one of the women. I noticed her name tag said ANGELICA.

"Hi. I'm here for Victoria Champagne," I said.

"Just a moment, miss." The lady nodded and picked up the phone. She dialed an extension, listened to it ring, then shook her head. "There's no answer."

"Oh. But I have a meeting. . . ." I said, double-checking the Post-it my dad had given me.

"No one's picking up. Why don't you have a seat over there and wait. I'll let you know if I get through."

"Thanks." I sat down on one of the white sofa chairs. I couldn't believe no one was answering the phone. Maybe this Victoria Champagne had forgotten all about me. Maybe this so-called Vicki hated New York and flew back to Los Angeles. Maybe she met some other girl on the sidewalk and hired her to be the intern instead.

There was a six-foot-tall woman next to me in brown thigh-high boots, flinging her platinum hair over one shoulder while laughing over martinis with an investment-banker type. She looked like a Swedish model. I was always envious of girls who were that tall. If I were six feet tall, I know I'd have a much easier time shopping for jeans.

"I love you, booba-boobie-head." She mumbled sweet nothings to him while playing with his tie.

"I love you, too, my sweet, luscious lambie-kins," he said, nibbling on her earlobe.

I wondered how much longer I would have to wait here and watch this public display of mushiness.

Suddenly a commotion erupted by the side entrance. The double doors flew open and a group of people entered the lobby. I spotted a young girl in the middle of the group. She was wearing a baseball cap, large sunglasses with black-and-white-striped frames, and an oversized red-and-black-checkered jacket that looked like it was stolen off the back of a six-foot-eight-inch lumberjack.

I had to look closely. Was that? No way! It couldn't be. But it was! It was *her*! Sabrina Snow! The girl of the moment! The actress every boy in my school had a crush on. And she was standing right in front of me!

It was strange that she was dressed in such a huge, unflattering coat, but then I remembered the article in *Party Weekly* magazine. It called this clothing style "schlumpy chic," and it was the latest trend among celebrities who didn't want to be recognized in public.

It didn't matter what Sabrina wore, though—I could see past her disguise. I had studied countless pictures of her in magazines strutting around in Michael Stars tank tops with her red-haired cockapoo puppy. And of course, I had examined the infamous picture of her flicking off the camera while dancing in a sequin-studded bikini at the after-party for the Rock the House Awards, New York City's notorious party where every top rock star and movie icon gathered to honor the year's best accomplishments in cinema and rock and roll.

It seemed to be the coolest and most exciting party that existed on the planet. And, of course, nearly impossible to get into.

Sabrina and her entourage hurried past the concierge desk over to the elevator bank. I waved to Angelica, the woman at the front desk, and got her attention. I pointed to Sabrina and mouthed, "Victoria Champagne, right?"

I stood up from the couch and wanted to run over and introduce myself, but then I stopped. I needed to make the right first impression. I realized it was probably best if I acted professional and waited for them to call down to the lobby for me.

A security guard let Sabrina and her crew into the elevator bank. I could hear Sabrina's voice now. She was talking to a short man with kinky black hair. I caught the words "Mini Cooper" and "chocolate-dipped strawberries." After seeing all her movies, Sabrina's voice sounded familiar, like a best friend's.

I watched as Sabrina and her entourage disappeared into an elevator, then I sat back down on the white leather couch and rubbed my palms together. The chance to assist Sabrina was the opportunity of a lifetime. It would blow the college-admissions committee at Brown out of the water.

As I sat there and waited, my knees started to wobble. I was scared that when I stood up, I would fall over and not be able to walk. I had to remind myself: *Do not say anything stupid. Talk in sentences that make sense. Be cool. Don't shake with nerves—it will only freak her out.*

"Are you Lily?" A voice pulled me from my inner pep talk.

I looked up. There was the short man I had seen walking

with Sabrina before. He ran his hand through his black, curly hair.

"Uh, yes, Lily is me," I said. *Sometimes I am so smooth. Yeah right.*

As he walked over to me, he pushed up the sleeves of his baby blue cashmere sweater. I was surprised to see a mess of black hair growing on his arms.

"I'm Bert Covitz," the short man said. "Sabrina's manager." He reached out his hand and firmly shook my sweaty palm. Then I saw him wipe his hand on his slacks.

"Thanks for coming by," he said. "There are a zillion things going on, but I want to find a summer intern for her pronto. We've been interviewing high-school kids all week and she hasn't liked anyone yet." Bert talked a mile a minute and with great authority like he had his finger on the Holy Grail.

"Thanks for meeting me. I am so thrilled to possibly work for Sabrina. I am a huge fan. She is such a versatile actress. The way she can play a superhero, a flamenco dancer, and a deaf girl all in one year." I was giving some great compliments here. I secretly patted myself on the back.

"She certainly is one of a kind," Bert agreed. "She's got the chops."

We stepped into the elevator. Bert pressed the button for the sixth floor. "Tonight's the New York premiere of Sabrina's new action movie, *Spinning the Wheel of Fire*. She's upstairs getting ready now. It's a bit chaotic, but we'll squeeze in a quick interview with you."

I couldn't help but stare at his thick eyebrows when he spoke. They looked like two bat wings hanging over his eyeballs.

The elevator beeped and the door opened on the sixth floor. I couldn't believe in just moments I would be meeting Sabrina. She would be looking at me, and from that moment on, she would know that I existed in this world.

We walked down the hallway, stopping outside suite #622. Bert slid his electric key card in the slot. My head started to spin. I wanted this internship more than anything. I had to get it. This was the chance of a lifetime. I could already see it printed on my résumé: *Lily Miles, Intern to Sabrina Snow*. I could even write my personal essay about how much I learned from her and call it "A Summer of Enlightenment."

The door swung open. Bert led me through the foyer of the suite and back into the living room. Sabrina sat on a stool in a red baby-doll dress with black knee-high stockings and gold shoes. Behind her was a floor-to-ceiling window overlooking an expansive view of the Manhattan skyline. Washington Square Park. Luxury skyscrapers. The Empire State Building. The view was like, *whoa*.

Sabrina took a sip from a porcelain teacup while two women fussed over her long brown hair. One wrapped her locks around a circular brush and another frantically dried it with a high-powered blow-dryer. Two other women gathered around her, one painting her fingernails and the other, her toenails. They focused while applying the red polish as if they were touching up an angel in a Renaissance fresco.

Everyone was in action. Another woman ran a steam machine over an emerald-green dress hanging from the door of a closet. A cater waiter lined up bottles of Evian on a snack table filled with fresh fruit, miniature sandwiches, and cheesecake. Bert grabbed a clump of green grapes from the snack table and headed over to Sabrina. I stood by the living room's entrance and watched.

"I have a few things to go over with you," Bert said, standing with his clipboard by Sabrina.

"Did you get the turquoise car I asked for?" Sabrina asked.

"Done. I also have the entire seventh row roped off for you and your invited guests. FYI, after the screening, there is a reception in the movie-theater lobby. They're bringing in ice sculptures, cherry blossoms, catered food, a dance floor—the whole shebang."

"Who's the DJ?" Sabrina asked.

"DJ Mad Shuffle."

Bert came over to the buffet and cut himself a sliver of cheesecake. As he shoved it into his mouth, I walked over to him.

"Is this a bad time?" I asked. "Maybe I should come back for the interview another day. She seems really busy."

"No, no!" he said, wiping the cheesecake off his lips. "It's gonna happen. Just hang out a sec—"

As soon as the stylist finished straightening Sabrina's long brown hair, Bert announced to the room, "Okay everyone! Let's take ten! Then we'll start the makeup." All the stylists listened to him and walked over to the snack bar to take a break.

Bert motioned me over to him and Sabrina.

"Sabrina, this is Lily Miles," he said.

"Hi," I said. "It's unb-b-b-believable to meet you." Apparently my nerves had given me a stutter. I had spoken smoothly for so many days of my life—why in this one important moment did I have to lose that ability?

"Likewise, I'm sure," she said skeptically. Sabrina eyed Bert and then turned back to me. "Let's go into my room so we can have some privacy."

I followed Sabrina as she opened the door to the bedroom. As soon as the door opened, there was a loud yelp, and Sabrina's red-haired cockapoo (a mix between a cocker spaniel and a poodle) greeted us, jumping up and licking Sabrina's ankles.

"Mercedes!" Sabrina said, sweeping the dog up in her arms. "Hey, baby!" She nuzzled her face into its red fur. "Lily, meet my puppy, Mercedes SL600. He doesn't like nail-polish fumes so I put him in here."

"SL600?" I asked.

"Like the car model. He is the cutest little puppy, except he pees when he's scared. Otherwise, he is perfect," she said, closing the door behind us.

Sabrina put the dog down in front of a tote bag filled with miniature clothing. "Now go pick out your outfit for tonight." She nudged the dog closer to the tote bag.

"Wow, look at all those fancy dog clothes," I said.

"No, no! I'm not one of those stereotypical girls that dress their dogs in fancy clothes. Only comfortable ones." Sabrina looked at me with a very serious look in her eyes. Then she became distracted by Mercedes pushing around a pair of overalls with his nose. "Ooooh, Mercie. You found your new OshKosh. See, overalls are comfy and practical."

"I used to have a pair of OshKosh," I said, starting to fidget, picking at the corner of the desk. "Except there was a Halloween pumpkin on the front pocket."

"And . . . ?" she said.

"That's it," I said.

"Oh, I thought you were going to tell me a story." Sabrina gave me a look. "Why don't you take a seat—you're making me nervous."

I sat down quickly in the desk chair and folded my hands in my lap. She sat on the edge of the bed, running her fingers through her long hair. It was the first time I had the chance to look closely at her. She had beautiful, porcelain skin and a presence that pulled you toward her. She watched me closely and I noticed that her eyes looked like holograms; each time she moved, they flickered and you saw new shades of blue and green. There was something timeless about her features. She could be in this century, two centuries in the past, or even a century in the future. She sat before me without any makeup on, and still, her face glowed and her lips appeared iridescent without lip gloss. As she turned in profile, I noticed her long swan neck. It was decorated with several strands of bright turquoise beads. I was so used to seeing her on a screen, it took my breath away to see her three-dimensional.

"I just love your hotel suite," I said. "It's so modern, and the linens on the bed look extra crisp. They must be a very high thread count."

"Whatever. I'm just living at the Mercer Hotel while I shop for a loft in the Meatpacking District. Once I find what I'm looking for, I'm out of here."

"You're going to buy your own apartment? That is so cool."

"I've been living with my whacked-out mom in Malibu. But now I want my own place in New York. I plan on doing some serious theater work this year. Unlike a lot of the other actresses my age, I actually invest all of my being into creating a role. I obsess over how the person would talk, move, wear their clothes, what music they would listen to. What they dream about at night. What scares the hell out of them. I live for stepping into a character's skin and breathing life into their words. It gives me an electric charge. So, what's your deal?" she said, switching gears. "Bert says you want to be my summer intern."

I had to say something brilliant. This was my chance to shine.

"I would *love* to be. I am a humongous fan of your work. I've seen all your movies. My favorite was *Too Cool for School*. I've watched it ten times. Everyone at my high school loves you, too. You were voted the most popular star in our yearbook."

"But I'm not a star," she corrected me. "Stars are twenty-one and over. I am only sixteen and therefore, I'm a star*let*."

"Oh, got it. Sorry," I said. Then I realized I just apologized. My dad told me I shouldn't apologize in interviews. "I mean I'm not sorry. I am sorry. Oh, skip it." What was I saying?

Sabrina gave me a weird look. Then she crossed her legs and loosened the buckle on one of her gold shoes. "So you're a huge fan of my movie *Too Cool for School*," she said. "What do I say in the last scene when I drive across the school campus in a Thunderbird?"

Umm . . . oh God. A pop quiz. I knew this. I knew this! This was so easy. My hand started to shake. I was so nervous to be put on the spot. I couldn't think. My mind shut down. I remembered the scene. She drives the Thunderbird into the front door of the school and screams—she screams—what does she scream? I couldn't remember for the life of me.

"I can't remember," I said.

"I thought you saw it ten times," Sabrina said.

"I did. I'm just really nervous," I said.

Sabrina sighed loudly. "Look, I'm not a human-resource chick so let's just cut to the chase. What's most important to me is I want someone I can trust. How do I know you aren't sent as a spy?" Sabrina crossed her arms in front of her chest, and the stack of gold bangle bracelets on her wrist went *clickety-click.*

"A spy? Who would I be spying for?" I asked.

"*The National Enquirer. Party Weekly.* My manager, Bert," Sabrina said. "The lady, Eleanor, my mom pays to check on me like a guardian."

"I am definitely not a spy."

"Okay. Then dump out your purse. I want to see if you have anything in there—like a tape recorder."

I looked at her for a moment. "Are you serious? You want me to dump out my entire purse?" I started to panic. I didn't have a tape recorder in there, but I had almost everything else. My purse was a huge mess. I carried everything inside of it and I hadn't cleaned it out in months. My friends always teased me that it was messier than my room.

"What's the problem? You have something to hide?" she said.

"No, not at all," I said. "I just wasn't expecting to have to dump it out."

"What's the big deal, then?" Sabrina said, grabbing my purse from me and dumping it over onto the bed. All of my things fell out. My wallet. My lucky vanilla lip gloss. Candy wrappers.

Loose change with gum stuck to it. Ticket stubs, receipts, pens, tissues. A rubber bouncing ball. My asthma inhaler. And then the worst of all—the embarrassing picture I had drawn of Max naked.

"Oh, no!" I said. I started to get upset. I couldn't help it. My bag was a pigsty, and now all of its contents were thrown across the bed. It was humiliating beyond belief. I was sure she would think I was crazy.

Sabrina's mouth dropped in shock when she saw the naked drawing of Max. She reached out to grab the napkin, but I snatched it back just in time.

"Did you draw that naked picture?" she asked. Her voice sounded accusatory.

Oh God, now I bet she would think I was a pervert or a nympho! I mean, how many girls keep naked doodles in their purses?

"Um, no way," I said, covering up. "My friend drew that."

Sabrina quickly changed her tone. "Wow, your friend is a fantastic artist," she said.

I was shocked. She actually liked it. "Yeah." I went along with it. "She's fantastic, and she's just starting out."

"The greatest painters of all time started out drawing nudes—Picasso, Renoir. . . . I love the way your friend just doodled some guy's naked bod on a napkin, too. It's such a statement. Sexy, yet casual . . . I want to buy it."

"What?" I asked, startled.

"As an investment. Who knows, your friend may blow up, and then I can say I bought this from her before she became big. See, I don't follow the trends. I create them. What's your friend's name?"

I had to come up with an answer quick. "Evie Nissen-blatt," I said, borrowing my best friend's name. *That's what close friends are for, right? To help you out in times of need.*

Sabrina jotted Evie's name down on a piece of hotel stationery. "And how much do you want for it?"

"For the napkin?" I asked.

"For the artwork," she said, correcting me. "Here, I'll offer fifty bucks. Okay?"

I stood there speechless.

She must have taken my silence as a "no" because she upped the offer to a hundred dollars.

"Sold!" I said.

Sabrina handed me the money and in return, I gave her the naked drawing of Max. "Just tell your friend," Sabrina said, "that the guy's schlong is completely out of proportion with his leg. And draw in some more pubes next time."

"Oh, right. Thank you very much," I said. "I'll let her know." Awkward.

Sabrina looked me up and down. "There's something I like about you. You're funny and you have guts," she said. "Why don't you come with me and my friends to my premiere tonight?"

"Premiere? Like a movie premiere?"

"Is there any other kind?" Sabrina laughed. "It will be a test. If you pass, you're in there like swimwear. And if you don't . . . get sauced, 'cause you lost."

"Where should I meet you?" I asked.

"Be back here at seven. Don't be late. When you're late, you embarrass your parents and your grandparents and your great-grandparents and every ancestor you've ever had."

"See you then," I said.

As I walked back through the living room of the suite, Bert ran over to me.

"How'd it go?" he asked, walking by my side.

"Good, I think. She asked me to come back for the premiere. "

"Positive sign," he said, giving me the double thumbs-up. "Meet us in front of the lobby tonight. Rock'n'roll, hoochie-coo," Bert said, turning around and getting right back to business.

As I let myself out of the suite, I overheard him instructing one of the stylists to sew up Sabrina's outfit for tonight. "Stitch the neckline so that the cleavage doesn't plunge down so low," he said.

I headed back down the hallway toward the elevators. I got into the elevator and pressed the lobby button. Although I was riding downward, I felt like I was climbing higher and higher.

Once I got outside, I called my dad on his cell. He picked me up on the corner of Broadway and Prince. As I got into the car, I couldn't contain my excitement.

"She wants me to come back for the opening of her movie tonight!" I yelled. "It's like an audition! If I do well, I get the gig!" Then I was so excited, I started singing the song that Evie and I like to sing whenever something especially good happens. *"Go me, go me. I rock! Get busy!"*

My dad smiled at me and gave me a high five. "Let's go grab some pizza and celebrate," he said.

Chapter

4

AFTER MY DAD AND I split a pepperoni, thin-crust pie at John's Pizza, we went back to the apartment. My mom had just come back with a load of groceries.

"I can see it on your face," my mom said. "You look happy."

"Guess who I met with? Sabrina Snow. The actress from *Too Cool for School*, remember? She invited me to her movie premiere tonight."

"Are you serious? Lily, how thrilling for you. Does this mean you got the position?"

"No, tonight's a test. I have to prove to her I can keep up with her wild and glamorous lifestyle. Which reminds me—I need a cool outfit desperately. Can I borrow something from your closet?"

"Come on in. Let's see what treasures we can dig up," my mom said, taking my hand and leading me to her closet packed with clothes. "You don't need a hanger for this closet. Everything is so jammed together, it stays up," my mom said, yanking out a dress.

"It's a little wrinkled," I told her.

"Don't worry," my mom said, throwing the dress on the bed and pressing it with her hand. "There," she said. "It looks great. I wore this with your dad in the Bahamas. You'll look absolutely beautiful in it."

"Thanks, but tonight I need to impress people who aren't wearing mom goggles."

"Ahh, too mature for you."

I spotted a more chic, silk, wine-colored dress. "How about that one?" I said.

"I wore that when I was in college," my mom said. "It hasn't held up too well."

We ripped apart her closet looking for the perfect pair of black heels she bought at the Shoe Inn in Easthampton. They were a little big because I am a 7½ and my mom is a 9. We didn't get discouraged, though. Instead, I used this trick I read about in a magazine article written by a renowned celebrity stylist. It said:

> Fashion Trick #230: If your shoes are too big, take a thin maxi pad and stick it in the shoe. This is even better than the tried-and-true toilet-paper-in-the-shoe technique because maxi pads come with a sticky liner that helps keep it in place.

I followed the article's advice and pasted a maxi pad in each shoe. I tried the shoes back on and they fit perfectly. Then I burrowed in my mom's closet like a little mole and discovered the purple vintage Dior dress she wore the night she met my father. I tried it on. It fit, but there was a small hole under the armpit. I closed the hole up with an inconspicuously placed miniature safety pin.

I thought of all the glamorous things Sabrina was doing to get ready for the premiere and I tried to copy her. I plucked

my eyebrows. I painted my nails red. I bought some fake tan-
ner from the drugstore and squirted it on my legs.

* * *

When I showed up at the Mercer Hotel, a turquoise stretch
Mini Cooper limousine was already parked outside. Bert was
leaning against the car. He smiled and waved at me. As I walked
over, I got a strong whiff of his citrus aftershave. I noticed there
was a clump of hair on his neck that he missed shaving.

"How's it shakin'?" he asked, looking me over.

"Doing great!" I said. "I am so excited to go to my first
premiere."

Bert's phone vibrated, and he checked the caller ID.
"Sabrina's going to be down in just a few minutes." He turned
toward me. "And I need to talk to you before she gets here."
His voice grew very intense and quiet.

"Yeah, sure. What's going on?" I was intrigued by his serious tone.

"Sabrina, you see, has been going through a lot lately . . .
because she had a falling-out with her mother before she
came to New York. This is between me and you, of course."

"Of course," I assured him.

"It happened last month at their home in Malibu. And
since then, she has been acting wilder and wilder. She has
also lost a lot of weight."

"What happened with her mother?" I asked. I was filled
with curiosity.

"Never mind the details," he said. "But they're not speaking, and I need you to keep an eye on her. You must let me
know if she is partying too much, drinking too much, or staying out too late. I am counting on you because you will see

more than I get to see. She doesn't trust adults. And you and she are the same age."

It suddenly registered what Sabrina was talking about earlier. She was right. On some level, she was surrounded by spies. Bert wasn't only looking for an extra helping hand—he was looking for a secret agent. What he was asking me to do somehow felt deceitful. I was new to this world, but I sensed that I needed to tell Bert what he wanted to hear. At least for now.

"If I see her acting out of control, I will definitely let you know," I said.

"That makes me feel better. You understand, it is my job to guide Sabrina's career and to make sure the world sees her in the best light. Also, I promised her mother that I would keep a close eye on her. I like to think of myself not only as Sabrina's manager, but as her friend, too. There is a reason I have the excellent reputation that I have."

I couldn't tell if Bert was genuinely concerned for Sabrina or if he was only looking out for his own career, which rested on her success.

The front doors of the Mercer suddenly flew open. I looked over as Sabrina walked out, throwing a large metallic-blue purse over her shoulder with DIOR written across the strap. She was wearing a short, green dress that wrapped around her waist like a silk robe and an emerald-and-diamond choker around her neck.

She sauntered over to us, followed by two girlfriends wearing spaghetti-strap cocktail dresses, and an adorable guy wearing a white linen suit. They all looked so polished and manicured, members of the Pretty People Posse.

"Lily," Sabrina said, grabbing the young guy's hand. "This is my main squeeze, Bronson, and my best friends, Valerie and Nikki." Sabrina flipped her long, silky hair over one shoulder. I noticed there was a white orchid tucked behind her left ear. I looked down at my mom's vintage dress and felt painfully ordinary.

"Nice to meet you guys," I said, trying to sound peppy and fun.

"Right back at ya," Valerie said, shoving past me to get into the stretch Mini Cooper. Valerie's face was framed with dark square bangs and a blunt cut to her shoulders. She had a cute button nose with a diamond stud and very full lips that seemed to scowl at me as she walked by.

"Hi there!" Nikki said, shaking her extra-high, blonde ponytail. Nikki's eyes were plastered with eyeliner and she had a few freckles scattered over her nose. She had a sharp chin, high cheekbones, and beady eyes. There was something about her that reminded me of a canary. "Wait for me, chica," Nikki called after Valerie.

"After you," Bronson said, putting his hand out for Sabrina to get into the humongous car. Then he helped me up, as well.

I crawled inside the car and couldn't believe what I saw. Soft leather seats, a side panel lined with champagne flutes, a bucket of ice, and bottles of every drink imaginable. A table filled with platters of milk chocolate–dipped strawberries and bowls of rainbow-colored jelly beans. On the inside roof of the car was the image of a night sky—just like my room, except the stars were made from yellow electric lights.

"Turn the stereo up!" Valerie hollered at the driver. "Let's get this party started!" She shook her dark hair so that it fell around her shoulders.

Through the partition, I watched the driver fiddle with the radio dial. Then the sounds of pulsating techno music filled the Mini Cooper.

"Louder! I want to feel the beat in my Jimmy Choo heels!" Nikki said.

"I *love* this song!" Sabrina said, starting to dance in her seat. Nikki joined in and started dancing, as well, snapping her French-manicured fingers in the air.

"Oh yeah, shake it, baby!" Sabrina said, teasing Nikki.

"Get down! Let's see what you got, chicas!" Valerie yelled, egging them on.

I just watched and smiled. I wanted to join in, but they would probably give me dirty looks if I tried to dance with them. I wasn't part of their crew.

The car pulled into the left lane and started driving up-town. Bronson slid in next to me.

"They like to get their groove on," he said, grinning at me. He had the most adorable dimples when he smiled. His eyes sparkled and twinkled like there were fabulous stories behind them.

Bronson leaned over to me, talking over the music. "When these girls get together, you never know what to expect. They've been best friends since kindergarten."

"They all grew up in L.A.?" I tried to speak as his eyes melted me like butter.

"Yeah, in Malibu. I did, too. Sabrina flew us all out here

to keep her company for the summer. She's subletting an apartment for Val and Nikki close to the Mercer. And my dad's uncle is letting me crash in his studio while he travels through Asia."

"That is a sweet deal," I said. I looked over at the girls. They were still busy shaking their hips and waving their arms in the air to the music. "Are Valerie and Nikki actresses, too?" I asked. This was a good opportunity for me to get some inside dirt.

"Nope. Nikki's parents own a restaurant. It's this high-end romantic spot with a view of the Pacific. At sunset you can see dolphins swimming by as you carve into your steak. And Valerie's dad is a real-estate mogul. He owns, like, a quarter of Ventura County."

"Nice. And you?" I asked. I tried not to stare at him too much, but every time I looked into his eyes, I felt an electric shock, even stronger than the one I felt when I unplugged my flat iron and accidentally touched the wall socket.

"I live with my parents near Burbank. My dad's a screenwriter so he likes to be near the movie studios. I'm actually going to help him write his next script. It's gonna be a thriller that takes place in Cancun."

"Wow, that is so cool," I said. "So you want to be a writer?"

He nodded at me. "I was reading one of Sabrina's magazines while she was getting ready. And it said if a guy says he's a writer, his sex appeal automatically goes up ten points."

I laughed awkwardly. I didn't know exactly how to react. In my opinion, from the first second I saw him, his hotness meter was already maxed out.

"Hey, pass those strawberries," Sabrina yelled. I was happy she had broken up my conversation with Bronson. I was starting to crush so hard, it hurt.

The girls had stopped dancing now and were starting to primp in anticipation of arriving at the premiere.

"I want one, too," Nikki said, grabbing a strawberry as Bronson passed the tray down. "But please let me know if seeds get stuck in my teeth," she said. "There's nothing like walking down the red carpet and smiling with brown stuff in your mouth."

"I'm so over the red carpet," Sabrina said, grabbing a bottle of tequila from the limo's bar area. She filled up a bunch of glasses.

"I like it sometimes, but I have to be in the mood," Valerie said, putting her arms out in front of her and cracking her knuckles. *Crack. Crack.*

"I mean, what if something very embarrassing happens?" Nikki said. "Like when You-Know-Who fell over and mooned a zillion cameras."

"And everyone could see she wasn't wearing underwear and had zits on her butt," Valerie added.

"You mean the Queen Biatch? Don't even say her name," Sabrina said.

"Who's the Queen Biatch?" I asked.

"Don't ask," Valerie said, putting her hand on top of her head and loudly cracking her neck. "Ahh, that feels good."

I didn't ask again, but I really wanted to know.

"Imagine if you were walking the red carpet and you farted really loud," Valerie laughed.

"Eww. Gross," Sabrina and Nikki said.

"Or how about"—I tried to get into the conversation—"if you walked down the red carpet and vomited everywhere!"

Suddenly the car went completely quiet. No one was laughing. Everyone stared at me except Sabrina, who was looking down at the floor.

"Red Alert. Can somebody say 'faux pas'?" Valerie said. Her mouth sneered again as if she smelled something terrible on her upper lip.

"We don't talk about that," Nikki said, playing with her diamond anklet.

I eyed her with confusion.

"Maybe she doesn't know," Bronson said.

"Doesn't know? Everybody knows!" Valerie said.

"Knows what?" I asked.

"All right already! *I'll tell the story,*" Sabrina said. "A few months ago, I ate, like, five hundred chocolate kisses and drank, like, thirty cosmic lemonades, a cocktail I invented. Then I got sick while walking down the carpet. I threw up on my dress and a high-ranking government ambassador."

"Oh, wow, I'm sorry," I said. "I didn't mean to bring up a sore subject. I never heard about that, though. It wasn't in the magazines or anything."

"That's 'cause it happened at the *Too Cool For School* benefit in Nigeria. There aren't many paparazzi in Nigeria."

The car suddenly braked outside the premiere being held at a movie theater on 68th Street and Broadway.

"Here, quick," Sabrina said, passing out the glasses filled with tequila shots.

"Isn't that a bad idea right now?" Bronson said, leaning toward her.

"Puh-lease. Loosen up," Sabrina said, jokingly messing up his hair. He pulled away from her.

"Now!" Sabrina said, raising her shot glass in the air. "I want to make a toast. To you guys. I love you! You've got my back! And I've got yours!"

Everyone clinked glasses and chugged their drinks. I took a quick swig, but the tequila burned my throat. I secretly dumped the rest of it under the seat. I could see how drinking thirty cosmic lemonades could make you throw up.

The driver walked around to open the car door, and as everyone climbed out, the crowd on the street erupted in cheers. Sabrina grabbed on to Bronson's arm and beelined toward the lineup of cameras. She stopped and posed, strutted and smiled.

I watched Sabrina and Bronson walk with Valerie and Nikki down the red carpet. They knew how to move and how to make the right faces. How to smile so it seemed fresh and real. How to throw their hair over one shoulder and pucker their lips.

The photographers started snapping pictures, their cameras flashing like machine gunfire.

I wasn't sure if I should walk down the carpet with them, but I didn't know how else to get into the theater, so I took a deep breath and followed behind. I tried to act confident. I put my chin in the air and strutted. I decided to think up a big secret—a secret that would make me powerful and important enough to be featured on the cover of magazines like *Cosmo Girl*, *Vogue*, and *Party Weekly*. I tried to come up with a secret that I actually had that would make me *that* important. But I couldn't. Nothing real came to me. So I decided to invent one. I pretended I was the youngest winner of the Nobel Peace Prize. No one knew what I looked like because no one ever really knows what famous humanitarians look like. If only these photographers knew who I was! They would not have enough film in their cameras!

"Sabrina! Sabrina!" the fans screamed. There were young girls and teenagers leaning over the barricades competing for her attention, waving and hollering for autographs. I tried to catch up to Sabrina, but she ducked inside the main entrance before I could and I walked the remainder of the carpet alone.

As soon as she was inside, I felt the cameras stop flashing. I looked over and caught the eye of one member of the paparazzi. He looked at me, yawned, and took a slow drag from his cigarette. Who was I kidding? Of course they didn't want to take my picture. I wasn't a starlet. I wasn't even a Nobel Peace Prize Winner. I was just an average prep-school girl from the Upper East Side. They had identified me as a nobody, and I could feel the coldness in their eyes.

I hurried as fast as possible into the theater, but before I made it to the lobby, I slipped on a cord that ran from one of the spotlights to the electrical generator. As I fell to the ground, my left shoe went tumbling across the red carpet and to my horror, one of the photographers looked over just in time to spot my shoe turning on its side—with the maxi pad exposed for all to see! The photographer scrunched up his eyebrows, confused.

"Is that a maxi pad?" he said, pointing and laughing at me.

I grabbed the pad and my shoe and ran inside as fast as possible.

Chapter 5

THE LOBBY WAS FILLED to capacity with movie-industry types. Everyone looked incredibly important, like they were high-powered studio executives, producers, and actors on the verge of skyrocketing to stardom. The guests waved at each other while grabbing cartons of free popcorn and soda from the concession stand. People screamed hellos at each other while blowing kisses from across the room. It was a rocking industry lovefest. And I was there to witness it. As an outsider.

I grabbed a carton of popcorn and headed toward the screening room. That's when I felt a hand grab me firmly on the shoulder. It was Sabrina.

"Grab this! Grab it!" she said, handing me her metallic-blue Dior pocketbook.

I took it from her. The bag felt heavier than I would have imagined.

Sabrina whispered to me intensely. "Be careful. Mercedes is in it. I promised him I would take him tonight, but they don't allow dogs in the theater!"

I held the purse with both hands.

"It would look terrible if I got caught. Everyone will ac-

cuse me of using a dog as an accessory. And more impor-
tantly, I am up for the lead role of Cowgirl Willie in this big
film called *Ladies of the Wild West,* and the director, Antonio, is
here tonight. I don't want any drama."

I was in shock. I didn't know what to say. "Okay. Well,
what do you want me to do with Mercedes?"

"Make sure he watches the movie. And get him some
licorice," she said.

Sabrina took off, linking arms with Nikki and Valerie.

I couldn't believe I was holding a real Christian Dior pocketbook in my arms. And on top of that, there was a dog hiding inside of it. I zipped the bag open. Mercedes looked up at
me. He had those little brown crusty things in the corners of
his eyes. I smiled when I saw him wearing the overalls.

I went over to the concession stand and ordered a pack
of Red Vine licorice. Then I headed for the ladies' room. I
sat down in one of the chairs in the women's lounge area and
waited for the last woman to leave. When the room was empty, I carefully opened up the purse and let Mercedes climb
out onto my lap. I opened up the licorice and he licked my
cheek. I held out a piece and he started to chew one end and
then yanked it out of my hand. When he was done eating the
piece, he ran around in circles and then I threw him another
piece like it was a stick and he fetched it.

"You better be a good boy," I told him. "I need this internship
more than anything. If you are a good, I promise I will bring
you a delicious bone tomorrow from Schatzie's butcher shop."

I felt silly giving a pep talk to a cockapoo. It's not like
he could understand me, but it was worth a shot. Mercedes

licked my hand as I put him back in the pocketbook. He was very accommodating, and I imagined that he must have been used to camping out in Sabrina's purse.

When I got upstairs to the movie theater, the lights were out already. All the seats were taken so I stood behind the back row. When my eyes adjusted, I spotted Sabrina seated in the front of the theater. She was leaning into Bronson and whispering in his ear. I wondered what it would be like to be her right now—at the opening of my movie with an adorable guy on my arm. I wished Max was here and I was sitting next to him, holding hands and sharing a super-size soda.

The movie started and the title flashed across the screen: *Spinning the Wheel of Fire.* When everyone seemed absorbed in the film, I slowly unzipped the bag so Mercedes could stick his head out to watch. He watched very attentively, and when he started to get restless, I fed him another piece of licorice.

The movie told the story of Sabrina's character who helps her parents, two volunteer firefighters, as they drop water out of helicopters in a desperate attempt to save birds, bears, and her love interest, a park ranger, from a growing brushfire at Yosemite National Park.

When the movie ended, there was a reception in the movie-theater lobby. It was amazing how they transformed the room into party central with loud music, a dance floor, ice sculptures of helicopters, and giant pots of chocolate fondue.

Sabrina ran up to me. "So? Did Mercedes like the movie?" she asked.

"I think so."

"Did he make that face with his eyes like this?" She opened

her eyes wide and looked up at me. She was able to imitate him perfectly.

"Yes! He made that exact face."

"That means he loved it!" A thirty-something-year-old guy came over and gave her a big hug. He had shaggy black hair and acne scars on his forehead and cheeks. "Antonio," Sabrina said, kissing him on the cheek and turning her back on me.

I grabbed a plate from the buffet and stood by the escalator. Just as I stuffed a pig-in-a-blanket into my mouth, Bronson brushed up beside me.

"Good stuff, huh?"

"I—yeah, delicious. Want one?" I tried to chew quickly, but a few crumbs spit out of my mouth and onto his shirt.

"Happens to the best of us," he said.

"I've never done that before. I promise," I said.

"It's okay," he said. "Here, you can make it up to me." He stole a mini hot dog off my plate. "There. We're even."

I noticed he was watching Sabrina. She was in the center of the party holding court with a group of young handsomes. I held the bag with Mercedes safely under my right arm.

"So what made you decide to work this summer?" Bronson asked. "You didn't want to run off on a teen tour through Europe or something fun like that?"

"I have to start applying to colleges soon. If I have an internship on my application, at least I can compete with some of the kids at my school."

"Do you know where you want to go to college?"

"My grandpa went to Brown. I really want to follow in his footsteps. I'll feel like a complete failure if I don't get in.

It's just so impossible to stand out at my school. You feel like you have to be a mayor at fifteen years old or start a best-selling magazine in preschool. Half the kids in my school have started their own companies or nonprofit organizations. I feel so ordinary next to them. I'm still figuring out exactly what I want to do with my life, you know?"

"You mean you don't have it all mapped out yet?" Bronson said, teasing me.

"Not completely," I admitted. "I might want to be an art dealer. A writer. Or maybe a librarian."

He gave me a look.

"It's still up for debate," I said. "But I do like to read. And I do like to do crossword puzzles. And play Scrabble. Isn't that dorky?"

"A little dorky. And a little . . . cute." He smiled at me.

I couldn't help but smile back. "So why aren't you hanging out with . . . ?" I asked.

"She's too busy for me now, sweet-talking that director guy, Antonio. The girl who was supposed to play the lead part in Antonio's next movie dropped out at the last minute. And they start shooting September first."

"Oh, wow. Why did the girl drop out?"

"A family emergency. Sabrina wants the part really bad 'cause she gets to play a wild cowgirl, but Antonio is deciding between her and Olivia Carlyle. Sabrina can't stand Olivia. That's why she calls her the Queen Biatch."

"Ohhh, got it." Now I knew who the mysterious Queen Biatch was. It was Sabrina's cinematic rival, the only real competition she had in Hollywood. Every teen blockbuster starred either Sabrina Snow or Olivia Carlyle.

I looked down at the food on my plate. I was really hungry and wanted to gulp it all down, but I got shy eating in front of boys sometimes. Especially crazy-hot ones like Bronson.

"I hate standing around," Bronson said. "Wanna dance?"

"Sure," I said, trying to hide my excitement.

He led me out on the dance floor. DJ Mad Shuffle was spinning eighties music, and we danced together in the middle of the crowd. It was hard to keep a perfect beat to the music because I was still holding the metallic Dior purse with Mercedes hidden inside.

"Have you ever seen the Bus Driver dance?" he asked. "I learned it at this Sweet Sixteen I went to last week." He started driving an imaginary school bus to the beat of the music, then opened the "bus door" and waved to "kids" as they boarded the bus. He made a funny face as he did it, and I laughed.

"How 'bout this one?" I said. "Can you do the Shopping Cart?" I danced while pushing an imaginary shopping cart and miming taking food off the shelf.

"You got the moves," he said, jokingly bumping his butt into mine and then twirling me around in a circle.

He was a great dancer and had his own style. He did this cool move with his fingers when he danced, as if waves from the music were rolling through his hands.

"That's very cool," I told him. "I've never really seen anyone move their fingers like that."

He smiled back and nodded. "I get it from too many years of piano lessons. And also," he said, "I believe in living to the edge of your fingertips."

I'm not sure exactly what he meant, but I liked the way it sounded. It seemed sexy and free-spirited.

The DJ put on a slow song. Bronson looked over at Sabrina. She was still in the middle of an intense discussion with Antonio. Bronson put his hand out to me. "Hey, why stop now?" he said, twirling me into him. "We're just getting warmed up."

He put his arm around me, and I leaned against his shoulder. It felt so nice to have my head on his chest. I looked at him and smiled. His lips were so close to mine now. Approximately six inches away, to be exact. Being close to Bronson made me think of Max. They were so different from each other. Bronson was clean-cut and smooth. He oozed charisma. Max was understated and down-to-earth, his charm buried deeper inside him. Also, Max was far away at camp. And Bronson was right here in front of me.

Maybe it was best if I tried to get over Max. How long could I go on pining for him? It had almost gotten pathetic. Perhaps it was time to open myself up to a new boy. Like Bronson. If only he wasn't Sabrina's boyfriend, I could fall for him right now on the dance floor—and if only I wasn't shaken from my love dream by something suddenly yanking on the Dior metallic purse that I was still holding. I looked down at the bag and there was Mercedes nudging the zipper open and jumping out onto the floor of the party. I was so absorbed by Bronson that I had forgotten all about Mercedes. "Oh, no!" I screamed.

"What's going on?" Bronson said, shaking his head, confused as Mercedes started running through the legs of the party guests. But then Bronson seemed to catch on pretty quick.

"Sabrina did not!" Bronson said, following me as I raced around the party trying to catch Mercedes.

Some of the guests seemed amused, laughing and pointing, while others continued networking, utterly clueless.

"You go by the buffet, I'll go by the bar," Bronson said. "Make sure he doesn't run out the front door and into the street."

I got to the buffet just as Mercedes ran underneath the long white buffet cloth. I got on my hands and knees and started crawling beneath the table, but just as I was about to grab Mercedes, he made a mad dash back out into the middle of the party.

Sabrina was in the center of the room still immersed in her conversation with Antonio. He was leaning in to her, rubbing his black goatee. She was gently patting him on the arm, fluttering her eyelashes when Mercedes ran over, lifted his hind leg, and took a leak right on the bottom of Antonio's designer pants.

"Ohmigod!" Sabrina screamed in horror.

"How disgusting!" Antonio scowled.

Sabrina grabbed on to Antonio's arm. "I am so sorry. I am so sorry. It was an accident."

"My pants are wet! I can feel it on my ankles!" Antonio made his way quickly toward the men's room, holding his pant leg out with two fingers so it wouldn't touch his skin.

I stood there helpless and humiliated. And then I felt it: the electrifying glare of Sabrina's eyes as they aimed to throw daggers—*bang, bang, bang*—at my head.

She squinted at me until her eyes were almost closed. And then she walked over to me. "You. Ruined. My. Premiere," she said.

"Sabrina, I'm so sorry. He jumped out of the bag. I ran to stop him. I tried my best."

"Your best blows," Sabrina said, turning her back on me as Valerie and Nikki ran over to her side. They ushered her into a nearby hallway. I couldn't believe this happened. Tonight was a test, and I had utterly messed it up.

I saw Mercedes in the corner of the room so I went and scooped him up in my arms. He was shaking a little bit, like dogs do when they get scared, but I told him it would be okay. I went to find Sabrina to desperately apologize again and give her back the dog. I did a few laps around the party, but she was nowhere to be found. Neither was Valerie or Nikki. Or Bronson.

I went out front and looked up and down the street. Then I spotted the stretch Mini Cooper speeding through a yellow light.

"Hey!" I screamed, waving at it. "You forgot M—!" I didn't know how to finish the sentence. You forgot Mercedes. You forgot me. But it was useless. The car had driven away.

"Let me grab that," Bert said, walking over to me and taking Mercedes from my arms. He petted the dog's head with his hairy fingers. "Are you all right there, puppy?" he said. Then he turned to me. "This is exactly what I was talking about before. I told you to tell me if she is pulling any of her antics. Now look what happened." Bert rolled his eyes, exasperated, and walked away from me.

"It was an accident. Please understand," I called after him. "I'm incredibly sorry. I feel terrible."

"As you should," Bert said over his shoulder.

As I walked back to my apartment brokenhearted, an image of Sabrina flashed through my brain. I saw her laughing at me while sitting on a throne with Bert, Valerie, and

Nikki feeding her chocolate kisses and cosmic lemonades. I pictured myself kneeling on the floor before her and begging forgiveness while she turned to me and said, "You failed. Zero points. Your game is over, girlie. Now get out of here." Then she would usher me out of the room with a flick of her hand. And as I walked away dejected, I would hear her sarcastic voice, screaming after me, "Get sauced, Lily, 'cause you lost!"

When I got back to the apartment, it was an hour before my midnight curfew. My dad was sleeping on his favorite reclining chair. A late-night talk show was playing on the television set. I noticed a stack of used books on Aristotle and Socrates next to his chair and a plastic bag from the Strand. I could hear my mom snoring in the bedroom.

There was a yellow legal pad with his handwriting on it, as if he was preparing notes for his class tomorrow. I tiptoed to the kitchen to procure a late-night snack.

My dad must have heard me, because he opened his eyes. "There she is," he said.

"Hey, Pops," I said.

He propped himself up with some pillows. A look of concern came over his face when he saw I was upset. "What's the matter?"

I came over and sat with him in the living room. "I don't think I can do this. I'm sorry. I'm just not hipster enough to fit in with hardcore celebrities."

My dad looked at me. "What are you talking about?"

"I know that I am letting you and Mom down. But there is no way I'm going to get this job. I messed up tonight. I guess I'm gonna be Xeroxing at Uncle Ted's insurance firm all

summer or filing papers for you and the philosophy department."

"So you're giving up?" he said.

"I'm not giving up. I'm accepting my limitations."

"There's no such thing. You have to stay out there and
keep pushing through. Keep fighting. You can get this internship if you really put your mind to it."

"Dad, you don't get it! You're not the one falling down the
red carpet, or spitting pieces of mini hot dog on a cute boy!
Or letting a dog take a leak on some hotshot film director's
expensive pants! You spent tonight safely eating ice cream
and watching TV while I was in the limelight, tripping like a
toolbox and embarrassing myself beyond belief! So don't talk
to me about getting out there and pushing through!"

My dad looked at me a bit surprised. "I was just trying
to help you." He got up to go to his room. "But next time I
won't bother."

As I saw him disappear down the hall, I suddenly felt
pangs of guilt—the terrible ones you get after being mean to
someone you care about.

Chapter 6

IN THE MORNING, I woke up and had to admit to my-self—even though I hated doing it—that maybe there was a tiny ounce of truth to my dad's words last night. I also had promised him that, now that I was older, I would try to follow through with my commitments. Besides, I would have to be an idiot to let an opportunity like this sail right past me. I had to step up to the plate and grab it by the *cojones* (that means "balls" in Spanish).

I needed to convince Sabrina that I would make a great intern, despite what had happened Friday night. I decided I would take the weekend to carefully think of the right strategy and get my confidence back up. Then first thing Monday morn-ing, I would return to the Mercer and lay it all on the line.

* * *

When Monday morning finally rolled around, I put on my game face and decided to head down to Sabrina's hotel suite. My dad was getting ready to go teach one of his summer philosophy classes at Columbia. He taught three different classes: Existentialism, Knowledge and Reality, and Top-ics of Ancient Philosophy. And my mom was making waffle toast for breakfast. She would take slices of fresh whole-grain bread and warm them up in the waffle maker.

"I can't believe I'm going back to the Mercer this morning," I said, sitting down at the dining table.

"You're my girl," my dad said. "You're my girl."

"Thanks," I said. "But the question is, will I be Sabrina's girl?"

"Of course you'll be," my mom said, handing me a plate of her special toast. "She would be so lucky to have you. Do you want some beach-plum jelly with that?"

"Sure," I said.

My mom passed the jar down the table.

"Confidence is key," my dad continued, trying to psyche me up. "See the goal in your head. Take your hand, ram it out there, and grab what you want."

"You make it sound so violent," I said.

"Yeah, Neil," my mom agreed. "Quiet it down."

"Not violent. Aggressive. Now is not the time to be timid. Get what you deserve and bring it home."

"Thanks for the pep talk." I took my last bite of toast and jelly and brought my plate into the kitchen.

I left the apartment to head down to Soho. On my way, I stopped by Schatzie's, the butcher shop on Madison Avenue, to pick up the fresh bone I had promised Mercedes. The butcher, Schatzie, gave me a tiny spare rib in a plastic bag.

I stared at the bone. It looked bloody and gross. "Don't you have something a little nicer?" I asked. "This dog isn't just any dog, you know. It's a famous person's dog."

Schatzie gave me a look. "Come again?"

"This bone is for the dog of a really famous person."

Schatzie's eyes grew intense. "I don't care if it's the Queen of Sheba's dog. It's a *dog* and all dogs—whether it is a homeless mutt or a purebred collie—enjoy noshing on raw bone marrow." Schatzie glared at me with intense bug eyes and then burst out laughing.

I looked up at him. "Uh, thank you, Schatzie." With no other option, I grabbed the package and slipped out of the door.

* * *

I showed up at around nine o'clock to the Mercer Hotel. I walked up to the concierge and spoke with Angelica. She recognized me from last week and called up to Sabrina's suite to get clearance for me to go upstairs. "Please tell them it's Lily Miles again about the internship position."

I waited anxiously as Angelica repeated my message into the receiver. Then she waved me on. "Go ahead," she said. I was relieved that whoever answered the phone had granted me permission.

I rode in the elevator to the fifth floor. As I walked down the hall, I recited to myself the song that Evie and I invented. *"Go me, go me. I rock! Get busy!"*

Then I practiced saying the key phrases I wanted to say to Sabrina when I pleaded with her to give me one more chance to be her intern.

When I got to Sabrina's suite, I knocked on the door. A woman with pale skin and too much blush opened the door. She looked about sixty years old, with short, curly, over-processed hair and thick teeth that looked like dentures.

"Hi, I'm here to see Sabrina," I said.

"Who are you exactly?" the lady asked with suspicion.

"My name is Lily. I met with Sabrina about the internship position last week."

"Wait a second. Let me tell her you're here," the woman said, shutting the door in my face.

A minute later, the woman came back and opened the door. "Fine. Sabrina said you can come in," she said.

"Thanks," I said, walking into the suite.

"I'm Sabrina's guardian, Eleanor," the lady said. She sat down by the desk in the living room and started playing a game of solitaire. "Sabrina's indisposed. She will be out shortly. Take a seat on the couch and wait."

I sat down and watched Eleanor flip through the deck of cards. She looked overly made up like an actress from the silent-movie era.

Mercedes ran over to me. He was wearing a yellow-and-purple Los Angeles Lakers basketball jersey. I put my arm out to pet him, and he licked my hand. I took out the bone from the plastic bag. I looked over to make sure Eleanor wasn't looking. Then I slipped it to him. He grabbed it in his mouth and ran into the bedroom to chew on it.

I noticed today's edition of the *New York Post* on the coffee table in front of me. It was opened to a picture of Sabrina with a caption that read, SABRINA DISSES MOMMY. I realized that the picture must have been taken on Friday. It showed Sabrina getting out of the Mini Cooper limo in her green robe dress, holding on to Bronson's hand.

There was a whole article about Sabrina and her mother. I picked up the paper and started reading it:

> At the premiere of her latest, *Spinning the Wheel of Fire*, Sabrina Snow looked fabulous, arriving in an Oscar de la Renta with a five-karat emerald choker on loan

from Cartier. The one accessory missing, however, was her mother, who just a year ago Sabrina thanked as her "mentor and confidante" while receiving a star on Hollywood Boulevard's Walk of Fame. The alleged fall out between the mother/daughter duo is proving to be true. But no one knows exactly why they are fighting. It is still a dark secret. All we know is the elder Ms. Snow has been spotted driving her yellow Corvette all over the place, from Sun Shadow's Restaurant in Malibu, to the exclusive LaBoomba Club at Hollywood and Highland, to an elite dinner party for twenty at the head of a movie studio's mansion. A close friend of Sabrina's told *Party Weekly*, "Sabrina hates her mom. You would, too, if you knew what happened." Another friend of Sabrina's, who doesn't want to be identified, said that Sabrina hasn't been eating lately. "Since the blowout with her mom, Sabrina moved to New York where she only eats carrot sticks, rice cakes, and sugar-free chocolate kisses. It's so depressing. She's gone down from a 34C to a 32A."

I put the paper down on the coffee table. That's when I heard Sabrina calling my name. "Lily! Lily!" she said. "Can you come here?"

Eleanor looked over at me. "I guess she wants me in there," I said, looking for approval. Eleanor nodded permission for me to go ahead.

I walked into the bedroom. The bathroom door was closed. I knocked lightly. "Hello? Sabrina?" I said.

I heard splashing coming from inside the bathroom. "Thank God you're here, Lily! I'm taking a bubble bath and I left my razor out there!" Sabrina hollered through the bathroom door. "It's in my beauty kit on the dresser. Can you bring it to me?"

I was surprised she was even still talking to me. This was a good sign.

I walked over and looked through her brown-and-white-striped Henri Bendel toiletry bag. It was overflowing with trendy, colorful bath salts, gels, and soaps.

As I grabbed her razor, I was startled to see a small silver frame showcasing the illustration I had sold her of Max. It was standing up on the dresser, next to her cosmetics. I couldn't believe she had actually framed it like it was a *pièce de résistance* on display at the Museum of Modern Art.

"I found it," I said.

"You can come in. I'm just taking a bubble bath. It's not like I'm doing yoga in the nude."

I pushed the door open. Inside, there was a humongous bathtub, the size of a Jacuzzi, filled with pink bubbles.

"Is that witch Eleanor still out there?" she asked me.

"Yeah," I said. "Busy playing cards."

"My mom pays her to swing by and check that I'm still alive. She thinks she's my guardian. Can you believe that? I don't know where my mom dug her up. She looks like she sailed in off the *Titanic*."

"Yeah, she looks a little antique," I said.

"She probably thinks you're here to corrupt me. As *if*." Sabrina started laughing and kicking her feet in the bathtub.

"Isn't this bathtub the coolest?" she said. "I got these bubbles in a GB last year. I love GBs!"

"GBs?" I asked.

"Gift bags. All the cool parties have GBs. But enough of the BS, we need to talk. You know what 'BS' stands for right?"

"Bullshit."

"Bingo."

I handed her the silver razor encrusted with purple crystals. Then I jumped up and sat on the bathroom counter.

"Yuck! I have so much dead skin on the bottom of my feet from wearing heels last night," Sabrina confided in me. "Wanna know a beauty trick?"

I nodded. I was hungry to learn as many of Sabrina's beauty tricks as possible.

"When I get out of the bath, I'm gonna rub Bag Balm on my feet. The stuff is used by farmers to soften cow udders, but it makes a great moisturizer for humans, too."

"Oh, I didn't know that," I said.

"Now you do," she said, starting to shave her legs. "Lily, you seem like a cool girl, but Friday night . . ."

"I wanted to apologize to you for that. Mercedes just jumped out of the bag. I promise I will do a better job from now on. I know I have what it takes to be an amazing intern." I began ripping through the buzz words. "I am organized, hardworking, detail-oriented, determined, and—"

"Okay, already," she said. "I've dealt with the dog situation. I sent Antonio fifty cupcakes to apologize."

I relaxed for a moment. I had a chance here. The window of opportunity was opening once again.

"What I'm *not* over," Sabrina said, "is the way you were acting with Bronson."

"How was I acting with Bronson?" I asked, thrown off.

"At first, I thought he was talking to you to save you from looking so awkward. But then I saw the two of you feeding each other pigs-in-a-blanket and bumping butts on the dance floor—that's when I realized you were actually flirting with him."

"I wasn't flirting. He was talking to me about you. And I was just trying to be polite by offering him some—"

"Shh. Shh. Lily, look, have you ever been in love?"

I shook my head no.

"Neither have I. I have been in 'like.' I have been in 'lust' and in 'crush,' but never the love thing. I'm just so picky and I don't know if it even really exists. Bronson is the first guy that made me think it might." Sabrina wiped a wad of bubbles from her hair. "I'm the happiest when I'm around him. I miss him the second he leaves me. I can't stop thinking about him all day. Whether I'm watching TV, studying my lines, working out with my trainer, Bronson's always on my mind. I can't imagine not having him in my life. When I think back to before I met him, everything seems darker and gray."

"But, Sabrina, you have nothing to be afraid of. I mean, look at you. Every guy in my school drools over you."

"Look, I know I can get almost every guy. But he's not like every guy. It's as if it barely fazes him that I'm famous. He doesn't buy into all that. I mean, his last girlfriend worked at a 7-Eleven on Ventura Boulevard. He actually cares about what's inside. That's the point, get it? So stay away."

"I promise." I looked down at the marble-tiled floor.

"You see," Sabrina said, "there are 'Girl's Girls' and 'Not Girl's Girls.' Girl's Girls stick by your side. Not Girl's Girls try to steal your boyfriends and put guys before their friends. I don't want them in my life. I'll tell you a secret. Olivia Carlyle, the Queen Biatch, and I used to be close friends—until I caught her trying to hit on my last boyfriend. Now, if she ever tries to come near me, I'll zap her with an electric cattle prodder." Sabrina leaned against the back of the tub. "So, are you a Girl's Girl or a Not Girl's Girl?"

"I am definitely a Girl's Girl," I blurted out. I certainly didn't want to be on her list of people to electrocute.

"Good." Sabrina dunked her head under the water and then popped up. "Anyway, enough of this mush fest—I need to get downstairs to my press conference."

I jumped up off the counter. "So does this mean I got it?"

"Got what?" Sabrina said.

"The internship."

"Yes—but only because I'm not normally around people like you, so it will be a great character study."

"People like me? What does that mean?" I asked.

"You know, normal, regular people."

I couldn't tell if this was an insult, but I didn't care. I just scored an internship with a major starlet and relished the good news. I got the internship! I got it. *I got it!*

"I am sooo excited!" I said.

Sabrina raised her eyebrows at me as if my excitement was strange and a complete overreaction. "But there are a few rules before you start. There's some paperwork you will have to sign. Bert will give it to you. The gig starts today, June twenty-ninth, and goes for the rest of the summer. Monday through Friday, nine in the morning until five at night. Some-times later."

I was flabbergasted. Touched. Overwhelmed. "This is fantastic. I'm your intern now!" I said.

"I expect a lot from the people who work for me. Play by my rules and you'll have no reason to worry about get-ting fired. You get a little stipend for being my intern of two hundred and fifty dollars a week. Plus a bonus if you do a mind-blowing job. What do you want for a bonus? A gift certificate to your favorite store? Dinner for two . . . tickets to an event . . . ?"

I thought about it quickly and then made up my mind. It was a no-brainer. "Tickets to this summer's Rock the House Awards would be unbelievable," I said.

Going to the R.T.H. Awards looked like the most fun ever. It happened every summer at the end of August. My whole life, I had dreamed of going. No one can even buy tickets. The only way you can get to go is if you're invited. And in order to be invited, you have to be famous, or ex-tremely well connected to the famous.

"You know how hard they are to come by, right?" Sabrina asked.

"Trust me, I know," I said. "Even the richest girl in my high school, Wendy Goldlocks, couldn't buy her way in."

"I get four this year," Sabrina bragged. "Obviously I'm us-ing two of them for me and Bronson. But if you truly work your ass off for me, I will hook you up with the other two tickets."

A jolt of euphoria rushed through my body. I imagined

getting dressed up and going to the black-tie reception where I would brush elbows with all the people I had always fantasized about meeting.

"I'm gonna work so hard for you," I said. "I'm going to be the best intern ever."

"Just what I wanted to hear." Sabrina climbed out of the bathtub. She wrapped herself in a towel, then she turned around and headed out the bathroom door, bumping into Bronson.

"Ahhh!" she screamed. "You scared me."

"Sorry," he said. He looked adorable in his cargo pants and T-shirt. I wished that he could have a twin. If only I could race up to a drive-through window at a fast-food restaurant and order, "One more please. Just like him. All for *me*."

"Eleanor gave me dirty looks again when I showed up," Bronson told Sabrina.

"She hates when boys get within ten feet of me," Sabrina said, running a brush through her wet hair.

"Do you want to grab a quick breakfast?" Bronson said.

Sabrina pouted her lips. "I'm sorry, babe. I'm running behind. The press junket for *Spinning the Wheel* starts in half an hour and I'm still buck naked. Rain check?"

"I was looking forward to some time—"

"I told you. Later. I have too much to do today."

"But we barely had a chance to hang out this last week."

"Ugh, you're stressing me out."

It felt strange standing in the middle of their fight. It was like I was on the couch at home, watching the latest episode of a reality show. Sabrina went to her closet and grabbed some clothes. Then she laid out two outfits on the bed.

"Now, help me, Bronsie. Which do you like better?" she said. "The Marc Jacobs dress or the Zac Posen?"

"Uh, the Marc Jacobs one, I guess," Bronson said. He rolled his eyes. It was clear he was still annoyed.

The phone rang and Sabrina grabbed the receiver off the nightstand. "I'm getting ready!" she said into it. It seemed as if she knew who it was before she even answered it. "That's ten more minutes. I'll send Lily down to help. I gave her the thumb's-up. She'll be working for me the whole summer so go over the details with her."

As soon as Sabrina hung up the phone, she turned to me. "That was Bert. Go to the Stellar Ballroom on the third floor and help him. The reporters start arriving in ten minutes for the junket."

"I'm on it," I said, heading out the door. "Oh, one quick thing," I added. "My school gave me a form that I need you to sign at the end of the summer. It says that I completed the internship and asks you to evaluate me."

"Yeah, sure, whatever. I'll take care of it in August."

"Thanks," I said.

Sabrina turned around to grab shoes from the closet, and as I walked past Bronson he looked over at me and secretly did the Shopping Cart dance from Friday night. I couldn't help but break out laughing.

"What's so funny?" Sabrina said, turning around.

I didn't know what to say.

"She tripped," Bronson said, saving the day. "On Mercedes's bed. She almost fell over."

"Yeah," I said. "It was really clumsy . . . in a funny sort of way."

Sabrina didn't laugh. "Well, watch where you're going. Mercedes's bed was handmade at a villa in Tuscany. It's one of a kind and impossible to replace."

"I'll be more careful next time," I said, leaving the bedroom. Bronson winked at me as I rushed past him, and I blushed. I just couldn't help it. You can't stop yourself from blushing, you know.

Chapter 7

IN THE ELEVATOR, I jumped up and down and screamed in celebration. When the door opened on the third floor, a woman in a business suit was standing there waiting to get on. She gave me a strange look over her glasses as I walked out. But I didn't care. I knew she would be yelling with joy, too, if she had just clinched the opportunity of a lifetime. Every ounce of my being smiled. *Success is so sweet and so savory,* I thought. I couldn't wait to tell the world that I was now officially Sabrina Snow's intern.

I ran over to Bert, who was standing by the entrance to the Stellar Ballroom in a black leather jacket with sunglasses tucked into his sweater vest.

"Congrats," he said.

"Thanks!" I said, overjoyed.

"I hope we don't have any more mishaps like Friday night, though."

"Perfect from now on," I assured him.

Bert took out a piece of paper from his briefcase and handed it to me. "Now that you'll be working for Sabrina, I need you to sign this."

On the top of the paper it said: "Confidentiality Agreement."

"Sign at the line," Bert said.

"What is this exactly?" I asked.

"A standard agreement. It's customary. It states that you will not talk to anyone about Sabrina's life and projects and that you will protect her privacy while dealing with the public. Or else, your actions are punishable by law."

I nodded. It sounded reasonable enough. I would be seeing the inside workings of Sabrina's growing empire. Bert needed security in knowing that I wouldn't appear on the E channel spilling my guts out about how she calls Olivia Carlyle the Queen Biatch behind her back. Or uses cream for cow utters to moisturize her own feet.

I signed the document and handed it back to Bert. He stuck it back in his briefcase. Then he handed me a clip-board.

"Here's the list of invited guests for the press junket," Bert said.

I looked down at the clipboard with a list of hundreds of people's names typed on it.

"You know what a press junket is, right?" he asked.

"No," I said, shaking my head, embarrassed.

"We invited several reporters and entertainment writers here to interview and photograph Sabrina and the other actors from *Spinning the Wheel of Fire*. In between stuffing their faces with free food, the reporters will be meeting with and photographing the cast members. In exchange, they'll write some nice blurbs about Sabrina in their magazines. At least, they better be nice or I won't invite them back next time."

"Understood," I said, absorbing all the new information.

"While I'm in there herding these reporters around like cattle, I need your help manning the front door. Only let people in who are on the list," Bert said. "Highlight the person's name in yellow and give them a blue wristband. Clear?"

"I got it," I said.

"Super. Welcome to the team. Oh, and here is a walkie-talkie in case you have any trouble." Bert handed me the device as a beautiful woman in her twenties with long, dark hair and turquoise eyes walked over to us.

"Violetta!" Bert said, giving her a kiss on the cheek.

"I finally have a moment to give you a proper hello. Everything under control with the door?" the woman said.

"Sabrina's new intern will be handling the list. Lily, this is Violetta, Sabrina's publicist. She works out of the New York P.R. office of Bradley & Stern."

"Great to meet you," I said.

"You, too," Violetta said, looking at her watch. "I have to go back inside. It's almost showtime." Violetta gave a warm smile and headed back into the main room. Bert followed her.

I stood at the door to the Stellar Ballroom proudly holding the clipboard under my arm. I couldn't believe I was the girl with the list standing at the door controlling who gets to come into the party.

A few minutes later, reporters and TV crews started to arrive. They came fast and furious in large groups, some of them carrying heavy video equipment. One by one, I scanned the list for their names and handed out wristbands as the crowd screamed out at me, "I'm on the list! Let me in! I'm late! Excuse me! Over here!"

I managed to stay on top of my game until a woman

came to the front of the line and introduced herself as Lucy Myerstone.

I looked up and down the list, but her name wasn't on it. "I'm sorry, but I don't see you here," I said.

"I am definitely on that list," she said. "There must be a mistake."

I asked her to repeat the spelling of her last name twice. "No, I'm sorry, but you're still not there."

She shook her head. "That's ridiculous. Just let me in. They must have made a mistake."

"I can't just let you in," I explained. "Give me one moment." I picked up the walkie-talkie and struggled with it for a moment, trying to figure out how to page Bert. Finally, I pressed the right button.

"Bert, are you there? It's Lily."

He picked up a second later. "I'm in the middle of something. I'll be out there shortly."

"I just have a quick name to run past you," I said.

"I told you. Not now!" Bert said abruptly.

It was clearly best to leave him alone. I turned back to the woman. "You'll have to wait until Sabrina's manager gets back here."

The woman smiled at me. "You're new, aren't you?"

"How'd you know?"

"I saw you struggle with the walkie-talkie." The woman laughed. "Look, I'm with *Glamster* magazine. They're expecting me. I need to get in there. I'm going to get in huge trouble with my boss if I don't cover this event."

I looked at her, trying to size her up. She looked nice enough.

"Here's my card," she said. "I have to get inside. If I don't, I might get fired. I'm a single mom. If I lose my job, I won't be able to buy food or pay rent."

I checked her business card out, and it definitely seemed legit. I looked over my shoulder at Bert ushering reporters in and out of the main interview room.

I weighed the options in my head. I certainly didn't want this woman to get fired.

"Go ahead," I said quietly.

"You're the best," she said, patting me on the shoulder and walking past me.

I stood outside the ballroom and continued to check people in until about ten minutes later when Bert ran over to me.

"What the hell?" he said. "That woman is stealing all the food from the buffet and shoving it in her coat. I saw her stick a wheel of brie up her skirt." He grabbed my arm and pointed to the reporter who wasn't on the list. "Did you let that woman in here?"

My heart sank. "She said she was with *Glamster* magazine."

"Was she on the list?" Bert said. "Was. She. On. The. List?"

I shook my head, ashamed.

Just then, Violetta, the publicist, walked by. "Is everything all right?" she asked Bert.

"Fine. Great," Bert said, covering.

"Hope so. You know I hate drama," Violetta said, throwing him a stern look, then walking way.

Bert pulled me aside. "There's no such thing as *Glamster* magazine," Bert said. It's more like Scamster."

"But she showed me her card," I said.

"It was fake. I told you not to let anyone in unless their name was on that paper. I'll take over the list. You go get security on her. Now. And be discreet."

I looked around. There was a security guard in a blue blazer standing at the periphery of the ballroom. I walked over to him.

"Excuse me," I said, "but we have a bit of a situation." I explained to the guard what was going on, then I watched as he walked over to the supposed *Glamster* reporter and grabbed her by the arm to escort her out.

"But I belong here! I belong here!" she said loudly as she was dragged out the front door.

I felt terrible watching her get thrown out of the junket. I had no idea what her story was. Maybe she was just hungry. She wasn't really doing anything to hurt anybody. She looked at me as he pulled her out of the room. And I mouthed to her, "Sorry."

Violetta looked over at the scene and shook her head in disgust. Then I eavesdropped as she walked to the front door and had some biting words with Bert.

"What's the dealio? You said that intern girl had the door under control. She's incompetent. Where'd you find her?"

"That woman must have sneaked right by her," Bert said, covering.

"Get it together. It's like amateur time here."

"I'm taking care of it," Bert said. "There won't be any more problems."

I felt ashamed. I looked at the ground and shook my head. Being the girl with the list at the door was harder than I thought.

After the event died down, I helped Bert gather the remaining press kits scattered on the tables.

"How can I trust you when you don't listen to me?' he said.

"She said she would get fired from *Glamster* if I didn't let her in."

"You have to be more careful. You're in the big leagues now. When I give you instructions, follow them. I am giving them to you for a reason. If you can't abide by orders, you're not going to last very long here. Violetta was furious, but I protected you this once. What would have happened if you let in someone who was dangerous today? Maybe this woman wanted to kidnap Sabrina and hold her for ransom." He packed up his bag.

"I think she was just hungry," I said.

"Well, the next person you snuck in might have been a serial killer who wanted to slash Sabrina's face. Stop being so naïve." He headed for the door. "You're done for today."

"But it's only one in the afternoon," I said.

"Go home and think about your mistakes. And how you will be more cautious in the future. See you tomorrow."

★   ★   ★

The rest of that week was orientation. I divided up my time between hours spent with Bert and time with Sabrina being trained on the particulars of the job. Bert assigned me a small table in the living room and said that it would be my workstation. There was a phone and a laptop computer. On the computer, there was a program with Sabrina's calendar and her address book. He also gave me a folder for organizing Sabrina's receipts, as it was my responsibility to do her expenses for the summer.

Bert showed me a memo pad where I was supposed to enter phone messages for Sabrina with specifics like the date, time, name of caller, and return phone number. He trained me on how to use the phone so I could get someone on the line and then transfer them to where Bert sat on the couch. He said sometimes when Sabrina was busy, he would have me roll calls for him. This consisted of quickly dialing a long list of people one after the next.

"As soon as someone picks up," Bert said, "you should say, 'Hello. I have Bert Covitz calling.' Then if the person is available, transfer the call to my extension by the couch. As soon as I am off one call, you should be already dialing the next. Keep moving down the list in a fluid motion."

He broke me in that Friday afternoon by having me roll over thirty calls for him. "Get the following people on the line in this order," he said. Then he rattled off what seemed like a never-ending list of names. I had to jot them down as fast as possible. "Kate Clifferd, Brian DeNapalois, Wyatt Sterling, Brandon Patterson, Julia Cooper, Greg Livingston, Dana Fields, Matthew Chow." And the list went on. I would guess the spelling and then try to figure out the proper lettering by looking through the address book on my laptop computer.

I started making the calls and transferring them to Bert. If I didn't dial fast enough, he would scream, "Hurry! Hurry! Roll! Roll! Roll!"

I was so nervous trying to please him that simple maneuvers like dialing a phone number and pronouncing someone's name accurately became challenging tasks.

Sabrina also sat me down and laid down the law. "Don't go through my things, take money from my petty-cash purse without permission, or steal any of my clothes. I caught my mom taking tons of clothes from my closet without asking—like my favorite Prada wrap dress and Gucci knee-high boots. It really ticked me off. Oh, and, of course, stay away from Bronson or I will hunt you down."

I nodded, absorbing all the rules and regulations. "I promise," I said. "I won't go near your clothing or your boyfriend."

"Also when I tell you to do something for me, I expect it to get done," Sabrina said. "I don't have time to ask you more than once. Mistakes slow life down and I detest people that get in my way. Oh, and I hate laziness. I didn't get where I am today by sitting around on my ass. Anticipate my needs and go the extra mile. If I want a glass of tea, you should have the pot brewing before I realize I even want it."

When 5 P.M. on Friday finally rolled around, my mind was spinning with all the new information. I was ready for the weekend and the Fourth of July festivities.

*　*　*

That Saturday night, my parents and I went to a friend of my dad's roof deck on 53rd Street and York Avenue. The man who owned the apartment worked as a professor at Columbia Law School. My dad walked around socializing with other faculty members. I overheard him talking to the host about the price of college tuition. "It's really out of control," he said. "Trying to put aside the money to send your kid through college these days puts on a hell of a lot of pressure."

I felt bad listening to my father stress out about money.

My mom noticed me listening to my dad's worries and led me to the railing. "Let's find a good spot to watch the fireworks," she said.

I started telling her more about my first week at the internship as a blast of orange Roman candles lit up the night sky.

"You're my working girl," my mom said. "They must have seen something very special in you."

"Thanks, Mom," I said. "But I can tell already it's gonna be harder than I thought. There are so many different ways I can get into trouble. Ways that I can't even think of yet."

"But imagine all the new things you're gonna discover. It's going to be a very stretchy experience."

"It's just Sabrina has this manager who is a complete control freak. He makes me feel like I'm walking on eggshells. One false move and I bet he'll tell Sabrina to get rid of me. And there's this guardian named Eleanor who gives me the evil eye. She glares at me like I've killed a dog or something."

"Glare at her back," my mom said half-jokingly. "No one's going to get rid of you. They're going to see how much you have to offer and appreciate you. The world isn't so scary out there. I mean, look how exciting your life has gotten in one week."

There was a loud whistling sound as glittering silver tails flew like rockets into the darkness, followed by an explosion of golden stars.

I thought about what my mom said. She was onto something. I took a second and stepped outside my skin and looked at my new life. *Wow*, I thought, *it was actually becoming something thrilling*. I just had to make sure I didn't screw up.

In the cab ride home, my dad told my mom that he wanted to have a budget powwow that night.

"I can hardly wait," my mom said.

When I got home, my parents stayed up in the living room arguing with each other over bills. My dad had his computer out on the table and was busy creating an Excel spreadsheet.

"I had a conversation tonight with Kenneth, one of the professors at the law school. He said he almost went bankrupt when he sent his son through college. I know he was exaggerating, but I'm getting anxious about next year."

"I have an idea," my mom said. "I want to start contributing more financially to the family. I've been wanting to talk to you about this for a while. And I spoke to Diane about it over Italian food last week. We want to start our own business."

"What kind of business?" my dad asked.

"A baking business that specializes in making only meat and vegetable pies."

"What?" my dad said. "Are you crazy?"

"I think there's a huge hole in that market. The industry is dominated by fruit pies. Diane and I were brainstorming, and we came up with some great ideas—sausage pie, fried meat pie, Jamaican jerk chicken pie, and ones with prosciutto and ricotta. We'll start small and try selling them to local bakeries and restaurants."

"Have you lost your mind?" my dad sad.

"You're always worried about money. I think this would be a nice way for me to start adding to our income. Plus, it'll be fun for me. I have been cooking as a hobby for decades, and everyone loves to eat what I make. Why not capitalize on my talents, Neil?" My mom quickly raised her hand up in the air. "Wait. Don't say anything. I just came up with a new recipe—applesauce and pork medallions weaved in a honey-mustard crust."

"Do you know how much it costs to start a new company?"

"I'm going to come up with a low-risk business plan."

"I'll believe it when I see it," my dad said, shaking his head. "And where are you going to do all the cooking?"

"I'll start in our kitchen and once the company grows we'll find more space outside our home."

"You never cease to amaze me. You better not turn our apartment into a disaster area."

"Just you wait," my mom said. "It's going to be a great success."

*　　*　　*

The next Monday when I arrived at the Mercer, Sabrina waved to me as she ran out the door with her personal trainer, Lorenzo. She was dressed in a sky-blue jogging outfit with white stripes along the side arms and legs.

"Bert has a special project for you," she said on her way out. "I'll be gone all morning. After my workout, I'm meeting my real-estate broker to look at some lofts for sale in the Meatpacking District near Little West Twelfth Street. Hope I find a winner."

"Good luck," I told her. "Call me if you need anything at all."

"Look at you," she said. "Lovin' the go-getter attitude." Then she was out the door.

Bert was in the middle of a call in the living room of Sabrina's suite. He held up a finger and told me to wait.

"You ate ten? It's the butter cream. It's absolutely addictive," he said into the receiver. "Yes, four o'clock works great.

I'll have her meet you downstairs. You're the best."

Bert rolled his eyes when he hung up. "What an ego-maniac."

"Who?" I asked.

"That director, Antonio. The town is buzzing about him because he's the new hot thing. So his head is blowing up. He's just a thirty-one-year-old punk who happens to be extremely talented."

Bert instructed me to follow him to the lobby. On our way downstairs, he said, "I just set up a meeting for Sabrina with Antonio for today at four o'clock downstairs at the Mercer Kitchen. He is going to tell her whether she got the part in his movie, *Ladies of the Wild West*."

"Very exciting!" I said.

I followed Bert over to the concierge desk, where he grabbed a bunch of heavy shopping bags from Angelica behind the desk.

He handed me some. "These will keep you busy all day. Take half of them," he said.

"What are all these?" I asked, pulling aside the tissue paper to reveal hundreds of sealed envelopes. The bags appeared to be filled with letters from around the world. They were stamped with exotic postage from Japan, Australia, France, Italy, and Morocco.

"Sabrina's fan mail," Bert said. I followed him inside the elevator and back up to her suite, where he started dumping out the letters onto the floor.

"Wow, there are hundreds of them," I said, sitting before the mountain of letters.

"They won't stop coming. Everyone loves her new movie."

Bert lined up a stack of papers on my workstation in the living-room area. "Here, sit down," he said, motioning me over. "These are pretyped form letters with Sabrina's reply to fre-quently asked questions," he said. "Forge her signature on the bottom of the page, stuff it in an envelope with a brochure for her upcoming makeup line, stamp and address it. Copy this," he said, handing me a piece of paper with Sabrina's ac-tual signature.

"You want me to fake her autograph?"

"Sabrina's too busy to sign all of these herself."

"But isn't that dishonest?" I asked.

He tossed me a black felt-tip pen. "Go with the flow." I couldn't help but stare at one long hair that protruded from his left nostril. "I'm off to a meeting, but I'll be on my cell if you have any questions." Bert took off, slamming the door behind him.

Alone in the suite, I sat down on the floor and spread all the letters out in front of me. Each one looked like a little present—something to be opened with a surprise inside.

It was amazing, really. So many people from around the globe were moved to write a letter, seal the envelope, place a stamp on it, and address it to Sabrina.

I picked up an envelope and tore it open. Inside was a note and a little yellow origami bird.

> Hello! My name is Makiki and I am a seventeen-year-old girl living in Aichi, Japan. Please come to Japan to promote *Spinning the Wheel of Fire*. Your Japanese fans all wait. Your great fan,
> Makiki

I decided to open an envelope from Kansas next.

Hi. My name is Joe Wavely. I live in Kansas, a little
above Wichita, the air capital of the world. I have to
write to someone famous for class, so I chose you.
You are super hot.
Peace out,
Joe

I looked down at the pile of letters. I had only opened
a few of them. There were hundreds more to go through.
Next, I opened an envelope from Ethiopia.

Dear our sister Sabrina,
My name is Aster. I am ten years old and live in
Addis Ababa in Ethiopia. I want to come to America
to be an actress. Can we be best friends?
Aster

Aster even included a few beauty shots of herself. I looked
at the girl's smile. I wondered what Aster was doing right now
in Addis Ababa, Ethiopia.

I forged Sabrina's signature on the form letter as I was
instructed to do by Bert. I couldn't help but feel a little guilty,
though. What if Aster knew that her note was just one of a
million other identical notes? What if she knew that Sabrina
never even saw it and that a girl named Lily Miles signed the
reply?

As I was writing Aster's return address on the outside of
the envelope, my cell phone rang. I picked it up. It was Evie
calling from soccer camp.

"Evester!" I screamed into the phone.

"Lilyrama!" she yelled back.

"You will never guess where I am!" I told her, then I filled her in on the latest.

"Oh, mamacita! I can't believe your new glamorous life!" Evie said.

"How is camp?" I said. "Give me all the dirt."

"Amazing. We are having the best time! But I needed to tell you something."

"Is everything okay?"

"Yep. It's better than okay. Surprise! I'm in the lobby of the dorm and there's someone who wants to talk to you."

I heard noise on the other end of the phone and then a guy's voice. "Hello?"

"What's up?" I said. "Is this Max?"

"Maximilian. Better believe it," he laughed. "Where the hell are you, little lady?" he asked me. "I need your advice on this tie-dye I'm making."

I laughed. "You're making another tie-dye? Just remember when you mix too many colors, it turns brown."

"Like that terrible one I made last year . . ."

"Just like that." God, I wish I could be in two places at once. Sabrina's suite and Ace Soccer Academy.

"Hey"—Max cleared his throat—"are you coming for the Disco Dance?"

"You know I can't—no non-campers are allowed."

"We could sneak you in. I'll find a way. I really want to see you. It's been too long."

"God, I wish I could go," I said. "But I'm really busy this summer with my internship. And you'll never guess who I'm working for. Sabrina Snow! Can you believe it?"

"You're breaking up," Max said. "I can't hear you."

"I was just saying that I'd love to go, but I have tons of responsibilities now that I'm working for Sabrina. I need to be here in case she needs me."

"Hello? Hello?" Then the line went dead.

I dialed Evie back, but it kept going straight to voice mail. Her cell phone must have run out of juice. For a moment, it felt like I was there hanging out at camp with all my friends. Then I looked out the window and was reminded that I was still in the city.

I spent the rest of the day tearing through all of Sabrina's fan mail. After my hand hurt from forging so many signatures, I decided to read one last letter. I leaned against the side of the bed and opened it up. Inside, there was a folded piece of loose-leaf paper. It said:

June 21st

For Sabrina:

I don't know who else to turn to. You are my favorite actress in the whole wide world. I need to tell you about something terrible that happened last month in school. I liked this guy named Mike in my math class and I drew him a picture with crayons of a rainbow and an ostrich (my favorite animal because they run fast and have long necks). I put the picture in his locker but didn't sign my name. Later that week, I saw him in the bookstalls of the library and asked him if he got my picture. His mouth dropped open when he realized it was from me. Then later that day, I was going down the stairwell and he and some of his friends followed me, screaming at me. They shoved me against the wall and said that I should never leave anything in Mike's locker again. Then Mike punched me in the arm and one of his friends shoved yellow chalk from the blackboard into my mouth and made me chew it. Now all the kids from my school make fun of me and prank-call my house. They call me "Ostrich Girl" and make birdcalls into the phone to scare me. Sometimes I lock myself in the bathroom and cry.

Sabrina, I really wanted to go to Six Flags this summer. All the other kids from my school go, but I have no one to go with. My parents said they will take me, but everyone will tease me more if I go with my parents. Could you please call me? It's really urgent. I feel so alone. I don't know how much longer I can take this. . . . Sometimes I wish I would die.

—Taylor, age twelve, Morristown, NJ

Below her name, she had scribbled a phone number. I felt a knot in my stomach. This girl sounded seriously messed up. After reading this note, there was no way I could bring myself to mail back the pretyped form letter with a brochure for Sabrina's upcoming signature makeup line and her answers to standard questions like, "What was your first big break?" and "When did you know you wanted to be an actress?"

I needed to speak to Sabrina immediately. I'm sure she would want to reply to this cry for help in a more personal way. I looked at the clock. It was almost five o'clock. Today had whizzed by. Sabrina was probably still in her meeting with Antonio at the Mercer Kitchen. I decided to go downstairs to check.

I saw her from afar, seated with Antonio in a side booth. She wore a shiny magenta blouse with a matching silk skirt. I watched as she flipped through the pages of a script. Then Antonio stood up and gave her a big hug.

They kissed good-bye on the cheek and went their separate ways. I walked over to Sabrina as she headed back into the lobby.

"Sabrina," I said, running up beside her.

"Hi!" she said as soon as she noticed me. "Guess what? Antonio just told me that I got the part. I'm gonna play Cowgirl Willie! And get paid millions for it!" She was so excited, bouncing off the walls. "I bet the Queen Biatch is crying in her bed! She lost! I *won*! This is the best birthday present ever."

"Congrats! That is awesome! You got the part!" I told her. "Wait—I didn't know it was your birthday."

"It's this Friday," she said, taking a sip from a bottle of Fiji water she was carrying.

"Happy early birthday," I told her.

"I'm turning seventeen and it's going to be the best year ever!" Sabrina said. "And this morning, my real-estate broker, Sagi, showed me the coolest loft with fourteen-foot-high ceilings and exposed brick. It's on Little West Twelfth and Ninth Avenue in the Meatpacking District. I'm considering putting in an offer to buy it. I fell in love with the neighborhood. A hundred years ago, the area used to be a meat market filled with butchers and hanging chunks of meat. Now it's this mixture of classic New York and modern times. There are so many new clubs and adorable boutiques. I ate at this amazing Pan-Asian restaurant called Spice Market."

I could feel the letter from Taylor burning up the back pocket of my jeans. I needed to take advantage of this alone time.

"Sabrina—I need to talk to you," I said.

"If you're gonna ask me for a part in my new film, I'll see about getting you a one-liner, but I'm not promising anything."

"No, that's not what I was going to ask. It has to do with this thing I found."

I took the letter out of my pocket and showed it to her.

"What the hell is that?" she asked.

"One of your fan letters. It's from this girl in New Jersey. She sounds really messed up. All the kids at school make fun of her. She completely idolizes you and just wants to talk to you. One phone call . . ."

"No way! I am not calling a stranger!" Sabrina shrieked. "Are you out of your mind?"

"Then maybe you could at least write her a personal note instead of one of those form letters," I said.

Sabrina looked at me like I was crazy. "Is this really the time or the place? I was in the middle of a total high. You're such a buzz kill."

"I'm sorry. I didn't mean to bring you down. It's just when I read the letter—I got worried."

"Let me teach you a lesson. Lots of those fan letters are fake. People pretend they are dying or in trouble just so they can get money or presents from me. Don't be so gullible."

"Really?" I said. "People do that?"

"People will do a lot of things to get close to someone famous. You'd be surprised. The person who wrote that letter is probably not a teenage girl at all. It's probably some psychopath guy who lives in a cabin in Nebraska playing the banjo all day with fifty photos of me taped to his wall! And when he's not playing the banjo, he's probably digging sock lint out from under his big toe or eating his own earwax. Now wash your hands right away! Who knows where that letter has been!"

"Wow," I said. "I didn't realize how far people would go to try and contact you."

"Here, dump this on your hands right away." Sabrina passed me her bottle of Fiji water. "You don't want to get some hand-eating fungus."

I dumped some of the water over my hands and wiped them dry on my jeans.

"I hope you learned your lesson," Sabrina said.

Back at the suite, Sabrina went into her closet and took out a shopping bag. "Now on to bigger, more important things. I have a present for you," she said.

"You got me a present? I can't believe you got me a present," I gushed.

"It was a kiss-up gift from one of the reporters at the press junket last week. I already have one, so I'm giving it to you. Besides it's a perfect token to mark this occasion."

"What occasion is it?" I asked.

"The start of your second week on the job. Don't you see how much opportunity lies before you? It's all there for the taking. Just dig into yourself and be the best you can be. Take advantage of everything in front of you."

I opened up the shopping bag and looked inside at a box with a photograph of a handheld electronic device.

"Your first BlackBerry," Sabrina said proudly. "We can be in constant communication. Now that I got the part of the cowgirl in this movie, the next month or so is going to be one of the most stressful of my life. Of *our* life. We have so many things to do to get ready for the part. I have dancing lessons, horseback-riding lessons, costume fittings . . ."

I sat on the edge of my chair. She was opening up to me. Things were getting intense.

Sabrina continued, "My mom used to be my right hand. My dad left us when I was five. He met some waitress at Sushi Mambo and moved back with her to Japan. My mom used to make sure I got to all my appointments and gave me tons of support—until this past year, when she became the Countess of Malibu. That is what I call her now. We stopped having our Wednesday-night dinners and going shopping together whenever one of us was in a bad mood. Now she's always at some event or luncheon because everyone is trying to kiss her ass because she's *my* mom."

"That sucks."

"Yeah, I know. We haven't talked since I moved out here two weeks ago. It's for the best. I can't wait until I'm not a minor anymore. Then I won't be stuck with all these old farts poking and prodding at me. Like Bert. And that ancient Eleanor. She pops her head in once in a while and stares at me. Then she runs off and calls my mom to report in. I just want someone

I can trust. I need a new right hand. Will you be it?"

I was blown away. "Wow," I said. "Not only will I be your right hand, I'll be your left hand. I'll be your third hand! I guess that would be weird because no one really has three hands unless they're born that way and—" I grabbed the BlackBerry out of the box. "How do I turn this thing on?" I said.

Sabrina smiled and pressed the button on the bottom right corner. The screen flashed on and it lit up our faces.

"Take it with you wherever you go," she said. "From now on, we're attached at the hip."

"I promise," I said. "Everywhere I go, it's by my side."

* * *

That night, I showed off my new BlackBerry to my parents. I passed it around the dining-room table while we dug into the dinner my mom made—two pies. One with meatballs and mozzarella and the other stuffed with spinach and artichoke hearts.

"Geez," my dad said, turning the device over in his hand. "You're more technically savvy than I am."

I told them I had no idea how to use it yet but that I would read the instruction manual before I went to sleep that night. Then I asked them for some advice.

"Friday is Sabrina's birthday," I said. "Do you think I should get her a gift? Or is it weird for an intern to give a present? I mean, she gave me this BlackBerry. But it's not really like she picked it out for me."

"I don't think you need to get her a gift," my dad said. "I'm sure she doesn't expect one." He took the last gulp from his glass of soda.

"I think it would make a nice gesture," my mom said.

"Obviously it would make be a nice gesture," my dad said. "But I'm saying that it isn't *necessary.*"

"I just want to do the right thing," I said.

"Get a gift. It shows how thoughtful you are," my mom assured me.

"What is she supposed to get her?" my dad asked. "It's probably not easy buying a gift for someone famous. They have everything."

"Just get a little token. It's a nice way to establish a warm connection between the two of them," my mom explained to my dad. "Lily, you can bring her one of my pies if you want. What did you think of them, by the way?"

"I love them," I said. "Especially the artichoke one."

"Have you sold any yet?" my dad said.

"Not quite yet," my mom said. "But we're still in the developmental phase."

✳ ✳ ✳

The next few days, Sabrina began texting me on the Black-Berry. Sometimes if Bert or Eleanor were in the same room as us, she would get a kick out of sending me an electronic message making fun of them.

After work on Thursday, I decided to pick up something nice for Sabrina. My mom had more of a natural flair for social graces than my dad, so I went with her advice.

I went to the Shakespeare & Company bookstore near my house. A saleswoman came over to help me. I asked her to recommend the newest and coolest coffee-table book.

The woman took me over to the new-releases section and showed me an impressive book called *Hollywood Stars &*

Rebels. It was filled with rarely seen photographs of old-time Hollywood icons. The book was very expensive, but I decided to use a chunk of my allowance that I had saved up. After all, I didn't want Sabrina to think I was cheap.

The saleswoman wrapped the book up in silver paper with a white ribbon, and I headed home. I have to say, I was proud of myself. This book weighed a ton and it was filled with cool photographs, like one of Marlon Brando playing the bongos, Steve McQueen driving a motorcycle, and Katharine Hepburn riding her bicycle through the studio lot. I was sure Sabrina would like it.

*　＊　＊　＊*

The next day when I showed up to the suite, Sabrina was going over the script for Antonio's movie. I gave her the wrapped present and she opened it.

"This is dope on a rope," she said, thanking me. She started to flip through the book.

"I also brought you a pie," I said. My mom had woken up early to make it before I left for the Mercer. "It's a vegetable pie with tomatoes and mushrooms."

"Sounds interesting," Sabrina said.

Just then there was a knock on the door. It was the bellhop with a huge bouquet of roses. Sabrina took the card from the flower arrangement. She read it and her face lit up.

"How sweet that they remembered," Sabrina said.

When she put the card down, I had a chance to glance at it. My eyeballs almost shot out of my head when I saw which celebrity couple it was from.

From that moment on, presents arrived for her all day.

My assignment was to make a list of who sent her each present and what the gift was.

Bronson, Valerie, and Nikki came at noon to take Sabrina out for lunch. I was instructed by Sabrina to stay behind to record her present deliveries. While Sabrina showed off her gifts to the girls, Bronson came over to me.

"Working hard?" he said.

"Have you ever seen so many presents?" I said.

"It looks like a department store in here." Then Bronson scratched the back of his head. "Hey," he said, lowering his voice, "we're going to the best place in Little Italy for lunch. Do you want me to pick you up something?"

I shook my head. "No, that's okay. Thanks."

"How about I bring you back a surprise?"

I felt touched, but I knew that wouldn't go over well with Sabrina. I grabbed a piece of torn wrapping paper off the floor so I didn't have to look him in the eye. "No, please. I hate surprises," I said, fibbing. "You don't have to do that."

"But I want to," Bronson said.

I glanced at Sabrina. She was still busy showcasing her gifts. "You *do*?" I said.

"Just you wait and see," he said, teasing me. Then he walked over to join Sabrina. "Ready to go?"

"We're out of here," Sabrina said, grabbing her oversized sunglasses and running out the door.

As soon as everyone left, I began typing up the "Birthday Gifts Received" list that Sabrina had asked me to create. I never imagined that some people got so many extravagant presents on their birthday. It blew my mind.

Here is an excerpt from the list. (I couldn't print the exact names of the celebrities because of the confidentiality agreement I signed. But I did grade the famous people A through D to give some idea of their caliber.)

A-list actress and her husband—five dozen red roses the size of footballs

B-list actor—leather bracelets from Fred Segal

D-list actress—the *Hollywood Stars & Rebels* coffee-table book (Ugh! Sound familiar?)

B+-list rock star—a six-foot-tall cactus plant with a red ribbon around it

The prime minister of Nigeria—a tablecloth

The mayor of Los Angeles—a handwritten note on his official stationery

A prince from Morocco—a silver spoon with Sabrina's initials on it

Valerie and Nikki—a gift certificate for spa services at Delicious Beauty Bar

Bronson—a Tiffany necklace with a star pendant and the letter S engraved on it

Bert—a Prada bag

Crazy Eddie—a selection of fine teas and tonics

Violetta—a designer T-shirt that said IF ONLY YOU COULD BE ME

The concierge at the Mercer Hotel—a huge gift basket filled with oranges, apples, and pears

Sabrina's mom—a pretty yellow dress (When Sabrina opened the present, she smiled to herself. I could tell that she liked the dress but didn't want to admit it. "Yellow was my favorite color *last* year," she said as she threw it in the drawer of her nightstand.)

* * *

When everyone returned from lunch, Sabrina, Valerie, Nikki, and Bronson sat around Sabrina's bedroom laughing and listening to music. Bronson came into the living room and passed me a small package wrapped in tin foil. I went into the bathroom and locked myself inside. Slowly, I unwrapped the foil to find hidden inside of it the most perfect looking cannoli. I took a bite. I wanted to enjoy it slowly, but I knew I had to eat it fast in case the phone rang with more deliveries for Sabrina. So I shoved almost the entire cannoli in my mouth at once. It was so delicious, and it tasted even better because it came from Bronson.

* * *

That afternoon after her friends left, Sabrina asked me to help her with the thank-you cards. I would go down the list and tell her the name of the person and what they gave her. Then she would handwrite a note in a silver pen on pale, pink paper.

"That's my signature style," she said. "Whenever someone gets a pink envelope with silver writing, they know it's from me."

I started reading names off the list and what present they gave her. When I got to the bottom of the list, I said, "And, of course, your mom sent you that pretty yellow dress."

"Oh, yeah," she said. "I don't need to send a thank-you note to my mom. Take her off the list."

After Sabrina had completed her thank-you notes, she sat

back in the desk chair. She shook her wrist because it hurt from writing so many letters. Then she said, "It's hard getting a million presents because now I have to remember all of their birthdays, too. Or else I look like a jerk."

As the last task of the day, Sabrina asked me to help her organize the gifts into three categories: 1. To keep; 2. To return for store credit; and 3. To regift. We piled them into groupings on one side of the living room.

After cleaning up the tons of loose wrapping paper thrown across the floor, I called the concierge and asked them to send a bellhop upstairs to take away our excess garbage. Sabrina told me to tip him with some money from the petty-cash purse. When the bellhop arrived I handed him the trash and a twenty-dollar bill. Then I walked back into living room. I was shocked to see that both copies of *Hollywood Stars & Rebels* had moved from the To Keep pile to the To Regift pile. Sabrina must have moved them when I was out of the room and wasn't looking. I have to admit, it was a bit heart-wrenching to see there was no sentimental value attached to my present.

I said good night to Sabrina, and on my way out of the lobby, I bumped into Valerie and Nikki. They were both wearing party dresses with their black bra straps peeking out.

"Not upstairs yet!" Valerie said, directing a messenger who was carrying a bouquet of turquoise and white balloons. "Here, just let me take them." She took the balloon bouquet from the man, accidentally whacking me in the face with one of them. It was the most amazing arrangement of balloons I had ever seen. One balloon had sequin studs pasted on it. Another one was in the shape of a flower. And in the center-piece was a gigantic swan made up of white balloons.

Valerie turned to a messenger carrying a two-tiered chocolate cake with fudge roses. "And you," she told him, "bring the cake straight back to the kitchen."

"Make sure it goes in the fridge or the flowers will melt," Nikki said as the messenger walked away.

"Hi, guys," I said. "What amazing balloons. Are they for Sabrina's—?"

"Shhh!" Valerie said sharply. "You should never *ever* say *her* name in public. You should always call her 'S.'"

"Why?" I asked.

"To protect her privacy! Duh!" Valerie said. I watched as her pouty, plum-lined lips opened in awe at my apparent stupidity.

"Yeah," Nikki said, chiming in, shaking her blonde ponytail. "You'd be surprised. Before we started using the code name, a terrible thing happened. I was on the steps of the Metropolitan Museum of Art talking with Valerie about how S bought her first water bra, and it ended up on Page Six."

"How mortifying," I said. "I bet Sabrina—I mean, S— must have been upset."

"You better believe it. From then on, we made a pact to protect her privacy," Valerie said, cracking her knuckles loudly.

"Got it," I said. "Thanks for the warning. I'll be more careful in the future."

"So," Nikki said, "are you going tonight?" She swung her blonde ponytail in the air so it bopped up and down. "It's going to be so much—"

I noticed Valerie quickly nudge Nikki in the arm, and she stopped talking mid-sentence.

"Going where?" I asked.

"Going home to rest," Valerie said. "If you're going to be S's intern, you're gonna have to keep up. She doesn't stop for anyone."

"Yeah," Nikki said. "Remember to wear comfortable shoes!"

"No heels, high boots, or stilettos," Valerie said.

"Only sneakers, flats, and wedges," Nikki added.

"Thanks for the advice, guys!" I said.

"No prob," Valerie said. "Well, gotta run. Bye." Then she turned to Nikki. "Come on, chica, we have tons to do!"

"Ta-ta!" Nikki said, blowing me a kiss in the air. And then they were off, leaving me in the dust of the swan balloons.

Chapter 8

WHEN I GOT HOME, my dad was off teaching at Columbia and my mom was busy cooking in the kitchen with her best friend, Diane. The apartment smelled like apricots and sausages.

"Hi, Miss Thing," Diane said when she saw me. "I heard you're hobnobbing with the rich and famous."

"It's a tough job, but someone's gotta do it," I said. "How's the new business going?" I said.

"Great," my mom said. "We spent today making flyers."

"Then we dropped them off at restaurants and gourmet shops in the neighborhood," Diane said.

"We're going to call it Pies & Surprise," my mom said. "Because it's not always what you expect beneath the crust. It's all about mixing and matching unexpected ingredients. What do you think?"

"Catchy," I said. Then I excused myself to my room. The meat aromas were so potent I felt like I was in a smokehouse.

I sat at my desk and decided to read Taylor's letter again. I had pinned it to my cork board. This time I looked it over more carefully. There was a return address on the back of the envelope for a street called Lime Orchard Lane in Morristown, New Jersey. I also recognized that the area code of the phone number—973—was legitimate for New Jersey. This was definitely not a psychopath in the Nebraskan woods. I guess it could still be a psychopath in the New Jersey woods, though.

I tried to listen to my instincts, and something deep inside me told me this was real. Taylor was an actual girl who needed help and somehow saw hope in a celebrity. This was my chance to touch someone else's life, the way Sabrina did every day on the screen.

I sat on my bed and looked out the window. They had posted a billboard for Sabrina's movie across the street. There was her face staring back at me now. I looked at the poster and the name of the film—*Spinning the Wheel of Fire*. In the movie, Sabrina's character went after what was important to her. She said "F-it" to convention and chased her dreams of being a volunteer firefighter. She took a huge risk, and by doing that, she discovered excitement and success.

Maybe somehow this billboard—with Sabrina's eyeballs the size of SUVs—was an omen calling to me. It was saying, "Spin the wheel, Lily, baby! Spin it!"

I grabbed the note and read it one more time. "I don't know who else to turn to. . . . It's really urgent. I feel so alone. I don't know how much longer I can take this. . . ."

Seven numbers and an area code were all that separated us now. She was that close. I let my fingers begin dialing. 1–9–7–3. Then I stopped. I couldn't. I didn't dare. I was out of my mind. What was I thinking?

Besides, what would I say? I would have to impersonate Sabrina's voice and expressions. I hadn't even practiced yet.

I looked in the mirror and listened to myself. I made my

voice sound extra perky, a little huskier, and more confident. "Hi, this is Sabrina," I practiced. "I got the letter."

I snatched my phone again. This time I dialed the numbers on the keypad. The other line began to ring. *Brrring. Brrring. Brrring.* I was on a roller coaster now. The seats were locked and I was going for the ride.

A woman picked up. "Hello," the voice said.

"Hi," I said. "I'm looking to speak to Taylor.'"

The woman sighed loudly. "Not again," she said. "I asked you to please stop calling. Stop calling and torturing my little girl."

"I'm not calling to torture your little—"

The woman cut me off. "If only all you kids would just leave her alone. Stop calling here. Last night you woke us up at three A.M."

"Please listen to me," I said. I could tell she was mistaking me for a prank caller. "I just want to talk to Taylor for a second."

"I'm not falling for this again," the woman said. "Last time I gave her the phone, one of you said her face looked like it had been whacked in with a frying pan."

"That wasn't me," I tried to explain. "I swear—"

Suddenly I heard a man's nasal voice in the background. "Is that one of the birdcallers?" he asked her.

"It's one of them," the mom said to him.

"Give me that," the man said. I could hear the phone changing hands now.

"Listen up," the man said. "I went to Radio Shack today and bought a voice recorder. I'm setting it up as we speak and if any of you call here again, I'm going to tape every rotten thing you say and turn it in to the police. You hear me?

You deserve to be locked up in one of those juvenile prisons and—"

I hung up the phone. I could feel my pulse racing. I wasn't prepared to have to fight my way through a blockade of over-protective parents. I would have to approach this situation much more carefully.

At least now I knew the letter wasn't a complete fake. Kids *were* phoning Taylor's house and terrorizing her with prank calls, tormenting her with names and making fun of her.

I wondered if Taylor had heard her parents yelling at me and was now lying in her bed afraid to fall asleep. If only she really knew who was on the other end of the line. It wasn't the real Sabrina, of course. But I was one degree away from Sabrina. And that meant I was pretty close.

Chapter 9

THE NEXT WEEK OF work started off with a loud beeping sound coming from my purse. I zipped open my pocketbook and took out my BlackBerry. I squinted my eyes as I looked at the screen. It was a message from Sabrina.

> STRLT4EVER: Leaving for costume fitting in 10 minutes. Meet me in Mercer Lobby NOW.

I looked at the clock. It was 8:50 A.M. My alarm hadn't gone off. I threw on a sundress, ran a brush through my hair, and sprayed on cucumber body spray. There was no way I could be at the Mercer within ten minutes. I was on the Upper East Side, and she was all the way down in Soho.

I tried calling her cell phone but she didn't pick up.

"Bye, Dad! Bye, Mom! I'm crazy late!" I yelled to them as I ran out the door.

Downstairs, I hailed a cab on the corner. We headed downtown, but around 79th and Lexington Avenue, we ran into gridlock traffic.

"Oh, no," I said to the cab driver. "Couldn't you have gone a quicker way?"

"This is the best route," the cab driver insisted.

My BlackBerry went off again.

STRLT4EVER: Need to leave in 2 minutes. Are you my right hand or not? You promised you were my right hand!

I wrote back.

L332203: Sorry. Stuck in traffic. Be there ASAP. Sorry!

She wrote back immediately.

STRLT4EVER: Whatever! Do whatever you have to do to get here. I HAVE TO LEAVE!

The cab cut over to Park Avenue and we sailed down to Soho. I gave the driver a wad of cash as we pulled up to the front of the hotel. I ran inside. Bert was sitting eating eggs benedict at the corner table of the Mercer Kitchen. He was wearing a linen shirt, and I could see tendrils of chest hair peeking out over the top button.

"Look who it is," he said, as I walked over.

"Sorry I'm late. I came as fast as I could. There was so much traffic."

"It happens," he said, cutting into one of his eggs so that the yolk melted down over the English muffin.

"Did she already leave for the costume fitting?"

"You missed her," he said, looking around to make sure no one was listening. "We need to talk, darling. What happened this past Friday night? You can tell me."

I gave him a blank stare.

"Sabrina's suite was trashed," he said. "There was choco-late cake smudged all over the mirror. The bedsheets were practically hanging off the ceiling. There were balloons tied to the showerhead and a tomato pie smashed on the floor. So why don't you tell me what happened?"

I couldn't believe my mom's hard work had ended up splattered on the carpet. "I have no idea," I said. "I wasn't with Sabrina on Friday night."

Bert looked at me, trying to decipher if I was telling the truth. "It's okay. You can talk to me. I'm on your side. Now, tell me everything."

"But Bert, I wasn't there. I promise," I said.

"The concierge said a bunch of their regular hotel guests complained that music was blasting from Sabrina's suite until four A.M. I've spent all weekend apologizing to them and promising it will never happen again."

"What would you like me to do?" I asked.

"You told me that you would keep me in the loop. Come get me. Call me if Sabrina is being self-destructive. If you don't tell me these things, then you are of no use—do you understand? Don't you get it?"

"I told you already. I will let you know if I see anything, but I wasn't there Friday night. I don't know what else to tell you. Give me a chance."

"I'll give you the benefit of the doubt. But you already have an imperfect record. The dog incident, the press-junket blunder, and now this." He took a sip from his coffee mug and leaned casually back in his chair. "Are you sure you can handle the responsibilities of this internship?"

"Definitely. I'm still learning the ropes, but I know I have what it takes."

"I'll keep my eye on you. If you don't get better soon, I

may have to suggest to Sabrina that we come up with another arrangement."

"What are you saying?" I asked.

"A lot of other girls wanted this position. My best friend's neighbor's niece, Annabelle, is one of them. She's a straight-A student and head of the yearbook committee at her school. She'd be here in a nanosecond."

"But I'm doing a good job," I said. "And I've only just begun." I wasn't going to completely back down.

"We'll see how good a job you do," he said. "Just remember, Lily. You are replaceable."

Just then I noticed Bronson across the lobby. He was walking toward us.

"Bronson," Bert hollered to him. "Show Lily where this costume fitting is. She was late, so Sabrina had to leave without her."

"Yeah, no problem," Bronson said.

"We'll talk more later," Bert said to me as I walked off with Bronson.

As soon as we got out of earshot, I turned to Bronson. "Thanks for saving me," I said. "Bert and his hairy chest were starting to freak me out."

"I'll tell you what's starting to freak me out—my stomach," Bronson said. "I feel terrible. I barely slept this weekend and I ate about ten steak burritos."

"What on earth happened Friday night?" I asked him. "Bert was giving me the third degree."

"Surprise birthday party for Sabrina."

"Don't you mean for S?"

"I don't buy into that pretentious crap. Why didn't you show up?"

"Wasn't invited," I said, looking away.

"The Strap Girls planned it," Bronson said. "They probably forgot to mention it."

"What do you mean, 'the Strap Girls'?"

"That's my secret nickname for Valerie and Nikki because they're always wearing tank tops with their bra straps showing."

I remembered running into the Strap Girls in the lobby on Friday. They didn't "forget" anything. It was obvious they didn't want me around.

"No, I think Valerie doesn't like me for some reason," I said as Bronson and I walked down the street. "And Nikki just follows her."

"Don't let it bug you," Bronson said, walking beside me. "Valerie's my least favorite of Sabrina's friends. She is probably just jealous because she feels like you're moving in on her territory. She doesn't like sharing Sabrina with other people, or having new people around." Bronson stopped outside of a Xerox store. "I need to pick something up here quick, okay?"

I nodded and followed him inside.

Bronson paid the cashier, who handed him papers in a plastic bag.

"Hey, I want to know what you think of this," Bronson said to me.

He took a white book held together by black binding out of the plastic bag and handed it to me. I opened up the book. On each page were typed lyrics from different songs.

"A little something extra for Sabrina, a belated part of her b-day gift. I put together a book of lyrics from my favorite songs," he said. "Then I wrote on each page what the song meant to me and how it reminded me of her."

I turned the pages of the book. On one page were the song lyrics to Led Zeppelin's "Thank You." In the margin next to it, he wrote about hearing it the day they met while he was surfing at Point Dume in Malibu. The song was playing on a car stereo in the parking lot.

"The day I met her, she was sunbathing on the beach with Val and Nikki. It's actually on this strip of sand where they filmed the beginning of the movie *Grease*. I came out of the water from surfing with some buddies and noticed her. She was wearing this iridescent silver bikini. I really wanted to talk to her, but I didn't want to be cheesy and go over to her. Because of who she is, you know. Anyway, we ran into each other in the parking lot. I was loading my board on top of my buddy's car and she walked over to me and said 'Hey surf boy, wanna party tonight in The Hills?' I guess the rest is history."

"Wow," I said. "This is so cool."

"Anyway, I like to do little things once in a while to surprise her. I hope she likes this."

"Of course she will. It's really personal. She's going to be psyched."

"I hope so. I've just never dated anyone quite like her before . . . and sometimes she's hard to please. Especially lately. Like nothing's ever good enough."

"Don't be ridiculous," I told him. "If a guy gave me a book like this, I'd be in ecstasy."

"Really?" Bronson said.

I nodded.

"Good," he said. "I hope she feels the same way."

He gave me a smile and for a moment I felt like I was going to fall over.

I wanted so badly to tell him about Taylor's letter and get his advice. This seemed like a perfect opportunity. But I wasn't sure if I could trust him yet.

I had to remember to call Taylor again. Next time, however, when her parents answered the phone, I would say Sabrina's name immediately and then *plead* for them not to hang up and to put Taylor on the phone.

We took the subway to Quixote Studios. When we got there, the security guard at the front desk had us sign in and gave us nametags. Then we went down a long hallway.

Sabrina ran into the hallway dressed in a jean skirt and a blue-checkered blouse. She saw us, smiled, and sprinted toward us.

"What do you think of this costume?" she said, throwing her arms around Bronson.

"Very sexy," Bronson said, then he kissed her on the lips.

Sabrina turned to me. "You're late. What happened to you?"

"I'm really sorry. My alarm didn't go off in time."

"Set more than one alarm. You should always have one that is battery operated, too, in case the electricity goes out." Then Sabrina whispered in my ear. "Do you think this costume makes me look fat?" She spun around in a circle.

"Not at all," I said. The outfit fit her perfectly. In fact, it made her look too skinny. Her ribs were poking out. For the first time, I could see why Bert was worried about her weight.

"You can't see any cellulite, can you?"

"You don't have any cellulite!" I said.

"If you saw me naked, you would see I have two little cellulite bubbles on my upper back thighs."

"I don't believe it," I told her.

"Which reminds me—I need you to do me a favor." She reached into her petty-cash purse and handed me some money. "There's this new diet pill I want to try. It's really just an herb. Crazy Eddie told me about it this morning."

Bronson was listening in. "Babe, you don't need that stuff," he said, interrupting.

"Shush up," Sabrina said, turning to him.

"You look great already. I think it's hot when girls have some curves."

"Bronson, the camera puts on ten pounds and I know what I need to do."

Bronson gave up. He walked over to a water cooler on the side of the room and filled up a paper cup. Sabrina continued giving me instructions. "They sell it at this fruit-and-vegetable bodega in the East Village on Ninth Street and Third Avenue. Pick me up some today."

"What's it called?" I asked.

"Tinyachea. Oh, and they sell it on the down low because it hasn't been passed by the president of the Health Association—or whatever that association is called."

"Are you sure those pills are all right for you? They sound dangerous."

"You both are driving me up a wall. I'll be fine. Just tell the person at the cashier you want to buy some 'Little T,' and they'll hook you up."

Sabrina led us into the main dressing room. She showed us the racks of costumes she had been trying on. A few women were busy tailoring costumes. They looked up and smiled at us from where they sat, hovering over their sewing machines. A few other stylists milled around the room, hanging up clothes and marking them with Sabrina's name. I recognized a few of the ladies from the day of my interview in the Mercer suite.

"So did you guys come here together?" Sabrina asked.

"Yeah," Bronson said. "Bert asked me to show her where you were."

"So you came here together," Sabrina said, throwing me a look. "How adorable."

I could tell she was annoyed. And suspicious. Then she stopped in front of one outfit—a rainbow snow cone–colored dress with three tiers of ruffles.

"I can't decide if I like this costume they want me to wear," she said. "I need to see how it looks on someone else. You know, get an objective perspective."

"But I'm not the same size as you," I said, trying to get out of it.

"Doesn't matter. I just want to get the idea. I have a wonderful imagination."

Sabrina took the dress off the rack and handed it to me. "You should try it on," she said, ushering me into the dressing room. "That way I can see if it's nice."

I went inside and tried the dress on. It was extremely short. It was also a size two, and I couldn't fit into it. I tried to close up the zipper, and I zipped up part of my skin.

"Ow!" I screamed.

"Is everything okay in there?" Sabrina asked.

"Fine!" I said. I could see through the slit in the curtain. Sabrina and Bronson were on the couch. She had just opened up his gift and was thumbing through the pages of song lyrics. She did not seem very impressed by his gift but then quickly tried to cover it by throwing her arms around him and screaming, "I love it, pumpkin face! I love it! I love it!"

I turned toward the mirror. I looked ridiculous. I couldn't go out there dressed like this. It was humiliating to model this outfit in front of Sabrina, let alone Bronson.

"Come on! Let's see it!" Sabrina hollered out.

"Umm, it doesn't really fit," I said over the curtain.

"Come on out," Sabrina said. "I'm sure you look fantastic."

I felt as if I had no choice. I had signed on to help her through thick and thin. I would just have to suck it up.

I took one last look in the mirror and pulled down the dress as far as possible—which wasn't very far at all. I looked at my legs. I had stubble. I hadn't shaved in a few days. I looked at my arms. They looked nowhere near as sculpted and polished as Sabrina's. I looked like I was a teenager shoved into a first-grader's party dress.

I pulled apart the curtain slowly and walked out. Bronson and Sabrina just stared at me. Then she ran over and gave me a big hug.

"Thank you, Lily! Thank you so much!"

"You're welcome . . . ?" I said.

"You have saved me from making the huge mistake of wearing that dress myself! Isn't it just hideous! It's atrocious, isn't it, Bronson?"

I looked over at Bronson. He shrugged his shoulders. "I'm gonna grab a soda from the machine."

I felt like "grabbing a soda" was Bronson's way of having mercy on me and saving me from another moment of this humiliation.

"Grab me a soda, too," Sabrina said. Then she turned to me. "Lily, if you want, you can have some of my diet pills when you pick them up. I'll be more than happy to share them with you," she said sweetly.

"It's okay," I told her just as warmly. "I wouldn't want to take any of them from you."

She never stopped smiling as I walked back into the fitting room. It was like a big wide-open fake smile. I couldn't believe that Bronson just saw me dressed like that. Now he would probably have a picture in his head of me as a pale weirdo with stubble on my legs, and he would carry that picture with him in his mind forever.

Sabrina continued trying on different outfits and spending time with the stylists who played around with her hair and makeup.

"The camera washes everybody out," Sabrina explained to me. "So they need to put on more makeup than usual so people don't look like corpses on the screen."

I watched as one of the makeup artists did Sabrina's eyes. First she applied cover-up to the lid, followed by blue eye shadow, and then painting on brown eyeliner with an angled brush.

"Look how that makes your eyes pop," the stylist said, excited.

"They look really good," Bronson agreed.

Sabrina looked in the mirror. "Actually, I'd prefer a different shade of blue and dark liner on the bottom."

When the makeup artist stepped away, Sabrina whispered in my ear. "I've learned you have to look out for yourself. Or they'll do whatever they want. Ultimately, it's my face on the screen so I need to protect myself. Got it?"

I nodded. Finally, after an hour of stressing over different colors and shades, we left Quixote Studios. Outside, Bronson said good-bye to me and Sabrina to go home and write. He was working on a scene and he wanted to e-mail it to his screenwriter dad by the end of the day for feedback.

Sabrina handed me a list of things to do. Then she ran off to meet her personal trainer, Lorenzo, for a workout. I read over her note:

Lily,

Pls. do the following for me:

1. Bring Mercedes to the Little Guy Groomers for a shampoo and haircut. Make sure they clip his nails. They didn't last time!

2. Pick up goat's milk from the health food store on Ninth and Broadway.

3. Make appointments for me using my pseudonym "Victoria Champagne" for the following private services at Delicious Beauty Bar (spa to the stars): A. toe-hair waxing; B. laser-hair removal of happy

trail; and C. "facial for down there" using the birthday gift certificate Valerie and Nikki gave me.

4. Buy a present for Crazy Eddie's birthday. Something unique and personal.

5. Order me all the music on the top 100 Billboard
charts. I need some new tunes to work out to!

6. Call Samantha at the Dior store on Fifth Ave. and
have her send me some more A-line miniskirts.

7. Get Bronson and me tickets to the Yankees game
next Monday night. The seats must be above the
Yankee dugout in the first two rows ONLY.

8. Order me new cross-trainer sneakers. Size 7.

9. Tell my pseudo-guardian Eleanor to stop looking
through my drawers! And to stop leaving her huge,
plastic Monday-through-Sunday-labeled pillbox on
my bathroom sink! Yuck!

xoxo,
Sabrina

Her demands kept me busy the rest of the week. I was
worn out and exhausted when the weekend finally rolled
around.

Chapter 10

THAT SATURDAY, IT SANK in how much I really missed my friends. It was sometimes fun hanging out with my parents, but a girl needs her bosom buddies. Evie and my other best ladies were away from the city for another five weeks. None of the usual suspects were around to grab frozen yogurt, go to the movies, or hang out in Central Park's Sheep's Meadow watching the cute boys play Frisbee.

That Sunday afternoon, I walked through the lobby and saw my favorite doorman, Damien. He mentioned that his son, Junior, was asking about me and really wanted to make plans. He handed me Junior's cell number on a piece of paper, and I went upstairs.

Then something odd happened. I actually began contemplating giving Junior a call and asking him to hang out. Yeah, his breath did smell like sour-cream-and-onion potato chips, but at least it was someone for me to have a little weekend teenage social interaction with.

I went to bed early that night to rest up for my fourth full week of the internship. In the morning, I took the subway down to the Mercer. I had taken care of almost everything on Sabrina's master list. Mercedes got a wonderful haircut at Little Guy Groomers, and I remembered to make sure they clipped his toenails. I stocked the fridge in her suite with tons of goat's milk, picked up the Tinyachea pills (despite the fact that I didn't think she needed them), ordered the latest model of Adidas cross-trainers, picked up every album from the Billboard Top 100, got Samantha to messenger over seven adorable A-line skirts from Dior, and asked Eleanor as kindly as possible (per Sabrina's request) to no longer leave her huge pillbox labeled with the days of the week on the bathroom sink. I could tell she was embarrassed because she said, "Sometimes when you get older, you forget where you leave things." I couldn't get up the nerve to tell Eleanor not to go through Sabrina's drawers, but I crossed it off the master list anyway. I got Crazy Eddie's birthday present. I came up with the very original idea of getting him a real live goat. I ordered it through a charity that sends the animal to a needy family in the developing world and provides Crazy Eddie with a donation certificate in the mail. Sabrina thought this was a great idea, and she sent Crazy Eddie a handwritten happy-birthday note telling him about it using a silver pen on her pale pink stationery. Also, I made Sabrina's appointment for Monday (today) at Delicious Beauty Bar to receive her secret spa treatments.

There was only one thing on the list that I had trouble tracking down. As soon as I arrived at the suite, I decided I had better tell Sabrina.

"About those Yankee tickets . . ." I said.

Sabrina was getting ready to take off for the spa. "Yeah, I want hard copies. What time will they be messengered here? The game starts tonight at seven. So I want them here by four o'clock at the latest."

It was hard breaking the news to her. "They're sold out in the sections that you wanted."

"Come again?" Sabrina said, throwing her electric key card in her purse and slipping into her Prada flip-flops.

"I couldn't get the tickets. Other people have already bought them. I could get you tickets in a different section."

She started laughing at me. "No, that's not the way it works. Do you know how embarrassing it would look if I wasn't sitting in the best section? Did you even tell them who the tickets were for?"

I shook my head. "I didn't," I admitted.

"Don't you think that would have been intelligent?"

"I was just protecting your privacy. I didn't know if you wanted me to name-drop."

"There is a time and a place for name-dropping. And this would be one of those times." Sabrina looked at me, annoyed. "I told Bronson I have a surprise for him tonight. If you don't get me these tickets, you are going to ruin my romantic date with Bronson."

"I called the box office. I called other ticket companies around the city. They told me those are some of the most popular tickets. They sell out before the season even starts. Some of them are held by season ticket holders, too."

"I want you to get on the phone now with one of the Yankee team managers and get me those tickets. I can't believe you are telling me this at the last minute. I'm about to run out the door to get a 'facial down there,' and you are dropping this bomb on me."

I hurried over to the desk and picked up the phone. Bert had downloaded Sabrina's electronic address book into my

BlackBerry last week so I now had a complete Rolodex of her contacts. I began searching under the word "Yankees."

"Billy Lopez," Sabrina said.

"Who's that?" I asked.

"My contact at the Yankees. Call him now and make it happen."

"Uh, okay. Sorry," I said. "I am getting right, um, on it." Sabrina's wrath was starting to shake me up.

"And don't stutter on the phone like that. You have to use charm to get what you want in this world. I am going to get on the extension by the bed and listen in to the way you handle this. You have to flirt a little. 'Hi, Billy, I'm Sabrina Snow's intern. I have a big, big, big favor to ask you, pretty please. I heard you are the coolest manager in Yankee Stadium. I just need two tickets tonight above the dugout for Sabrina. It would mean so much to her. You're the best.'"

I sat by the desk and dialed the number. Sabrina grabbed the phone by the bed and listened in.

A man's voice picked up on the other line. "This is Billy," he said, sounding all business.

"Hi, is this, uh, Billy Lopez?" I asked.

"Yeah, I just told you that," Billy said. "How can I help you?"

Sabrina glared at me.

I took a deep breath and then tried to turn up my charm volume. I just had to pretend I was playing a role like Sabrina does in the movies.

"My name is Lily. I'm Sabrina Snow's intern."

"Oh, how is she?" His voice warmed up. "Send her my love."

"I will," I told him. "Look, she's trying to get some tickets for the game tonight. If it's not too much of a hassle, do you, uh, mind getting her two?"

I looked over at Sabrina. She was shaking her head in adamant disapproval and biting her lip.

"Be charming or else—" Sabrina fiercely whispered to me.

I forced myself to get over my nerves. "Billy," I said, lightening up my tone, "I know it's a big, big, big favor, but I would appreciate it if you could help me out. Pretty please. Sabrina would adore you forever."

"Just tell me what she needs. Her wish is my command," Billy said.

"Two tickets by the dugout in the first two rows."

"They're hers," he said, and agreed to messenger them over to the Mercer right away.

"Thanks a million," I told him. Then I hung up.

Sabrina hung up her phone receiver, as well. "Okay. Better," she said. "But being charismatic is a skill you still need to work on. See, you are my first line of defense. You deal with the world for me. Therefore, you represent me. If you act dorky or awkward, it reflects badly on me. If you act cool and smooth, it makes me look great." Sabrina looked at the clock.

"I'm out of here," she said, heading for the door. "Stay on top of those tickets."

Alone in the suite, I realized I had just become Sabrina's marionette. I was like a dummy and she was pulling the strings and telling me what to say.

But maybe I needed a lesson on how to speak with more ease and charm. Perhaps the ability to be a smooth talker and BS had become a vital skill in today's society. If so, Sabrina had just helped me develop an important ability that I was lacking.

Perhaps charm and BS skills would be important when writing my college essay, and the title I had been throwing around in my head, "A Summer of Inspiration," wasn't enough of a head-turner. I needed something eye-catching, like "Uncensored: Forty Days with a Starlet—Sweat, Tears, and Charm." A title like that would really wake up the members of the Brown admissions committee.

That afternoon, I met with Michelle, the assistant of Antonio, the director of Sabrina's upcoming cowgirl movie. She was a sophomore in college and was working for Antonio just for the summer. Bert brought her upstairs and introduced her to me.

"I need you both to go over Sabrina's schedule for the next few weeks. Then when you're done, I want you to show me a copy," Bert said, taking off and leaving us alone.

"First things first," Michelle said. "Let's order lunch." She grabbed the hotel menu. "I'm starving."

We ordered up room service, and Michelle said she had permission to stick it on Antonio's credit card. It felt very nice to be treated to lunch.

Michelle told me she was enjoying working for Antonio because he was so passionate about film. She said he had his own eccentricities, though. For example, he farted when they were alone together, he only liked eating raw foods, and he insisted on having at least ten small-pointed black fountain pens at his disposal at all times.

I told her how paranoid Sabrina was about spies, but how there was some truth to it because her strange guardian,

Eleanor, snooped through her drawers, and Bert insisted on knowing all about Sabrina's social life. Then I picked up the silver frame on Sabrina's bureau and showed Michelle the doodled picture of Max naked.

"I did it myself!" I confessed, laughing. "And she framed it because she thinks my friend drew it and might be famous one day."

Michelle laughed so hard she snorted. Then she started telling me about college life. I was shocked when I found out she went to Brown University.

"Oh my God! Do you love it?" I said.

"It's really great," Michelle said. "I adore not living at home. There are all these great madrigal groups that stand and sing on the street corner. I'm double-majoring in English and theater. And the professors are unbelievable."

It was great to hear about the university from someone who was currently going there. I had heard lots of stories from my grandpa, but he had attended Brown more than fifty years ago and his stories recalled a long-lost time.

While eating our delicious lunch (a three-course meal of shrimp salads, Kobe beef cheeseburgers, and strawberries with whipped cream), Michelle and I went over the scheduling.

"*Ladies of the Wild West* starts filming the first week of September," Michelle said. "But before that, there are additional costume fittings and classes that Sabrina needs to attend, like horseback-riding lessons, Country Western dance classes, and sessions with a speech coach to learn a Southern accent."

Michelle also told me that on the second-to-last Friday of August, Antonio was hosting a party to welcome the cast and crew and introduce everyone to each other before the filming began. He would be throwing the party at a Country Western–themed restaurant called Rodeo Ranch, where there was a sawdust floor, a bluegrass band, and a mechanical bull.

After Michelle and I were done with the calendar, she took off. Bert came upstairs shortly after, and I showed him our work. His kinky hair looked wetter than usual, like he had stuck extra globs of gel into it.

He looked over the schedule and said, "This makes no sense. It's just terrible."

"Michelle and I went over it together, though. She said it looked great."

"Well, it doesn't. You know, Sabrina likes to work out with her trainer for at least two hours every day. You don't leave enough room for that on Wednesday, July twenty-first. And how is she going to get from a fitting downtown all the way up to a dance lesson on the Upper West Side in ten minutes on July twenty-eighth? That doesn't leave much time."

"I'll call Michelle and make the changes. Just let me know what they are."

"No, I'm going to call Antonio and go over this directly with him. If you want something done right in this world, you have to do it yourself."

Bert dropped more bags of fan mail on the desk and left me to address envelopes and sign form letters. I started thinking about Taylor and wondered how she was doing. I hoped the kids from her school hadn't terrorized her lately. I needed to try calling her one more time. Maybe if I used some of my newly acquired phone charm, I could convince her parents that I was Sabrina Snow and they would put Taylor on the line.

Later that afternoon, the Yankee tickets arrived. I picked

them up from the front desk and brought them upstairs. When Sabrina came back from the spa, she grabbed them and stuck them in her purse.

"Oh, here," she said, handing me a piece of paper. "The spa gave me a free gift certificate. You can have it."

I looked at the green slip of paper from Delicious Beauty Bar. "Wow," I said. "I've never had a spa treatment."

"Go get a free massage, haircut, or a facial down there," Sabrina said.

"Thank you," I said. I wondered if she was giving this to me because she felt guilty for giving me a hard time about the Yankee tickets. "I'll really enjoy this. Can I ask you a question, though?"

"Shoot," she said.

"What exactly is a facial down there?"

"They do a bikini wax and then apply a hibiscus peel to make your VG smell like flowers."

"Oh, got it," I said, completely embarrassed now for asking.

"I feel so fresh and clean from head to toe," Sabrina said, dancing around the room.

At the end of the day, Bronson showed up to meet her for their evening out. When she told him she was taking him to the Yankees game, they started making out in her room. I didn't want to disturb them, so I slipped out the front door without saying good-bye.

* * *

At the end of that week, I accompanied Sabrina to the Clare-mont Riding Academy on the Upper West Side. Antonio's assistant, Michelle, had called ahead and arranged lessons with one of their horseback-riding instructors. Michelle had told me that Sabrina was not expected to be an Olympian equestrian, but she had to become familiar with the basics of riding a horse, as there were several horseback-riding scenes in *Ladies of the Wild West.*

As soon as we walked inside the riding academy, I felt as if I was entering a museum. A plaque hanging on the wall read: BUILT IN 1892, THIS BUILDING IS THE OLDEST OPERATING STABLE IN MANHATTAN. On the ground floor, there was a small arena. To the left and right, there were horses tied inside stalls. I was excited to see, in the back corner of the room, an old carriage left over from the horse-and-buggy days.

I had walked past the Claremont Riding Academy many times but had never ventured inside, mostly because of what happened the last time I rode a horse seven years ago with my family in Martha's Vineyard. I had an allergy attack, and my face and arms broke out in nasty hives. It was a long time ago, but I still remember how ugly I looked. I didn't want to tell Sabrina I was allergic to horses because I didn't want to cause a scene. Also, I thought it might make me sound incredibly dorky. I prayed I had outgrown the horse allergy like I had outgrown my allergy to lobster.

A woman came out of one of the stalls and waved. She looked like an overweight hippie with a long, loose salt-and-pepper braid hanging down to her waist.

"Hello, gals," she said. "I'm Pat. I hope you got here all right."

"Oh, yeah," I said. "I've lived in New York my whole life. I knew exactly how to get here."

"I'm not talking about directions." Pat shook her head. "I'm talking getting inside the building. About five men with cameras have been camping outside of here all morning."

"Ugh, paparazzi," Sabrina said. "I can't stand them!" She shook her head in disgust, and her black-and-white-framed sunglasses almost fell off her head.

"How did they know you would be here?" I asked.

"They're like an infestation of cockroaches. They never seem to die and they keep multiplying. See, the paparazzi have all these computer geeks working for them. They drive around in unmarked vans and have high-tech satellite systems that try and hack into our private e-mail exchanges and phone calls. That's why Bert is so good about making sure our e-mails are all on a private, secure computer server. But it's not foolproof. Also, the cockroaches know the hot spots where celebs like to go, and they infiltrate those places. They'll pay big bucks for a juicy tidbit a bellhop overheard while delivering luggage or a waiter caught while eavesdropping and serving breadsticks. Or—" Sabrina stopped as a new idea suddenly occurred to her. "Maybe someone from *here* called one of the magazines directly and let them know that I was coming."

Pat's face contorted in shock at Sabrina's accusation. "Neither I nor anyone else at the Claremont Riding Academy has compromised your privacy. In fact, the owner of the stables came out personally and lied to paparazzi. He told the men outside that you had canceled your appointment with us. It took a lot of convincing, but finally, they believed him," Pat said.

"Kudos to the owner of the stable," Sabrina said, relaxing a bit. "Anyway, let's get started." Sabrina put her hair up under a Yankee baseball cap. It looked brand-new, like she had just bought it at the game this week with Bronson. "I don't want to be flooded with attention while gallivanting on a horse all around Manhattan," she said. "Especially with psychorazzi on the loose."

Pat corrected Sabrina and said, "We will not be gallivanting. We will only be taking one bridal path in Central Park that goes around the reservoir."

Pat taught us how to properly mount a horse and hold both the single and double reins. Then Sabrina and I climbed onto our horses and followed Pat out onto the city streets and then into the park. It felt wonderfully unusual riding a horse through Manhattan. We rode like a lineup of baby chicks—one after the next after the next.

We had just entered the park on 96th Street when I started sniffling. Then I sneezed three times in a row.

"Are you sick?" Sabrina asked me.

"Not at all," I said, secretly wiping my nose on my shirtsleeve.

"Good. Because I can't go catching someone's cold now. I have too much work to do."

We followed Pat onto the bridal path. That is when I started scratching my arm. And there it was—a hive on my left wrist. It looked as if a big, mutant mosquito had bitten me.

Then another itchy sensation. This time on my right tricep. I had to scratch that one, too. And then on my thigh. And then on my right shoulder. And then—the worst of the worst—on my forehead.

I was riding behind Sabrina, and I hoped she wouldn't turn around to see me scratching myself.

"It's important when riding to pay attention to the horse's body language," Pat said. "The way they move their head tells a lot about what they're feeling. They're very humanlike in that way."

A group of little girls on a play date stopped to watch us ride by. They started "ooh"ing and "ahh"ing at seeing horses in the park. Then the girls recognized Sabrina. They got excited and started jumping up and down. Clearly her baseball cap and grungy sweatshirt disguise didn't fool her true fans.

"Mommy, look!" a girl with a red headband screamed as she yanked on her mother's hand. "It's Sabrina Snow!"

"Can we please get your autograph?" the other little girl said.

"How do I stop the horse?" Sabrina asked Pat. "I can't turn these little girls down."

"Just pull the reins tighter," Pat instructed.

We all slowed down for a moment. The girls walked carefully over to the side of Sabrina's horse. The mother handed Sabrina a pen and paper. I watched as Sabrina signed her name, carefully, and dotted the *i* with a star.

Then the girls turned to me. "Can we have your autograph, too?" they asked me.

I was shocked. "Me?" I asked. "You want my autograph?"

"Yes! Pleeeeease!" the girls begged.

Why on earth did they want my autograph? I was touched. My ego was climbing to a state of euphoric bliss.

"You're with Sabrina, so you must be famous, too!" the girls squealed.

Wow, I couldn't argue with them. I mean, fans were begging for my autograph for the first time—and possibly the last time—ever. I couldn't disappoint them. I took the pen from the girls and signed my name right below Sabrina's. And then I drew a little daisy next to the *L* in my first name.

As I handed the paper back to the girls, I looked over at Sabrina. She was rolling her eyes at me in disbelief. "Whatever," she said. "As *if.*"

I suddenly felt incredibly silly. My face became flushed and I hung my head down. Then I sneezed very loudly. I was transported back to the harsh reality where I wasn't famous at all. I was just an ordinary girl suffering from a horse-induced allergy attack.

"Up ahead, by those rocks," Pat said. "Let's stop, and we'll run through a few drills."

"Lily," Sabrina said over her shoulder. "I think I'm ready to go all the way with Bronson."

I noticed Pat shoot a quick look over her shoulder at Sabrina. She could clearly hear our conversation. I didn't know what to say. In fact, I could barely speak because it felt like my mucus membranes were about to explode.

"Have you ever gone all the way?" Sabrina asked. "I mean, do you even have a boyfriend?"

"No," I said. "I'm single." Then quietly I whispered to Sabrina, "You know our instructor can hear everything we say. Maybe we should talk about this later."

Sabrina whispered back, "It doesn't matter. I bet she could use a little racy talk. She looks a bit uptight, if you ask me." Then she raised her voice again. "So there's no one you even have a crush on?"

"There's this guy Max. He's really cool, but he's away all summer with my best friend at soccer camp." And, of course, there was the adorable Bronson, too. But telling her that part would be like committing suicide.

I sneezed again. My entire face was itching now. I felt my lip swelling up like a balloon. If my lip got too big, I would start talking weird.

This girl who went to my high school had to be rushed to the emergency room when she had an allergic reaction once to bees and her entire throat closed up. What if that happened to me and I died today a martyr, as Sabrina's right hand?

"If I sleep with Bronson, I want lots of vanilla candles around and Frank Sinatra playing. What else do you think would be cool?"

"Vicks VapoRub."

"Huh?" Sabrina said.

"I need Vicks VapoRub. And Benadryl." My horse pulled up next to Sabrina. I couldn't hide anymore. She looked at me and gasped.

"Ohmigod! Are you okay?" she said. "Your face looks like a pepperoni pizza."

"I'm allergic to horses," I admitted. "I didn't want to say anything because I knew how important this lesson was to you. And I wanted to be here for you."

"Lily, that is ridiculous. You look like a cartoon character. I'm calling Bert now. You need medicine waiting at the hotel after we're done with our lesson."

"Thanks," I said. "That's really nice of you. But I don't know if it can wait that long."

Sabrina's face got very serious. "What are you saying, Lily? You want to stop our training early? We just got here."

"I'm not saying I want to. I'm saying I might need to."

Pat looked at me. "Oh, my, you look terrible," she said. "Are you okay?"

Before I could answer, Sabrina chimed in. "Can my intern ride her horse back without us? She wants to quit early."

"No, we have to stay as a group. She looks very ill. We should all head back together. There's no reason to make anyone uncomfortable."

My entire body was itching now. Sabrina gave me the once-over. My nose was running like crazy.

"Fine," Sabrina said. "This is making *me* uncomfortable. Let's go back."

"Thank you so much for understanding," I said.

"But I if I fall off a horse while filming and break my neck," she added, "it'll be all your fault."

"Lily, I need you to get down from the horse," Pat said. "In your condition, it's no longer safe to keep riding. I'm responsible for your well-being."

"Okay, I'm getting off," I said reluctantly. Then I followed Pat's instructions on how to properly dismount.

Walking back to the stable was dreadful. I started to wheeze. As soon as we got there, Pat showed me to the bathroom, where there were all sorts of emergency remedies. I took a hit from the asthma inhaler in my purse and then popped a Benadryl from the cabinet.

In the cab back to the Mercer, Sabrina called Bert and told him to have some meds ready for me at the hotel room. When we got there, on the counter of her bureau was a bottle of calamine lotion. Sabrina insisted on helping me apply it with a cotton ball.

"Can't I just wait till I get home to put this stuff on?" I asked.

"No, you need immediate attention," she said. "Your hives are getting bigger by the minute."

"I know, but now I have to walk down the street like this. Everyone will stare at me."

"Don't be silly," Sabrina said. "Health before fashion. I'll play your nurse."

Sabrina kept painting my face until it looked like I was wearing a mask of pink polka dots.

When she was finished decorating me so I looked like a freak, she announced, "Done!" She jumped up from the chair. "Now, I need to get ready for my hot date. Bronson will be here any minute to take me to a dinner on the roof of the Empire State Building."

"Any minute?" I asked.

"Yeah, at six o'clock. I texted him in the cab and told him to come by early since the lesson was botched. You should stay and say hi to him." Sabrina dove into her closet and picked out a Shoshanna tank top and a Nina Ricci blue-and-white-striped skirt. Then she put a pair of large black Fendi sunglasses on top of her head.

I couldn't believe Bronson would be here in minutes. What would I say to him? *Hi, Bronson. My face looks like a plantation of zits. But they're not really zits. They're just hives. And hives are better than zits, right? And did I tell you that I couldn't stop thinking about you today?*

"I feel really ill. I have to go right now," I said. "I'm gonna go home and rest up for work tomorrow."

"Keep me company while I get ready!" Sabrina said, putting on a necklace with foreign gold coins and the signature Chanel logo dangling off of it.

I looked at the clock. It was 5:57 P.M. "Would love to, but I feel too sick," I said, grabbing my things, heading for the door, and tripping on Mercedes's Tuscany bed.

I looked back to see if Sabrina had caught me, but she was too consumed lacing up a pair of knee-high brown boots.

"Whatever," she said.

I grabbed the handle of the door and opened it, then I looked up and down the hallway. The coast was clear. I raced to the elevator and hit the *down* button. Suddenly I heard a chime and the *up* arrow lit up above one of the elevators.

The *up* arrow. Not the *down* arrow. This was probably him. I looked to my right. There was a stairwell. I ran for the stairwell, but I was stopped by a voice.

"Lily?"

It was Bronson. I didn't turn around. I just froze with my hand on the stairwell doorknob.

"Oh, hey, Bronson. What's up?" I said as casually as possible, still not looking at him.

"What are you doing?" he asked. "Are you taking the stairs?"

"Just getting some exercise," I said, still not turning around. "Real stairs are better than the StairMaster."

I could hear him walking over to me. "Why won't you look at me?" he asked.

"Just focusing on the stairs and trying to get psyched up."

He grabbed my arm and gently turned me around.

"Wow," he gasped. "What happened to you?"

I was *busted*.

"Long story," I said. "Don't look at me, please. It's too embarrassing for words."

But he didn't turn away. It felt like he was counting the calamine dots on my face. "That looks painful," he said. "How'd it happen?"

"Let's just say it involved horse hair and saliva," I admitted.

"Don't worry," he said. "I'm allergic to things, too."

"You are?" I asked. "Like what?"

"Like cinnamon gum. Whenever I chew it, it makes my nose red."

"Umm, not the same," I said.

"I guess you're right," he said. "Look—"

"I gotta go," I said. There was only so long I could suffer this torment.

"Lily, wait—" He grabbed my hand. Then he gently touched my chin with his other hand. "You have a big glob there," he said, wiping it off. "It looked like it was going to fall onto your shirt."

"You're a lifesaver," I said sarcastically.

Then he took the glob and stuck it on his face in a few different places. "See—now I have some, too. You can't be the only cool one around here. Pink dots are the latest trend. Haven't you heard?"

"Yeah, it's a great look. I want to keep them on my face forever."

"Hey," he said.

I looked down and realized he was still holding my hand.

"Feel better, okay?" he said.

I smiled a little. "Look, I gotta go. Have fun at the Empire State Building."

I ran into the stairwell and down the five flights of stairs to the lobby. When I walked past the concierge, I noticed Angelica at the front desk staring at me.

"Are you okay?" she asked me.

"I'm fine," I said, trying to get out of the lobby as quickly as possible.

Several hotel guests milling around turned and gaped at me. Then my phone started ringing loudly. It was Evie calling from her cell phone. I wanted to pick it up and talk to her, but I didn't want to bring more attention to myself, so I quickly silenced the ringer. As soon as I got outside, I tried to answer it, but I had missed the call.

Out on the street, people turned their heads to look at my calamine polka dot–covered face. In the subway, a teenage boy in a blue ribbed tank top couldn't take his eyes off of me.

I realized this must be what Sabrina feels like when she goes out into the world. Strangers staring at you like you're an object. For Sabrina, it was because she was famous and beautiful. But for me right now, it was an entirely different story.

Chapter 11

BACK AT MY APARTMENT, I took a hot shower. Then I drank three glasses of tap water and plunked down on my bed. No one was home. My dad was up at Columbia and my mom had left a note saying she was cruising the neighborhood with flyers trying to drum up business for Pies & Surprise. She still hadn't made one dollar off her new endeavor.

When my dad came home from teaching, he was concerned when he saw me. I told him everything that happened.

"Lily, this is serious," he said. "This is your health. You shouldn't put yourself in dangerous situations like that. What if something happened to you?"

"I was just trying to do my job," I told him. "Sabrina needed me. I'm her right hand."

"But it's not worth dying over. Or going to the emergency room. Your throat could have closed up. Your asthma might have kicked in. You didn't take care of yourself today, Lily. I'm really disappointed."

"But, Dad, I made them stop early. Now if Sabrina falls off a horse during filming, she said it's all my fault."

"And if you stopped breathing today, that would have been all your fault, too."

"You're being dramatic, Pops."

"How do I know I can trust you to take care of yourself? You have to take responsibility for your own well-being. If something happened to you . . ."

"But nothing did."

My dad got quiet. He shook his head and went into the other room.

I lay down on my bed. *Boy, he can do a great job at making me feel terrible,* I thought. If my mom was here, she would sit on the edge of my bed, tickle my back, and make me feel better.

I turned on my side and looked at my desk. That was when I saw Taylor's letter sitting next to my computer. I had been meaning to call her again. But one thing had led to the next and I had gotten wrapped up like a mummy in Sabrina's world.

I looked at the clock. It was only seven o'clock and thankfully not too late to call. I picked up the phone and dialed the number.

I focused and thought strategy. *Be confident! Think before you speak. Don't talk too fast. Carefully choose your words. Remember— you're Sabrina now.*

The phone rang and rang. Then the father picked up. I gulped.

"Hello," he said.

Now was my moment to shine.

"Don't hang up!" I said. "This is Sabrina Snow. I need to speak to Taylor. This is not a prank or a joke Your daughter sent me a letter and I can prove it."

"Now that's original," the father said incredulously. "You're Sabrina Snow, huh? The star of *Too Cool for School* and *Spinning the Wheel of Fire,"* he said, clearly not believing me. "The tape is rolling so make it good."

I had to prove it to him. Now was my chance. *Go!* "I'm serious," I said. "Please. Just put her on the line. You can stay on, too. I need to speak to her."

"The police are really going to get a kick out of this one," he said. "Taylor, you can pick up. Sabrina Snow's calling," he said in a mocking tone. "It's safe. We're taping the conversation."

Click. I heard another line pick up.

"Taylor, is that you?" I asked.

"Hello?" a young girl's voice said.

I reminded myself to think carefully. "Taylor, I need you to listen to me. What I am about to say may blow your mind. This isn't a prank. I got your letter. This is really Sabrina," I said.

There was silence.

"How do I know you're not messing with my head?" Taylor asked.

"Yeah, how do we know you're not messing with her?" the father said, skeptical.

"Your letter was written on three-hole-punch paper and had a rip on the bottom left corner. There was a Marlon Brando stamp on the envelope. You signed your name in all caps. The first two words are 'For Sabrina.' You told me all about the picture you drew of an ostrich and put in some guy's locker."

"Dad, can you get off the phone?" Taylor said.

"Is this why they do those birdcalls?" the father said.

"Dad, get off the phone!" Taylor said.

There was a beat of silence. Then a clicking sound. Taylor waited a second then whispered into the receiver, "My dad doesn't know about that."

"Oops, sorry," I said.

"I can't believe this. I can't believe this. I can't—You got my letter. And you read it. And you're really calling me."

"Read every word," I told her.

"Wow . . . wow . . . You're the first person to really call me since this past May and not prank me and . . ." Her voice trailed off.

"Are you all right?" I asked.

"Yeah . . . sorry," she said.

I heard little gasps on the other end of the phone. "Are you crying?" I asked.

"Maybe, um, no . . . Can you . . . ?"

"Can I what?" I tried to get the words out of her mouth.

"Can you please . . . ?" she tried again.

"Come on," I said. "It's okay. You can say it."

"Can you please, um . . . ?"

"You can say it," I encouraged her. "Go ahead."

Then suddenly it burst out of her mouth. "Can you please come here and take me to Six Flags?"

"Is that what you wanted to ask me?" I asked.

"All the other kids from my school go. It's only twenty minutes from my house. That's all I want to do this summer. Please. I'll do anything. I really want to go like the other kids, and not with my parents."

I didn't know what to say. I couldn't flat-out say, "No." That would destroy her.

"I'll try my best," I said. "I want to, of course. It's just . . ."

I started to stammer, then my mouth started running a mile a minute. "It's just, um, everyone watches me like a hawk. And they . . . they track me like I'm a stolen car, and even though I have my own suite at the Mercer, it's like I have no privacy, and if I even make one move—"

"What's the Mercer?" Taylor asked.

"What?" I said, caught off guard.

"You said you're staying at the Mercer."

That's when I realized I probably should not have given out that information.

"It's just this place in the city. . . . Anyway, bottom-line"— I changed the topic as quickly as possible—"I don't know when things will settle down because I'm getting ready now for my next movie, but as soon as a window opens, I promise I will come see you."

"But you don't know when?" she said.

"Soon. I will certainly try my best to make it happen soon." I tried to cheer her up.

"You will?" she said.

"I promise," I said.

"Oh, thank you. Thank you so much. Thank you."

"Of course," I said.

"Look, I gotta run to a rehearsal, but I'll call you again," I said.

"When?" Taylor asked. "Today? Tomorrow?"

"Um, in a week or two," I said.

"Great!" Taylor said. "Talk to you then."

"Yep," I said. "Good night. Sweet dreams."

As soon as I hung up, I started to panic. I had dug myself

into a hole. There was no way Sabrina would take this girl to Six Flags. No chance in hell. In fact, she would be appalled if she knew that I snuck behind her back to make the call and impersonated her voice.

But now I felt like there was no turning back. I had made contact, and entered into this girl's life.

Chapter 12

THE NEXT FEW WEEKS SPUN like a man-made tornado on a Hollywood movie set.

My parents fought about my mom's new business. Dad didn't like all the pots and pans lying around and he thought the kitchen sink was always messy. He was also annoyed that she never had time to go for their walks to the Great Lawn in Central Park anymore because she was so busy trying out new recipes.

"You've turned our apartment into a factory," he said. "And you haven't even sold one thing."

"I will. I just need a little more time to get our name out there," my mom said, reaching out and giving him a kiss. "I'm onto something good here. Trust me."

At my internship, Bert was busy running around as if he were a cartoon character with his head cut off putting together a leather-bound book containing all of Sabrina's new publicity clippings sent to him by Violetta. He also started taking potential meetings about how else he could market Sabrina as a brand. She could have her own clothing line, high-end restaurant, online matchmaking service, and national spa chain. The possibilities for stamping Sabrina Snow's name on products were endless. I imagined Bert staying up late at night, counting money in his mind.

The big news was that Sabrina decided to buy the loft she fell in love with in Meatpacking District. She called her real-estate agent, Sagi, and put in an offer. A few days later, her offer was approved and she started filling out forms and speaking to her business attorney. The process would take quite a few weeks, and she wouldn't be able to move into her new home on Little West Twelfth Street until early September.

"That means one more month staying at the Mercer," Sabrina said. "I am so over living in a hotel!"

Sabrina sent me out to buy every magazine on the newsstand that had to do with interior decorating and furniture. I picked up twenty-three total. The Strap Girls came around to look through the articles on modern design with Sabrina.

"Ooh, I just love that recliner," Valerie would say, pointing at a page filled with Eames chairs. Then she'd arch her head backward to crack her back. *Crack. Crack.*

"So do I!" Nikki would say, cleaning the black liner smudged under her eye.

"And this bed is to die for. It looks so comfy and cozy for you-know-what," Valerie would say.

"Yeah, it does!" Nikki would say, laughing and scrunching up her freckled nose.

They convinced Sabrina to use them as her interior-design team. Every day, Valerie and Nikki would run around Manhattan and come back with new ideas for the loft. Expensive beaded curtains from Morocco. Lanterns made of blown Venetian glass. Twelve-foot-tall palm trees to emphasize the high ceilings. Sculptures priced over six figures that they saw in an upcoming Christie's auction catalog.

When they ran in and out of the suite, Valerie and Nikki would often ignore me as if I didn't exist. Except once in a while, Nikki would talk to me if she needed something—like to call and see how late ABC Carpet was open. I think the only time Valerie said something to me was to comment on my hair.

"Lily," she said, playing with her diamond nose stud, "it's really strange, but I noticed that your hair never moves."

I didn't know what to say back to her. I didn't even understand what she meant. I think she was poking fun of the fact that I wear the same hairstyle every day. Down and parted in the middle, then tucked behind my ears.

One afternoon, scary Eleanor stopped playing solitaire for a few minutes to give Sabrina a speech about getting back in contact with her mother. Eleanor asked me to leave the room, but Sabrina said, "Lily can hear anything that has to be said. She is my intern and I trust her completely."

I sat there in silence and listened to Eleanor plead with Sabrina to get back in touch with her mom.

"She really misses you," Eleanor said.

"She should have thought about that sooner," Sabrina said, acting tough. "When I was home, she stopped caring that I was around. You should tell her that all those 'friends' only want to spend time with her because she is *my* mom. They don't really like her at all. It's not my fault she never had a fulfilling childhood and is trying to re-create one now by riding on my Dolce & Gabbana shirttails."

That shut Eleanor up.

The other piece of gossip I overheard had to do with Sabrina and Bronson. She invited him to move into the loft with her. She said she planned on staying in New York quite a bit, except for the six weeks when she would be filming *Ladies of the Wild West* in Canada. Bronson said he had planned on going back to L.A. at the end of the summer. He still had a year of high school to finish up. Sabrina offered to hire him a private tutor like the one she had during the school year, but Bronson said he enjoyed going to a normal high school, and his parents said he was way too young to move in with a girlfriend anyway.

I have to admit that I was still thinking about Bronson a lot. Ever since the day he held my hand while I had calamine polka dots all over my face, I felt a connection surging between us. Whenever he saw me—and Sabrina was in a meeting or out running with Lorenzo—we would sit down and talk. Bronson told me that he felt really comfortable around me. He loved music and started teaching me about his favorite bands. I learned about these groups that I never even heard of. The style of music was called "intelligent indie," and one day when Sabrina wasn't looking, he gave me a mixed CD that he had burned for me. It contained songs by this amazing new band he had found called Split Seconds. Bronson said the band was like "undiscovered gold."

I opened up to him and told him about how my parents had been fighting lately. That my dad seemed extra stressed about money since I was leaving for college in a year. And that my mom had started her own business. "I can't tell if my dad just doesn't want her spending money on groceries and other supplies. Or if he doesn't like the idea of her changing," I told Bronson.

He told me that his parents were still happily married

but that he often felt like they were the exception to the rule. Bronson told me he thought the key to a happy relationship could be found in all the little things.

"The way my dad still offers to get a drink for my mom after work and knows how to put in four ice cubes for her. And my mom always picks up my dad's favorite snack, peanut-butter pretzels, when she goes to the supermarket," he said.

It was after that conversation that I started dreaming about Bronson. He would just show up and we would go scuba diving together in Australia or for a casual stroll outside a castle in Scotland. In the real world, I knew he was with Sabrina, but my subconscious had a mind of its own.

Then there were a few days when he was holed up in his studio trying to finish the screenplay he was working on with his dad. I started to miss him tons. All I wanted was to see him again.

You can only imagine how happy I was when I went to check on Sabrina sunbathing on the roof of the Mercer, and there was Bronson, shirtless, lounging next to her by the turquoise pool.

Bronson with his shirt off was like *whoa*.

"Bronsie and I had a sleepover last night and we're both super hungry," Sabrina said when she saw me. "Could you get us lunch?"

"Sure," I said. "What are you in the mood for?"

"Something yummy. Did you get me some more diet pills, by the way?" she said, adjusting her red bikini strap.

I took them out of my purse and handed them to her. Sabrina had gone through three bottles already. It was making me nervous, but if I didn't have a new bottle ready for her the day she ran out of her stash, she would give me dirty looks and be mean to me. One day she was in a bad mood, and she threatened to fire me over it.

She took the sealed blue container from me. "Thanks," she said.

"So, food ideas," I said. "There is a great noodle shop down the street—Kelley and Ping's, or, what about Balthy's?"

"I don't think so. More suggestions," Sabrina said.

"How about this yummy French place, Patissimo? Or do you like Indian food? There's a place nearby called the Curry House—"

"I can't decide. Just figure it out. And we need it here in twenty minutes because we have to leave for my dance lessons." She handed me her credit card, and I headed out to Prince Street.

"Just remember," she called after me, "no carbs, cheese, or butter. Always broccoli with my salad. Extra ketchup. Only whole-grain mustard. White meat is a must. And if you pick a fish, I only do trout."

I decided on this Italian restaurant my mom had brought me to once a few blocks away. After buying a variety of entrées—herb roasted chicken, steamed spinach, salad with broccoli, and gourmet Italian sausages—I headed back to the hotel.

I ran the food back up to the roof. Bronson and Sabrina were swimming in the pool now.

"Thanks, Lily," Sabrina said, swimming over to the edge. "It smells delicious. But where's the tray?"

"The tray?" I asked. "What tray?"

"When Bert orders me lunch, he always serves it to me on

a leather tray. It's probably downstairs in my suite."

"Do you really need that? Let's just be casual and eat out of the take-out containers," Bronson said, climbing out of the pool and then diving off the edge.

"Babikins, that's kind of tacky," she said.

Bronson gave me a look. I could tell he felt bad for me. He was so smoking hot with wet hair that it was hard to look him in the eye.

"I'll go get it then," Bronson offered, swimming toward the ladder.

"No, Lily's the intern," Sabrina said.

"You're in the pool," I said. "I'll go get it." I ran downstairs to the suite with the bags of food. Bert was in the living room talking a mile a minute on the phone. It sounded like he was doing some hardcore wheeling and dealing.

"*Spinning the Wheel* already made over fifty million," he was saying into the phone. "No, I'm not making it up. It was reported in *Variety*. Don't you read the trades anymore, you lazy nitwit?"

"Do you know where the leather tray is?" I said quietly to him.

"Can't you see I'm busy?" he covered the phone and whispered. "Go look. It's somewhere in her room." He motioned toward the doorway of Sabrina's bedroom. Then he went back to ranting into the phone. "That is solid box office. It opened at number one playing at two thousand movie theaters across the country. Look, I gotta go. Have your people call my people."

I listened to Bert throwing around the Hollywood jargon

as I went into Sabrina's bedroom for the first time that day. I found the tray on the counter with her leftover breakfast on it. Then I grabbed some plates from the bar area and dumped the cartons of food onto the plates. I noticed the Italian sausages didn't resemble the shape of hot dogs the way I was used to. Instead, they were mini-links coiled in a circle like a curled-up snake. I tried to make them look as aesthetically pleasing as possible, but it was hard.

As I carried the tray out of the suite, something unusual in the bedroom caught my eye. The windowsill was lined with white votives in red glass holders. The candles' wicks were blackened from flames, and the room still smelled from their vanilla scent. Then I looked over at the bed, and there on the nightstand next to the stereo was the case for a Frank Sinatra CD.

I also noticed a bunch of Bronson's shirts and jeans shoved under one of the nightstands. It was like he planned on spending lots of nights at the suite and having plenty of changes of clothes.

Did that mean what I thought it meant? While horseback riding weeks ago, Sabrina had mentioned she might go all the way with Bronson. I guess she actually went through with it. I ran back upstairs.

"Put it over there." Sabrina pointed to a wrought-iron table with a blue-and-white-striped umbrella. She and Bronson were drying themselves off with towels.

I placed it down in front of one of the chairs. I felt like I was her butler.

"There was only one tray," I said, looking at Bronson.

"Don't worry about me," Bronson said.

"Baby, we can both share this one."

"No, it's all right," he said. "I'll just eat out of these." He grabbed the remaining take-out containers and carried the leftovers and plastic utensils over to his seat at the table.

"Don't you want to share mine?" Sabrina asked.

"No, really. I'm fine," Bronson said.

"Bronson, I'm not stupid. I can tell you're giving me a hard time because I'm using a tray, but I worked hard in my life to get to this point. I have a million other things to worry about. Why shouldn't I have this little luxury? I deserve it." Sabrina placed the napkin on her lap.

"Whatever makes you happy," he said, digging into his to-go container with a plastic fork. There was a tense silence between them.

Sabrina turned to me. "Lily, what's in these sausages?" she asked.

I felt dumb. I had no idea. I worried that they weren't appropriate for her low-calorie diet. "I'm not sure," I said.

"Take a guess," Sabrina said.

"Turkey?" I said. It really was a guess. I hadn't the faintest idea.

She picked up her fork and knife and started cutting. Then she called my name again. "Lily!" She pushed the tray out in front of her. "I can't eat this. The sausages look too weird. And the chicken is dry and gnarly. And the vegetables are contaminated by the chicken juice."

"But it's from a very nice restaurant," I said, trying to save face.

"Just order me some lettuce," Sabrina said, rolling her eyes.

* * *

After the lunch fiasco, Sabrina, Bronson, and I grabbed a cab to the Broadway Dance Center on 78th Street, where we had an appointment with Millie to learn how to country dance. Sabrina insisted I go with her for moral support. Lately, I noticed how difficult it was for her to do anything alone. It was almost like she was becoming dependent on me. I had been woven into her security blanket.

Bronson sat in between us, and when his arm rubbed against mine, I could feel his body warmth. He was wearing khaki cargo shorts and a soft white T-shirt. His shirt tickled my arm, and I imagined how nice it would be to spoon with Bronson under bedsheets made of the same material, his tan hand resting on my stomach.

He looked over and smiled at me.

I smiled back.

There it was again. I felt it. Sparks were starting to fly.

Sabrina was busy putting green eyeliner on her bottom eyelid while staring in the mirror. I felt a pang of guilt. If she knew what I was thinking about her "Bronsie," she would imprint my forehead with her three-karat Tiffany right-hand diamond ring.

"Thank God for makeup," Sabrina said. "My eyes look redder than a rat's ass."

"Didn't sleep much last night?" I asked.

"Uh, yeah. You can say that again," Sabrina said. I could only imagine what they were up late doing.

"I can't believe you are dragging me to a dance lesson," Bronson said.

"We've been over this ten times already," Sabrina said. "It will be fun. Besides, I need a dance partner."

"Fine, but if the teacher tries to make me prance, I'm out of there!"

Sabrina nuzzled in to Bronson. "Baby. I realize you are doing me a favor today. But if you go along like a good sport, tonight I will give you . . ." She looked at me. Then she leaned into him and whispered in his ear.

God only knows what she whispered to him. But if you could see the way his eyeballs went falling onto the floor of the cab, you would have known there was definitely lots of dirtiness involved. Mud piles.

The cab pulled up at the Broadway Dance Center, and Sabrina grabbed some cash out of her mint-leaf petty-cash purse and handed it to the driver. We took the elevator up to the second floor. Sabrina didn't want to walk the one flight because, as she said, "I swear my Givenchy stiletto heels are wobbling like dreidels! I knew this morning I should have put on my wedges."

"How are you going to dance in those shoes?" I asked her.

"I'm dancing in jazz shoes, silly," she said.

Inside, there were several dance studios. I could see a group of young girls taking a ballet class in one of them. Across the hall, a group of middle-schoolers was taking a salsa and merengue class. They were ripping into a dance number and didn't notice Sabrina passing through the lobby.

Millie, the dance instructor, came out of a doorway dressed in loose, stretchy gray pants and a blue leotard. She was wearing a bunch of long necklaces, and you could tell she was still sporting the same haircut from ten years ago. She had brown curly hair past her shoulders, sparkling eyes shooting out above crow's-feet, and magenta lipstick.

"Hello there!" she said, hustling over to us. "I have so much planned for you three. Today is going to be a great lesson. Giddy-up!" She was brimming over with energy. It was like she had just done a keg stand on a barrel of Red Bull.

She ushered us into a private studio. The wall was lined with mirrors and ballet bars. Sabrina took off her shoes and threw them in a corner. Bronson and I followed her lead.

"It's so nice to be able to teach country dancing. None of the city girls seem to care about it. They are more interested in learning to tango and salsa."

Of course they are, I thought to myself. I wouldn't be caught dead doing a do-si-do at a friend's house party.

Sabrina sat on the floor. She put on her jazz shoes and started stretching her legs. She looked like a professional dancer. Bronson leaned against the wall and gave her a skeptical look. She blew him a kiss.

"The things I do for you," he said, shaking his head.

"Love ya, mean it," she said.

Millie stood by the stereo and put in a CD. "My boyfriend gave me this CD for Valentine's Day—Willy M. Fox Live at the Derby." She pressed PLAY, and a song started blaring out of the speakers.

The song she played was called "First Love in Georgia," and it went like this:

In the South, near the Mason-Hoochie Line,
That's where I fell in love with Miss Susie Divine.
We laid rubber on the soft, green grass,
I was her true love, and she, my sweet lass.

I listened carefully to the lyrics. I knew that a "rubber"

was a condom, and I was kind of surprised Millie busted out such a racy country song.

> *Up near the lake on a Tuesday night,*
> *One kiss with Susie and I knew it felt right.*
> *Talking 'bout life and kissin' while we're in it,*
> *Didn't have a plan, but enjoyin' every minute.*

"On your feet!" Millie said, starting to bounce up and down. I could see she was deeply feeling the beat of the music in her long Rockette legs. Then she said excitedly, "Who's ready to learn the Texas two-step?"

Sabrina and I walked to the middle of the room. Sabrina summoned Bronson with her index finger, and he sauntered over to her, dripping with attitude.

"The two-step is danced with two quick steps and two slow steps." Millie punctuated the rhythm of the dance moves with her hands. "There is a leader and a follower."

"You're the leader," Sabrina ordered Bronson.

"Whatever you say, missus," he said.

Millie walked over to me. "We will be dance partners so you won't feel alone," she said.

I looked at Millie. *Great,* I thought to myself. *I am sixteen years old and I don't have a real dance partner. Instead, I am dancing across from a middle-aged firecracker while Sabrina is dancing next to a complete hottie.* This was truly depressing.

Will I ever have someone to do the Texas two-step with? Or will I graduate from high school a total toolbox and end up one day like my history teacher, Ms. Hamback, living alone with fifteen cats. Except—wait! I am allergic to cats. They make me wheeze and sneeze. So I won't even have any cats. I will be completely and utterly by myself.

"Stand with your feet together facing your partner. Grab your partner's hand. Then there are five different beats." She wrote them on a blackboard as she said them aloud. "And warning: This is not as easy at it looks!"

The steps were easy enough. The hard part was the timing—when to go fast and when to go slow. And, of course, when to pause. It was hard to make all the moves happen continuously and smoothly so that it became a dance.

"I don't get it!" Sabrina said. "How can you move fast and slow to the same beat?"

Millie demonstrated the routine while using me as her dance partner. Sabrina tried to follow, but she was surprisingly uncoordinated.

"What the hell," Sabrina said. "You must be teaching us wrong."

I, on the other hand, was surprising myself with my dance skills. If I didn't think about the beat so hard, it came more and more naturally.

"Good, good. You're getting it." Millie looked over at me and smiled. "Why don't you dance with Bronson for a while. Sabrina, come here. Let me help you."

I watched Sabrina move away from Bronson, his arms letting go of her waist. She looked unhappy.

As Millie gave Sabrina private coaching in the center of the room, Bronson and I danced our best rendition of the Texas two-step around them. We actually almost started to get it. And he began laughing and jokingly singing along with the song like he was a hillbilly.

"Yeeeehaaaw! Way down yonder by the Mason-Hoochie

Line! That's where I fell in love with Miss Susie Divine!" Bronson said.

I could feel Sabrina getting angrier and angrier. She was pissed because she couldn't learn the dance. And now she was even more angry because I was dancing circles around her with her man and looking into his blue-gray eyes.

"Giddy-up! You two look magnificent!" Millie said to Bronson and me. "Now add this move." She starting bringing her knees up high in the air like wild, Western stomping.

Bronson cracked up, and we started stomping together.

Millie applauded. "In a year, I could see you both winning a Western pair dance competition! You make a great team!"

I knew she was exaggerating. We weren't that good, but it was nice to hear, and I enjoyed the compliment until I felt a hard push on my arm. I looked up, and there was Sabrina.

"That move is easy," Sabrina said. "Anyone can do that." She started stomping her legs to the beat. "Look how high I can do them," she bragged, admiring herself in the mirror. She brought her knee up high and then kicked out her leg wildly. She was on a roll until she kicked her leg up and smacked into Bronson's groin.

Bronson grabbed himself in between his legs and fell to the ground.

Sabrina crouched down next to him. "Baby, I'm sorry. I'm so sorry. Are you okay?"

He looked at her with squinty eyes. "Do I look okay? I told you I didn't want to come to a stupid dance class."

"I know. I'm sorry. It was an accident. It's not like I meant to kick you in the nuts! If Lily hadn't gotten in my way . . ."

"Don't blame it on her." Bronson shook his head. "You never watch where you're going. You're always looking at yourself in the mirror. You don't even see anyone else around you."

"That is not true!" Sabrina said.

"Do you want to put some ice on your groin?" Millie said, running over to them with an ice pack.

"This is not happening." Bronson's face turned red. "Thanks. But no thanks." He stood up, straightened his shirt, and stumbled out the door.

Millie continued the lesson, but I could tell Sabrina was distracted by her fight with Bronson. She couldn't pick up any of the dance steps.

As soon as the lesson ended, Sabrina ordered me to buy her twenty instructional videos on country dancing, as she would prefer to practice in the privacy of her own suite than with such a lunatic instructor.

When Sabrina saw Bronson was not waiting for her outside with a bouquet of stargazer lilies, as she had said he might be, she took off her sunglasses and said, "I feel as if the world is ending."

Then we spotted him sitting on a stoop across the street, and she said, "I changed my mind. I feel as if the world is just beginning." Sabrina walked over to him while I waited in the corner deli, spying on them through the window.

They stood across from each other, and I could tell by the distraught look on Sabrina's face that they were in a heated argument. Then Bronson got fed up and walked away. Sabrina stood there looking dazed, shaking her head and covering her mouth with her hand.

By the time I got outside, Sabrina was hiding in the alcove

of a brownstone building. She waved me over. "I don't want anyone to see me crying," she explained.

"Are you all right?" I asked her.

"Bronson is such a jerk!" Sabrina said.

"It's okay," I said, putting my hand on her arm. "I'm sure you guys can work things out."

"No way!" she said. "I hate him! I never want to speak to him again."

"What happened?" I asked her, pulling out a napkin from my bag so she could use it as a Kleenex.

"I told him I've been pissed at him lately. I just don't understand why he won't stay in New York and move in with me. I told him if he really adored me, he wouldn't go back to Los Angeles at the end of the summer. He got mad and said that nothing he does is right and that I can't be pleased. So he wants to take a 'break.' And then he said—" Sabrina's voice quivered. "He said that . . ." Then she collapsed her face in her hands. "He said that he is falling for someone else."

"Someone e-e-else?" I said, filled with fear.

"You heard me." Sabrina turned to me. "Do you know who it is?"

I shook my head adamantly. "No."

"Because if you do, now would be the time to tell me."

"I have no idea. I promise."

"You better not be lying. You're part of the inner sanctum now. Get it? If you break my trust . . ."

My heart froze. Then it started beating again very fast.

"I don't think you understand," Sabrina said, "what this feels like."

Her tone sounded slightly condescending, but maybe

she was right. I had never been in love before.

Sabrina turned to me. "It feels like death. Like the bubonic plague."

I couldn't remember what the bubonic plague was, even though I recall writing it down on a flashcard for Ms. Hamback's history class.

"Never fall in love, Lily. Ever."

I listened to her, but I didn't care what she said. I still wanted to. Even the anguish of it all seemed romantically tormenting.

"Everything will be okay," I told her. "I am sure Bronson and you will get through this. You're just having a fight."

She looked at me. I saw a twinge of hope flash like a comet across her eyes.

"Do you really think so? You think we'll get through this?"

"You guys have a connection. It's obvious. That can't just go away overnight."

"I hope you're right. . . ." She took her purse from me and held it under her arm. "I think what I need is a day off from all this hard work," she said, wiping the tears from her face.

"That's the spirit," I said.

"We need to have a Girls' Day. Like my mom and I used to do. As soon as we have a free afternoon, we're going shopping," she said, then blew her nose with a Kleenex.

When Sabrina grabbed a cab back to the Mercer, she seemed more optimistic. I imagined her caught up in a daydream of making up with Bronson while dressed in brandnew jewelry and designer couture.

As I walked home, I started brainstorming a mile a minute.

I was madly curious about who Bronson was falling for. I decided to be very rational about this and make a list in my
head. He could be falling for 1. Nikki; 2. Valerie (not very
likely); 3. Someone I had never met. And then I had to add 4
because if I was going to complete this game of logic, 4 *had*
to be part of the list: 4. Me, Lily Miles.

I knew, of course, that 4 was unlikely. It didn't matter that
some of the guys at school said that I was "kinda cute." And
Josh DeMarco, the boy with the number one cutest butt in
my grade, told me that I was like the girl-next-door type—
but in Paris. Still, in a lineup, every guy would pick Sabrina
over me. That was just the way of the world, and I had to deal
with it. I was on the earth while Sabrina was in the sky. I was
made of grass and trees and she was made of that celestial
matter that makes the stars sparkle.

Chapter 13

THAT FRIDAY AFTERNOON, SABRINA announced it was finally Girls' Day! We jumped in a cab and headed over to East 60th Street. A group of tourists in bright pink-and-green jogging outfits stared as we walked past the Plaza Hotel on our way to Fifth Avenue. Sabrina pretended she didn't notice their eyes on her as she adjusted the thick red belt that clasped around the waist of her white sundress. She had tied a giraffe-printed scarf around the strap of her Dior metallic-blue bag.

"The television in my suite stopped working," Sabrina said as we walked past a hot-dog stand. "Make sure it's fixed today. Sometimes I like to leave it on when I'm out, to keep Mercedes company. He just loves Nickelodeon. Also, I need to start watching those how-to-country-dance tapes, and I want to watch Animal Planet. They have a cool show on tonight about dog breeders."

"I'll let the concierge know," I said, jotting down her request in my pocket-sized notebook. Sabrina would throw out assignments to me as soon as they passed through her head. I always needed a pen and paper handy to write down her never-ending demands.

"Also get me more toothpaste, Q-tips, and tampons. And

I want you to start checking Page Six every day to see if I'm on it."

If I didn't write all the little things down, I would forget something. I learned this the hard way. One day, I forgot to pick her up an antiwrinkle cream she wanted. She blew up at me.

"What's your problem?" she said. "Are you a bobble-head doll? Or a human being? Sometimes you really astound me."

It was hard to predict Sabrina's reactions. Sometimes she would get very angry over something little like the face cream. And sometimes a bigger thing would happen, like when I forgot to make a reservation at Nobu for eight P.M., and it would just fly off her back like she didn't care.

"Here's our first stop," Sabrina said outside the famous Harry Winston diamond store on 56th Street.

The white-gloved doorman spun us through the revolving doors. My mouth dropped open as we walked into the room filled with chandeliers and what I guessed was more than a billion dollars' worth of jewels. Cages of diamonds, rubies, and emeralds were sparkling as if they were about to come alive.

A brunette woman with a perfect bobbed haircut ran over to us. "Sabrina, how nice to see you," she said, adjusting her pastel pink suit. "Perfect timing, too! I just walked in the door from an auction at Sotheby's."

"Ooh, that is great timing," Sabrina said.

"I think I have a necklace you will just die for. Let me go in the back and get it."

"Can't wait!" Sabrina said, flashing one of her "cute faces" as the woman ran to the back.

While we waited, Sabrina and I walked around, admiring a cameo locket from the turn of the century, an eleven-karat emerald-cut diamond engagement ring, and an Italian gold-and-cultured-pearl bird brooch.

"Here we go," the woman said, walking out of the back. She was carrying a silver box that she opened slowly. Inside, I saw a flash of hypnotic color. There was a delicate chain filled with diamonds and rose and blue colored sapphires. It looked like a necklace I had seen in the Museum of Natural History that had belonged to an Italian princess.

"I'm going to faint," Sabrina said. "That is the most beautiful thing I've ever seen."

"It really is unbelievable," I agreed.

The woman ran the necklace through her fingers. "Designed as a series of fringes alternating in length, decorated with numerous pear-shaped sapphires in various colors, completed by small round diamonds, and mounted in white gold. It's one of a kind."

"Let me try it on right now," Sabrina said, holding up her hair.

The woman helped fasten the clasp around Sabrina's neck.

Sabrina spun around and looked in the mirror. Her face lit up. "What do you think?" she asked me.

"It's spectacular," I told her. I was dying to see how it would look around my neck, too.

"Yeah," Sabrina agreed. "I'm going to take it. Done."

I could only imagine how much the necklace cost. It had to be at least six figures.

The woman helped Sabrina take the necklace off and put

it back in the silver box. Then she placed it carefully into a shopping bag and handed it to Sabrina.

"Wear it in good health," the woman said.

Sabrina took the bag, thanked the lady, and sauntered out the revolving doors, grinning from ear to ear. As I spun through the doors out onto the street, I realized Sabrina never handed over a credit card or any money.

Once we got outside, I turned to Sabrina. "Do you realize you forgot to pay her?" I said.

"Duh," Sabrina. "Of course I noticed."

"Shouldn't we go back? I mean, they're going to figure it out at some point. It's not like a five-cent piece of candy."

Sabrina shook her head. "I don't have to pay! They gave it to me! It's 'swag.'"

"Swag?" I asked.

"Yeah, tons of designers give me free stuff because when I wear it around town, everyone copies me. And their sales go way up!"

"So when you shop, you don't pay for anything?" I asked. That seemed too good to be true.

"Most of the time I don't pay a cent. Harry Winston probably would have given you a little something, too, just because you were with me," Sabrina added. "You should have asked."

"Are you serious?" I asked. "Can we go back? I'll go back right now."

"No," Sabrina said. "You missed your chance. That would be tacky. Besides, we have another store to get to."

Sabrina led us to the latest, trendiest cosmetic boutique a few blocks down called My Mademoiselle. "This place has been begging for me to come by for months," she bragged.

A man ran over to us, flashing his perfectly bleached teeth. "Hi. I'm Danny. Take whatever you want, honey," he told Sabrina.

Sabrina picked up a basket and started walking around the store.

"I just love your work," he gushed after her. "Would you sign this picture of you?" He handed her a magazine page ripped out of *Party Weekly*.

"I guess it's a fair exchange," Sabrina said, signing and handing back the photograph. Danny gleefully took it and immediately taped it on the wall above the cash register.

I noticed a few other shoppers in the store recognized Sabrina; however, they tried to play it cool by pretending they didn't even see her. I knew the shoppers were just trying to respect her privacy. I assumed it was because we were in a hoity-toity store.

While Sabrina made her way around the boutique, I decided I might as well get in on the act. After all, Sabrina said earlier that she thought it would be okay if I took a few things.

I grabbed a basket and walked around, passing the most beautiful color of lipgloss I had ever seen. I snagged a tube of it. Next I saw this sparkly body lotion that smelled like fuzzy peach and threw that into my basket, too. Then I snatched some nail polish and some expensive perfume that was supposed to make me irresistible to guys.

Suddenly I looked up and there was Danny. Sabrina was on the other side of the store busy at the "Make Your Own Perfume" counter. She looked fixated on smelling the different types of fragrant oils.

"Finding everything?" he asked.

"Yeah, thanks," I told him.

"So how do you know Sabrina?" he asked me. He was super friendly.

"I'm Sabrina's intern."

"That is so neat," he said. "Golly gee!"

"Yeah, it is pretty cool," I said, trying not to sound too cocky.

"And look at that gorgeous stuff in your basket," he said, looking down at my beauty supplies. "You're really going to enjoy that, I bet. It's going to look perfect with your coloring." He was the nicest guy ever.

"Yeah, I can't wait to try it," I said.

"Come to the front. I'll get everything ready for you."

I followed Danny to the register, where he took my basket and started ringing up all my cosmetics on the cash register.

"All right. That will be eight hundred twenty dollars," he said.

"What?" I said, shocked. "I thought it was swag."

"That's for invited celeb guests only. Not for you," he said.

I felt so embarrassed. I couldn't afford spending that kind of money on makeup. "I guess I'm not going to get anything then," I said. "Next time, though."

"So you want me to put all this back?" Danny said, looking down at the basket filled with items.

"Yeah," I said. "Sorry about that." I left the store as quickly as possible and waited for Sabrina outside. I could see Danny glaring at me as he started putting the products back on the shelves.

A few minutes later, Sabrina ran over to me, holding shopping bags from My Mademoiselle overflowing with goodies.

"What an awesome day!" she said, taking the same lipgloss that I wanted out of one of her bags and putting it on her lips. "Isn't this sooo much fun?"

We spent the afternoon racing around Manhattan going to all of Sabrina's favorite stores. We shopped for shoes (black high boots, furry slippers, Mary Janes, alligator-skin square-toed heels), underwear (G-strings, low-riders, mesh, and sequin-studded), stockings (control top, sheer toe, fishnets), and sleepwear (flannel pajamas with a scottie-dog design, silk nightgowns, lace teddies).

While we were lingerie shopping, Sabrina confided in me that Bronson was coming over later that afternoon and they were going to have a "talk." She seemed very optimistic. She said he had called her that morning to say that he needed to see her today. "I was so happy to hear from him," she said. "I miss him so much. It kills me inside. All I want is to be next to him again."

I told myself that I should be happy for her, but part of me felt disappointed. I was dying to know who Bronson had his eye on. Was I delusional to think it might have been me? That I had a chance? It didn't matter anymore, though. Apparently, Bronson had thrown his mysterious crush on the back burner. And I might never have a chance to find out exactly who she was.

Chapter 14

WHEN SABRINA AND I got back to the Mercer, the bell-hop ran over to help us with all of her shopping bags. As she got into the elevator with him, I noticed Angelica at the front desk was waving me down.

"I'll meet you up there," I said, walking over to the concierge.

"Sabrina's manager left some things for you," Angelica said, holding out two bags filled with fan letters. I grabbed the bags and thanked her. There was a note with the package from Bert telling me to go through this new batch of mail and respond to the letters.

As I was waking away, Angelica called out, "Also, I have a message for Sabrina. A girl named Taylor called fifteen times, but she didn't know Sabrina's pseudonym so I couldn't put her through. I told her I could hold a message at the front desk, though; it seemed important."

What was she doing calling the hotel? Clearly, I had made a huge mistake when I mentioned that Sabrina was staying at the Mercer.

"What is the message?" I asked.

"She told me to tell Sabrina, 'Please call as soon as possible. It's an emergency.'"

"Are you *sure* you didn't connect her to the voice mail in Sabrina's room? Not even once?" I couldn't believe this was happening. What had I gotten myself into?

"I am positive that I didn't," she said, slightly put off. "But I suppose, during my lunch break, the new guy may have. . . ."

I nodded, freaking out inside. "Right . . . I'll be sure to pass the message along."

What happened if the new guy *did* put one of Taylor's calls through? Taylor would have left a message on the room's voice mail—the same voice mail that Sabrina could be up in the room now checking!

I ran to the elevator bank, banged on the fifth-floor button, and ran to Sabrina's suite. When I got inside, Eleanor was reading a book in the living room and Sabrina was throwing her shopping bags around her bedroom. She kept dumping out all of the contents into a pile by her closet.

"Is everything okay in there?" Eleanor asked.

"Peachy," Sabrina said to her.

"I spoke to your mom again today." Eleanor came over and stood in the doorway. "She'd really like to hear from you."

"Maybe she should have thought about that sooner," Sabrina said.

"Let me know if there's anything you want to talk about," Eleanor said. "I'm here for you."

"You'll be the first to know," Sabrina said. Eleanor sensed that Sabrina wanted to be left alone and walked away.

I looked at the phone. The light indicator was *not* blinking. Which meant there were no messages, or she had checked them already.

"Mercedes, stop licking my leg," she said, shaking him off of her. "Look at this pile of swag," she said, as if annoyed by it.

"What's the matter?" I asked, utterly paranoid.

"I'm pissed at you," she said.

I swallowed hard. "What did I do?" I asked, playing the innocent card.

"The TV still isn't working! I asked you to get it fixed today," she said. "And I'm missing Animal Planet. I wanted it to be on the TV when Bronson came over. That's one of our things. We like cuddling together, watching the animals, and pretending we're on safari."

I sighed with relief. I could handle this one. "I called the concierge and they promised they would fix it." It was true. I had called the front desk while we were out shopping. I tried to fiddle with the TV dials, but all I got was static.

"It doesn't matter what people promise. They often don't do what they say. If you asked them to fix the TV, you should have followed up with them this afternoon and asked again if they actually had. And even if then they still said it was all taken care of, you should have come up here to the room before I got here, turned the TV on yourself, and seen with your very own eyes it was working."

"But, Sabrina," I said, "I was with you all day. When was there time to check the TV?"

"If you were a hardcore intern, you would have found a way."

I started to get frustrated. "But we were attached at the hip all afternoon."

"Sit down, Lily," Sabrina said. "It's the end of the day, but we need to have a talk before you leave."

I slumped down on the couch.

"What is going on with you? I thought you said you were going to be a fantastic intern for me. You oversold yourself. Right now you're fine, but you're not unbelievable. Have you read *All Right, Not Awesome?*"

I shook my head no.

"You should pick the book up. Right now, you're all right, but you're not awesome. I need an intern who is awesome. How much of your potential are you living up to on a scale of one to ten?"

"Um, a seven?" I said.

"A seven! You think you're a seven. I think you're more like a four." Sabrina continued, "I, myself, am at a four, as well. That's why I need you to be at a nine or ten. To bring me up!"

"I want to do a good job," I said, worried. "What can I do?"

"Focus!" Sabrina said. "Prioritize! Be on time! Dig deeper into yourself. Be the best you can be!"

"I know I have it in me to be awesome. I swear," I said. "I want to be the best intern you ever have."

"It's not about words," Sabrina said. "It's about actions. Show me."

"I will," I said. "Don't give up on me, please."

"And it goes beyond that," Sabrina said. "Don't you want to make something of your life? Don't you want success? I got where I am today because I went above and beyond. I pushed myself. I want that for you, too. Pay attention to the little things, because they are the building blocks for big things. You don't want to be an intern forever, do you?"

"Definitely not," I said.

"Then now's the time. I wasn't always famous. I didn't

always have as much money, but I went after my dreams and I went after them hard. What makes you tick? What do you want to be?" she asked me.

"I'm still figuring it out," I said. "Maybe an art dealer, a writer, or a librarian."

"Great. Well, once you decide which one it is—focus and work hard. Don't compare yourself to your friends or other people. That will only slow you down. Concentrate on your own goals and charge toward them. Lily, I only want great things for you."

"I'm going to go buy that book right now and prove to you I can be a ten." I gathered my things and headed toward the door. I felt terrible that I had let her down.

As soon as I got out on the street, I called Taylor immediately. I had stored her number in my cell phone and I needed to take care of this situation ASAP. Then I could go to the bookstore and buy *All Right, Not Awesome*.

Taylor picked up the phone on the first ring.

"Hi," she said.

"It's Sabrina," I said, imitating her voice.

"Sabrina! Sabrina!" she said, delighted.

"Taylor, please don't call the hotel again. I'm not supposed to be taking calls at the hotel." Then I made up an excuse. "It's for security reasons. You don't want my life to be in jeopardy, do you?"

"Of course not. I'm sorry. Are you mad?"

"No, not at all," I said. "Just don't do it again, okay?"

"I won't," Taylor said. "I'm sorry. Please don't be mad at me. Please." She was starting to get worked up. "It's just you said you would call and it has already been a few weeks and you hadn't called. And I was listening to our taped conversation because my dad left the tape running and heard you mention your hotel. So I called information and tracked it down. Because I wanted to let you know that some kids from school toilet-papered my front yard," Taylor said.

"What?" I asked.

"The trees in front of our house are covered in toilet paper."

"That's terrible," I said.

"They did it last night," Taylor went on. "And when they were done, they threw a basketball at my window and screamed that I was flat-chested and ugly and that I shouldn't come back to school next year because it makes them want to puke when they see me in the hall. And then some boy—I think it was Mike's best friend, Evan—said he had a number for a modeling agency and I should call it. But I know he was just making fun of me."

"They said all that?" I said. "Who are these people? Who do they think they are?" I was starting to get really mad. It sounded like she was surrounded by a bunch of bullies.

"The school used to pick on this guy Teddy, the plumber's son. He talks with a lisp and has a huge birthmark on his leg. And he peed in his pants once during a spelling bee. He moved one town over this year, and since he left, everybody started picking on me. It's like I'm the new Teddy." Taylor sounded so sad. "I don't want to be the new Teddy. I don't want to be Ostrich Girl, either. I just want to die."

"Don't say that," I said. "Don't say all those things."

"I'm so alone. Can I come stay with you? I'll take a bus to the city. I'll figure out where the hotel is. You're my only real friend."

I was hit by her words. I really had gotten in deep now.

"Taylor," I said. "Do *not* go anywhere. Just stay put. Stay right where you are." Then I made a quick decision. "I'm coming to visit you," I said.

I imagined Taylor showing up at Sabrina's doorstep with false hopes of being accepted as a refugee into the hotel suite. That would *not* go over well. I would definitely get fired and lose all chances of Sabrina signing my school's form that said I completed the internship.

"You're coming to visit me?" she said. "I'm so excited."

"Yep, I'm coming. It's only a matter of time," I said, suddenly realizing the weight of my words. "And I'll take you to Six Flags. As soon as there's a window, I'll be there."

Just then, I looked up and noticed Bronson crossing the street on his way to visit Sabrina. He saw me standing outside the hotel entrance and waved.

"Look, I gotta go," I said. "Just don't go anywhere. And give me a little time."

When we hung up the phone, Bronson was standing next to me. He had heard the end of my conversation.

"Just give you a little time, huh?" he said. "Is that your boyfriend or something?"

"Oh, no," I said. "I don't have a boyfriend."

"That's good news," he said, smiling. Then he lowered his voice. "I have to run upstairs."

"Yeah, I heard. She's up there waiting for you. Reconciliation time," I said.

"Not so much," he said. "I left tickets to a concert in the back pocket of a pair of my jeans. And they're stuffed away underneath one of her nightstands."

"So you're just here to get tickets?" I said, surprised.

"They're for tonight. It's that band I put on your mix called Split Seconds. They're playing at Roseland. You should come with me and check them out. I have an extra ticket. You like music, right?"

"Music. Uh, yeah, music is good. I, um, think I like music." That sounded ridiculous.

"Is that a yes?" he said, teasing me.

I wanted to go, but realistically, I couldn't go. Sabrina would slaughter me. It was too risky. I tried to make the "no" word come out of my mouth while looking in his eyes.

"Yes, I think that was a yes. . . ." I said. (I couldn't help it.)

He laughed. "Meet me outside the club at eight o'clock."

"Wait!" I said. "I don't know if I can." I looked up at the hotel.

"She's not spying on us," he said, catching on. "I think you should come. You deserve a little fun. She keeps you on a short leash."

I looked at him. What the hell? You only live once, right? "Okay," I said.

"See you then."

As I walked to the bookstore, it felt like I was an astronaut walking on the moon. Gravity had changed, and now I was floating. Did Bronson just ask me out on a date?

But then I thought up all the reasons I shouldn't go. I was Sabrina's intern, after all. If she found out, I could get fired. And on top of that, even though they were on a break, didn't

Sabrina and Bronson just light vanilla candles and play Sinatra? It didn't matter how adorable he was. I couldn't go. No way. No how. It just wasn't right.

At Shakespeare & Company, I picked up Sabrina's recommended read. As soon as I got home, I plopped down on my bed, and read the back jacket of *All Right, Not Awesome*, which said that it had sold millions of copies and was one of the most recommended books on successful business skills and leadership.

I had just started reading page one when my mom knocked on the door.

"We've both been working so hard," she said, walking into my room. "I feel like we haven't caught up in days."

I put my book down. "Yeah, being Sabrina's right hand is demanding."

"You look so tired," she said. "I don't like it when you're so beat up. Are they overworking my little baby? I'll have none of that. Give me the telephone. I'm going to call and have a word with them."

"You would not, Mom. That would be utterly embarrassing."

"Only kidding," my mom said. "Anyway, I'm running out to meet Diane for a late coffee to discuss strategy. We still haven't sold a thing. I'll see you later."

"Bye, Mom," I said, picking my book back up.

After finishing the first chapter, I walked out into the living room. My dad was watching TV by himself.

"Hi there," he said. "Wanna join?"

"Actually, I think I'm going out for a while," I told him.

"Where are you going?" my dad asked.

"There's a concert I was invited to," I said. "By someone from work."

"No name? How mysterious," he said. "Between you and your mother, I feel like everyone's jumping ship. It's an empty house these days."

"I know, Dad. We'll hang out soon. Promise."

"Yeah, see if you can pencil me in," my dad said, turning his attention back to the TV screen. "Be home by curfew. It's a dangerous city out there. And you know how I worry."

Chapter
15

WHEN I GOT TO Roseland, I saw Bronson standing outside by the front entrance. It cheered me up to see him. Just then, my cell phone rang. I answered it.

"L-Girl!" Evie yelled into the receiver.

"How's it shakin', E-Mama?" I said.

"Where have you been?" she asked. "I've left you a bunch of messages. I have so much to tell you."

Bronson was walking over to me now. I didn't want to be on the phone when we said our hellos.

"Evie, I gotta jump. At a concert with a hottie," I said.

"But I have so much to tell you—"

"I'll call you back later," I said, then hung up.

Bronson gave me a big hug. "You showed," he said. "Wasn't sure if you would."

"I wasn't sure, either," I said. "But I'm here."

"Want to go inside?" He led me past a huge bouncer and into the large ballroom.

Bronson and I squeezed our way through the crowd so that we could stand by the front of the stage. The audience went wild when the band charged onto the stage dressed in matching red suits with black button-down shirts.

The lead singer leaned in close to the microphone and looked out at the audience. "How you doing tonight?" he said.

The fans screamed and hollered.

"You sound good." The lead singer looked away and laughed as if embarrassed by the adulation. "I read this blurb recently online. Some critic was saying we're gonna be the next big thing. But you know what? We're already as big as we want to be because we have fans like you."

Everyone cheered even louder. One kid in the mezzanine took his jacket off and started spinning it around in the air over his head. "We worship you, man!" the kid screamed out.

The room laughed.

"Let's make some music," the lead singer said. Then the band burst into their first song.

Bronson and I danced with the crowd, but I started having nightmares that members of the paparazzi were lurking in the audience, trying to snap pictures of us. I had this vision of Sabrina opening up the next issue of *Party Weekly* and, to her horror, discovering a photograph of me out on the town with her boyfriend.

I tapped Bronson on the shoulder. "We have to talk. Do you think there's stalkarazzi at this concert?"

He laughed at me. "Probably not," he said. "Why? Are you scared?"

"A little," I said.

"I wouldn't worry about it," he said. "I have strong paparazzi radar. I usually see them a mile away."

"I hope so," I said.

"You're safe with me," he said. "Come on. Let's have some fun."

Bronson and I danced around for a bunch of songs. I recognized some of the tunes from the mix Bronson had given me. It was fun to sing aloud, throw my hands up in the air, and let loose.

Near the end of their set, the lead singer said, "Now, we're going to change things up a bit. I wrote this song last year hanging out in Jamaica. It has more of a reggae vibe to it. I want to see all the pretty girls out there shakin' it up."

The bass guitarist started to play a few chords. Bronson turned to me. "This is one of my favorites," he said, reaching out to hold my hand. He squeezed my fingers with his, and my palm tingled. I held on for a few seconds more, but then I let go. I had to pull it away and remind myself that this was not a date. We were just two friends enjoying an innocent night of rock'n'roll.

Then he put his arm around my waist. I let his fingers linger for a moment, but I knew if Sabrina saw me, I would probably get poisoned with cyanide or wake up one morning with an ax in my forehead. So I decided to move a little to the right. Away from him. And then a little farther to the right. And then even farther.

"Is everything okay?" he asked. He gave me a weird look.

"Yeah, it's great!" I said, pretending everything was. "Why?"

"You're just acting a little odd," Bronson said.

"It's just . . ." I said. The music was so loud. I felt like I was screaming in his ear. "I don't want to get in the way of you and Sabrina."

"You're not. We're over. I'm free to do what I want."

"But Sabrina thinks you're just on break. And besides, I know about what happened the other week."

"What happened?" Bronson said.

"You know," I said, trying to indicate with my eyes that I knew exactly what happened.

"I don't know. Really," he said.

I whispered in his ear. "I know that you and she—"

"I can barely hear you over the music. Can you talk louder?" Bronson said.

"That you and she—"

"I still can't hear you," he said.

"*That she and you had sex!*" Just then the band stopped playing in between songs. There was silence and my voice was heard shouting, "*Sex!*" over the crowd. Tons of kids turned and stared at us, stifling laughs.

The lead singer of the band even heard me. He laughed and said into the microphone, "Wow! Someone out there knows what she wants!" The crowd burst into cheers.

Completely embarrassed, I ran for the door. Bronson followed me out onto the street.

"I can't believe that just happened," I said, covering my face in humiliation. "Of all the words I could have screamed at the top of my lungs."

"Lily, listen to me." He grabbed my chin in his hand. "We didn't do that. That didn't happen."

"But I saw the blown-out candles and Sinatra's greatest hits. . . ."

"All we did that night was fight. We weren't getting along. It wasn't the right time, you know. . . . Besides, she acted so crazy at the dance studio that day. It was the last straw. Nothing I do is ever good enough. She's impossible to please."

"Today when you saw her, did you guys talk about getting back together?" I asked.

Bronson shook his head. "No, I told her it's over. There's a lot of great things about her. She's gorgeous. Her life is so exciting. I see the way she acts around other people, but she's different with me. Nicer. She told me that she was miserable without me, and she would just die if I didn't go with her to this party Antonio's throwing at Saddle Ranch. It's just sometimes I feel like I'm tagging along."

"I know about Antonio's party. It's a week away."

"I'm not going. I think it's best if Sabrina and I don't talk for a while. I need to do my own thing now. And she's obsessed with asking me who this other girl is that I like."

"You didn't tell her?" I asked, worried.

He shook his head.

Then I had to ask for confirmation. "Do I know her?"

"No. Not at all," he said.

Of course. I never should have gotten my hopes up. . . .

Then Bronson broke into a smile. "Yeah, maybe you know her just a little bit," he said. By the way he kept looking into my eyes without blinking, I realized that he meant me. I felt a rush of excitement.

I wanted to tell him how I felt back, but Sabrina's face flashed through my head. And I could hear her voice saying, "You're part of the inner sanctum now. Get it? If you break my trust . . ."

"I should get going," I told him, starting to walk down the street. "It's getting late."

He followed me. "It's only a little after eleven."

"I have a midnight curfew. It's the one thing my crazy dad's strict about. Otherwise, he stays up and gets worried that I've been kidnapped or mugged."

"We still have at least half an hour. Besides, I'll be gone soon," he said. "I'm going back to L.A. on September first."

"That soon?" I said. It suddenly sunk in how fast the summer had flown by.

"School starts on the seventh. Plus, my dad set up some meetings for us. We're just about done working on that Cancun thriller I told you about. Early September, we're gonna start showing it to producers and trying to sell it. It would really change my life if it gets made." Bronson looked me in the eyes. "Look, we don't have to *do* anything. I just want to hang out and talk with you. Let me, at least, walk you back to your apartment. We can stop and get gelato on the way."

I knew I should go home. But it was hard to not enjoy this time together. "Okay. Fine," I said. "But only for a little bit."

He linked his arm in mine and we started walking toward Broadway. We stopped at a gelateria and ordered waffle cones stuffed with cookie dough and mint chocolate chip. As we walked down the street, I couldn't help but check for paparazzi on the loose. There were so many dark corners and alleyways where they might be hiding out, stalking Bronson and me with their powerful zoom lenses. So far, thank goodness, the coast was clear.

"I can't believe school is starting again soon. There's a back-to-school party at this girl in my grade's house. Her name is

Wendy Goldlocks. Her family has Picassos and Matisses in their apartment. The rumor is that even though we haven't started senior year, she's already gotten into Harvard. Her parents donated a few million to build a new building."

"Nice life," he said.

"Yeah," I said. I realized that as soon as the summer ended, I would have to start filling out all my college applications. And then I would have to keep my fingers crossed for months while I waited for the deciding word from Brown.

"It's funny. The same people have been popular since fourth grade. It's like they've been put on pedestals and my class has been engrained to see them a certain way. Almost like celebrities, I guess. They're raised above the rest of us, and the rumor mill—the New York Private-School Gossip Circuit—supports that. It helps keep the popular people up and the rest of us down."

"I wasn't always the coolest, either," Bronson said. "When I was in middle school, I slept with one of those huge retainer things for my teeth."

"You mean headgear?" I asked.

"Something like that. Until one day, I woke up in the middle of the night and the metal device had fallen down around my neck and it was, like, choking me. I told my parents there was no way I would wear it ever again. So now I'm stuck with this small gap between my two front teeth."

"What small gap?" I asked.

He smiled, and I examined his teeth. "I can't see any space there at all," I assured him.

"Well, I can," he said.

I laughed. "Do you think Sabrina ever went through an awkward phase?" I asked.

Bronson thought about it and then shook his head. "No," he said. "I know that she didn't."

"How can you be so sure?" I asked.

"I've seen all her photo albums—pictures of her since she was a baby. She was beautiful and cool at every stage. But that's not always a good thing," he said.

"Why not?" I asked.

"I think everyone who goes through an awkward phase is kinda lucky," Bronson said. "Even if it only lasts a few months."

"It doesn't feel lucky at the time."

"But when you snap out of it, which hopefully you will, that awkward time will always keep your ego in check. The pain of being teased and tormented helps keep you grounded."

When he said that, I couldn't help but think of Taylor. I hoped that she would outgrow her awkward phase, too, one day and life would become happier and easier.

★ ★ ★

When Bronson and I arrived outside my apartment building, I looked up and saw Sabrina's face on the billboard across the street advertising *Spinning the Wheel of Fire*. Then I looked at Bronson.

"Nice apartment building," he said.

"Thanks. I live on the twenty-second floor with my nut-job parents," I told him.

He leaned into me. I could smell the cologne he was wearing. This was the opportunity I had been waiting for—a kiss with Bronson.

But then I looked up and saw Sabrina's face again on that billboard. It looked like she was glaring down at me.

Bronson's lips were so close to mine now. I could almost feel them.

"Can I see you tomorrow night?" Bronson asked.

This was killing me. I wanted to spend every second with him until he left, but I knew that I couldn't. We were like Shakespeare's Romeo and Juliet. Bronson and I were two potential lovers star-crossed by an actual starlet.

"Bronson." I pulled away. "I can't do this. I'm sorry. I gave Sabrina my trust. I've worked so hard all summer to get this far. It's the whole reason I didn't go to soccer camp. I gave up being with my friends. If she found out . . ."

"She won't," he said.

"It's just," I continued, "I can tell how important you are to her. She really cares about you. She acts crazy sometimes, but deep down you mean a lot to her."

"But Sabrina and I are over now," he said, going in to kiss me.

I turned my head.

"Denied," Bronson said, shaking his head and laughing softly.

"It's just not right. It would tear her up if she knew you were out with me right now."

"Are you going to tell her?"

I shook my head.

"Then she'll never know." He went in to try to kiss me again.

I could feel his breath on my face. I wanted to make out with him so badly.

"But *I* would know." I turned my head again. "She's been

so depressed lately about you. And I hate seeing her that way. Even though she's mean and bossy sometimes, I still care about her and—"

"Did you ever wonder if she cares about you?" he asked.

I looked down. I hadn't really thought about it before. *Did* she care about me? Even a teensy weensy bit? Or maybe I was just the girl who answered her fan mail, logged her birthday presents, took her to appointments, and handled her schedule—this summer.

"I have a prediction," Bronson said. "When you leave in two weeks, she won't miss you one bit. It's business. You're just her intern. Nothing more, nothing less."

"That's harsh," I said.

"I'm not saying that to be mean, Lily. I just don't want you to get hurt."

But the damage was already done. Something about what he said made me feel sick inside, I think because I knew that there was a big possibility that he was right. I remembered the way she just recycled the birthday gift I gave her and the way she liked to order me around: *Get my lunch. Get me more tampons. Make me another appointment at Delicious Beauty Bar.*

"Lily," Bronson said. "Don't get upset."

"I can't help it," I said, embarrassed that what he said was affecting me so much.

"I just wanted to remind you," he said. "She'll take you for all she can. Don't forget to take something for yourself along the way, okay?"

"I'll try," I said.

Then he wrote on a piece of paper all of his contact information in Los Angeles. "If you ever want to get out of New

York and take a little vacation," he said, "I'll show you all my favorite spots."

"You promise?" I said.

"Yeah, come crash with me and my parents in Burbank. There's a Bob's Big Boy just up the street. They make the biggest burgers. And I'll take you to the best karaoke lounge. We can dance some more together. Do the Shopping Cart."

"And the Bus Driver?" I asked.

"Absolutely," he said.

Bronson and I hugged good-bye.

"And let me know if you change your mind before I leave."

Then he took off. I watched him as he disappeared around the corner. I couldn't believe I had passed up my chance to kiss him. As I went back upstairs to my apartment, I missed him already. But then I realized something in the elevator. There was one thing and one thing only that I felt good about. Tonight, despite all its wild temptations, I proved that I was a Girl's Girl.

When I walked in the front door, my dad was waiting up for me.

"You're late," he said. "It's past midnight."

"Sorry," I said.

"No you're not," he said. "You knew what you were doing. I don't ask much of you, Lily. I give you a lot of freedom. I just ask that you follow this one rule."

"Sorry. I didn't know if you would be staying up for me."

"I always wait up for you," he said, shaking his head. "You have a cell phone. It only takes a minute to pick it up and call me to say you're running late."

"I said I was sorry," I said.

"What should I do here?" my dad said. "Any suggestions? You don't seem to like to follow rules."

"Please, Dad. I'm exhausted. I had a long day at work and I just had to say good-bye to one of the most amazing and cool guys I have ever met. So let's talk some other time because I'm going to bed." I turned on my heels and walked to my room.

"I'm not done talking to you," my dad said.

"Have your people call my people," I said, dropping some Hollywood lingo. Then I shut the door.

*   *   *

The next morning, I woke up and had that amazing experience. You know the one when you open your eyes, and as you come back into consciousness you remember something . . . and you take a moment to distinguish if it's a dream or if it really happened? And then you realize—to your wonderment—it really happened.

That's how it felt when I woke up and remembered hanging out with Bronson last night. It was hard knowing I wouldn't see him again this summer. I pulled out the piece of paper from my jean jacket with his contact information. Maybe I would go visit him in Burbank one day. I'm sure we would keep in touch. Besides, it was nice knowing I had a super-hot guy friend out in La-La Land.

When I went out into the living room, my dad was lying on the ottoman chair highlighting passages from a book on ancient Greek philosophy.

"Where's Mom?" I asked him.

"Who knows anymore? Making a pie, eating a pie, selling

a pie," he said. "So have your people called my people yet? It's been almost nine hours."

I took a bowl from the kitchen and filled it with milk and Cheerios. "They've been busy rolling calls all morning, but you're next on the list." I played along.

"Great," he said. "So when they call, I'll give them the big news."

"What big news?" I asked him.

"I've decided to ground you," he said, highlighting another passage from his book.

"Ground me?" I asked. "But you've never grounded me in my whole life. Isn't that what parents did in the eighteen hundreds?"

"I've been too much of a pushover," my dad said. "It's not fair to you or to me."

"You can't ground me," I said. "I'm a working girl with a job to do."

"Your internship is during the day. You can come and go as you please during that time. In fact, I'm all for it."

"But sometimes Sabrina needs me at night. If there's a party in the evening, I have to be there for her."

"You're only sixteen years old. How many parties do you need to go to?"

"You can never have too many parties. Especially ones with free appetizers and GBs. Plus, going to parties is now technically my job."

"What's are GBs?" my dad asked.

"Gift bags. Only the in people know that."

"'In' people? Are you an in person?"

"Now I am," I said proudly.

"What exactly are you inside of? I don't get it."

"The scene. What's happening. The pulse. What's cool. What's not cool. Where to go. Where to be seen. How to stand. How to smile."

"What the hell are you talking about?"

"Ugh, Dad," I said. "You're so out of touch. Get with the program," I said. Then I grabbed my bowl of cereal and went to eat it in my own room.

★　★　★

On Monday morning, I got ready for work and went down to the Mercer. When I got to the suite, Eleanor was sitting in the living room, crocheting a scarf. She actually said hello to me.

"Morning, Eleanor," I said back. I realized then that she was just trying to do her job and make Sabrina's mom happy. It was her responsibility to be a guardian and size people up to make sure they weren't a bad influence on Sabrina, just like it was my job to be Sabrina's intern and take care of her day-to-day needs.

I went into the bedroom and found Sabrina in a chair by the window, brushing Mercedes's hair. He looked content curled up in her lap. She had him dressed in plaid boxers and a white T-shirt. Sabrina smiled and waved at me when I came in. Her eyes were puffy as if she had been bawling her eyes out all night.

"Are you okay?" I asked.

"I'm great. Why? Do I not look okay?" she said defensively.

"Your eyes are very red," I said.

"So are yours."

I glanced at my reflection in a hanging mirror. My eyes looked fine.

"I had a long talk with Bert today. They want me to play Laura in a revival of Tennessee Williams's *Glass Menagerie* this December. It's gonna be a stretch for me playing such an introverted, shy girl, but I'm up for the challenge. I just love Tennessee. His words read like poetry."

"I studied the play in school and loved it," I said.

"Times like this, I want to call Bronson and tell him the good news," she said. "I bet he was with another girl this weekend. I could feel it in my bones. I couldn't stop bawling just thinking of him on a date with someone else."

It was ironic. Sometimes Sabrina seemed paranoid. But then other times, her paranoia turned into extremely perceptive intuition.

"If I find out who she is, I swear—"

"What would you do exactly?" I said, suddenly petrified.

"Punch her in the mouth and hold her down while a dentist gave her all gold teeth."

"Ouch," I said.

"Maybe I should rebound with Antonio. He is cute, don't ya think?"

"In a slickster, pockmarked-face, too-old-for-you sort of way," I said.

She thought about it for a second and then nodded her head. "Yeah, you're right," she said. "I'm sure I'll meet someone else wonderful soon. Maybe an East Coast guy for a change." Sabrina picked up an envelope that was on the table. "Oh, guess what arrived this morning?" Sabrina opened the envelope and counted aloud, "One-two-three-four tickets to the Rock the House Awards."

My eyes lit up. "Wow!" I said, starting to drool.

"They're coming up next week," she said. "August thirty-first, your last day working for me."

"So soon," I said.

"You haven't been perfect, Lily. I still don't feel like I can depend on you completely," Sabrina said, shaking her head.

I was worried she was going to take back the bonus she had promised me.

"But I can see," she continued, "that you've been trying to step up to the plate. So here. As promised." Sabrina separated two of the tickets and handed them to me.

My hands trembled as I placed my fingers on the tickets. Finally, I was holding them in my hands. I stood there fixated, reading every inch of the fine print. Radio City Music Hall. Eight P.M. August 31. Orchestra center. Seats C401 and C402.

"I'm taking Antonio this year since Bronson and I are obviously Kaput. Anyway, I'm jumping in the shower. You should get to work doing my expenses from July. I need you to input them into a spreadsheet on the computer. Let me get you the stack of receipts." Sabrina stood up but quickly lost her balance and started to sway back and forth. She dropped back down into the chair.

"Are you all right?" I asked, concerned.

"I'm fine. Just a little dizzy spell. All better now." She stood up again. This time she successfully walked to the desk drawer and pulled out an envelope overflowing with receipts.

I looked over on the counter and saw the bottle of diet pills. There were only a few capsules left. Maybe the pills were responsible for making her dizzy. When she ran out of this bottle, I would make no more trips to the vegetable bodega in the East Village. Even if she yelled at me. It was important to please her, but not when it involved playing a part in her hurting herself.

As Sabrina took a shower, I went through the stack of receipts that had piled up from July and entered the information on to a spreadsheet.

Henri Bendel $4,562.34	Pocketbook, shoes, and jeans
Wearable Art Clothes $399.23	Designer one-of-a-kind T-shirt
Amore Restaurante $989.22	Dinner w/Bronson
Little Guy Groomers $2,002.10	Fluff & dry visits for Mercedes
S&T Wireless $1,245.03	Cell phone bill
Susan Ying $550.00	Private masseuse
Limousine Service $5,086.00	Car service
Yellow Cabs $2,417.00	Taxi rides
Mercer Hotel Bill $89,050.22	Hotel suite & room service

I was blown away by Sabrina's expenses. I couldn't imagine going out on a dinner date and spending almost a thousand dollars for two people, or running up more than a thousand dollars for one month's worth of cell phone charges. It must be quite a life to be able to spend without thinking twice.

I was still working on the spreadsheet when Sabrina got out of the shower. She put in one of her Country Western dance tapes and practiced the Texas two-step around her bedroom. Then she spent a few hours working with a speech coach on perfecting a Texan accent.

At the end of the day, I showed Sabrina the spreadsheet with all her expenses. She glanced at it and told me to send it along with the receipts to her accountant. I looked up her accountant in my BlackBerry, stuck the receipts and paperwork into a FedEx envelope, and left it, on my way out, at the Mercer front desk.

* * *

That Friday Sabrina wanted to spend the day with her agent, Crazy Eddie, who was in from Los Angeles. He was taking her to lunch at the Palm and then they were seeing a matinee of a Broadway show. That evening was Antonio's big party at Saddle Ranch, so Sabrina told me I should rest up because it would be a late night.

I lay in bed most of the morning plowing through more chapters of *All Right, Not Awesome.* I decided to send Sabrina a very nice e-mail on the BlackBerry:

> I'm really enjoying the book. My favorite part is how its says that All Right is the enemy of Awesome. Because once people are All Right, they become lazy and don't work extra hard to become Awesome. I hope to always make the leap from All Right to Awesome for you! Lily

It was a total kiss-ass e-mail. I was saying exactly what I knew she wanted to hear.

She didn't write back for an hour. Finally, my BlackBerry went off. I grabbed it and read the message:

> At intermission of Broadway play. Happy you liked the book. Remember it's important to make the leap

for YOU, too. Not just for ME. See you tonight.

xoxo, Sabrina

I walked out into the living room. My mom was in the kitchen with Diane. She was putting pies into white boxes and passing them to Diane, who was tying red ribbons around them.

"Morning," my mom said. "Guess what? The Rosier Café wants three pies delivered weekly. Our first customer."

"Congrats," I said. "That is awesome."

"Hey, Miss Thing," Diane said when she saw me. "Any juicy Hollywood stories?"

"I'm still waking up," I told her. "I'll tell you tons later."

I headed into the living room, passing my dad, who was on the couch doing the crossword in the *New York Times*. He looked up at me.

"Pops, we have to talk," I told him. "There's a huge party tonight and I have to go. I'm officially asking permission ahead of time."

"You're grounded, remember? Besides, I thought it would be fun if we had a family night and rented a movie. I already spoke to your mom and she thought it was a great idea. We can even rent one of Sabrina's flicks if you want. I'd like to see what all this fuss is about."

"But I have to go to this event. Sabrina needs me."

"I think you can skip one event to be with your family," my dad said.

"Mom, did you hear that Dad's grounding me? This is so not fair!" I said.

"I'm not getting into the middle of it," my mom said. "We've been through this before."

"Look, Lily, I'm concerned. I was at the faculty club yesterday, and one of the TAs said she heard on the radio that Sabrina no longer speaks to her mom. Did you know that?"

Diane suddenly jumped into the conversation. "Is that true?" she asked.

"Yes, it's true, and of course I know that. I spend twenty-four-seven with her. I know lots of her secrets."

"Do you know why they don't speak?" my dad said.

Diane just stared at me and my father and listened to our conversation.

"This is so 101. Her mom has been piggybacking on her celebrity status," I said. "She has become a party mom. Sabrina calls her the Countess of Malibu."

"Ooh, that sounds fun. I want to be the Countess of Malibu," Diane said.

"That's not what the assistant heard on the radio," my dad said. "She heard that Sabrina punched her mom in the face. She socked her and gave her a black eye. Then she tried to light their Malibu house on fire. Did you know that?"

"I don't believe it," I said. "That's not what she told me. That's just the tabloids."

"Holy cow, did she really sock it to her own mother?" Diane said.

"Could you stop butting in?" my father said. "I'm trying to have a conversation with my daughter."

Diane shut her mouth and looked away, offended. "Touchy," she said.

"Come on," my mom said, "let's get these over to the Rosier." They piled the pies carefully into a large bag and headed out the door.

"Be back in an hour," my mom said. "And I wish the two of you would stop fighting."

"Me, too," Diane said. "And I want to hear more celebrity gossip later."

My dad ignored both of them and kept talking. "This actress is a wild card. I want you to be careful. I don't care if she is some big-time star."

"Star*let*, Dad."

"Excuse me?" he said.

"Stars are twenty-one and over. Sabrina's only sixteen now and therefore, she's a star*let*."

"Call her whatever you want, she's out of control. She tried to set her mother's house on fire."

"Dad, she gets worked up sometimes, but she would never do that. You're buying into the BS just like everyone else. I promise you, I really know her."

"Tonight, you're staying in. One night off from schmoozing with Hollywood types won't kill you. We haven't had any time together lately. Tonight, you are just going to be my normal daughter again."

"No, Dad! Stop telling me what I am or am not going to be. It's the same way with Mom. I'm sick of it. You don't want Mom to start her own business. And you don't want me to go out in the world and become famous and successful in Hollywood! You just want everything to stay the same! And it's not going to! It's changing every second. So deal with it!"

"Lily, do not talk to me like that. I will not let you treat me this way. I have to be honest—in these last few weeks, I haven't liked you so much."

I stopped in my tracks. And looked up at him. Tears started welling up in my eyes. I couldn't help it. "Excuse me?" I said.

"I just don't like who you're becoming."

I couldn't believe my ears. I could feel the flood gates start to open. *Don't cry. Don't cry.* I tried hard, but I couldn't fight off my tears.

"Then why would you want to watch a movie with me anyway? If you don't like me, then have fun by yourself!" I said. I went into my room and packed up some of my things in a big purse. I threw it over my shoulder and headed for the front door.

"Lily, don't walk out of here. Get back here," my dad called after me.

But it was too late; I was out in the hallway and running for the elevators.

*   *   *

I didn't want to go home the rest of the day, so I was stuck getting ready for the Saddle Ranch party on the streets of New York. I used the gift certificate Sabrina had given me to get my hair done at Delicious Beauty Bar. The stylist gave me some sexy, side-sweeping bangs and made my hair blonder in the front.

Next I went to Bloomingdale's. Off the sale rack, I bought myself a cocktail dress with a lace trim. I also found a good deal on a pair of black heels. Then I hopped from one makeup counter to the next, testing eye shadows and lipsticks. Some of the nice beauticians offered to give me free ten-minute makeovers, and by the time I walked back out onto 59th Street, I was done up like a Gucci model.

Part of me wanted to go home and show my parents how I looked all dressed up. But I knew my dad and I were still in a big fight. And if I went home, we would just end up arguing more. Plus, he would certainly not let me back out of the house. That afternoon, I sent my mom a text to her cell phone saying that I didn't care what Dad said—I was going to a huge party tonight and no one could stop me. She sent me one back calling me a little troublemaker but telling me to have fun and be safe.

* * *

When I got down to Soho that evening, the Strap Girls were standing in the lobby.

"Your hair looks so much better, chica," Valerie said when she saw me.

"Way to clean up your act. You look good," Nikki said.

I couldn't believe Valerie was finally calling me "chica." Like I was part of their group now. Even though she was such a witch, in a strange way, it was horribly gratifying to finally feel accepted by them.

"Where's Sabrina?" I asked.

"She's already in the limo. She didn't feel well, so she's lying down on the backseat." Valerie twisted the diamond stud in her nose.

"Gotcha," I said. "What's the matter?"

"She fell down in the bathroom," Nikki said, straightening her ponytail.

"Ouch," I said. I wondered what happened and if she had another one of her dizzy flashes.

The Strap Girls and I went outside and climbed into the back of the limo. Sabrina was sprawled out on the backseat.

"Are you all right, Sabrina?" I said to her. "I'm worried about you."

"Shhh! Be quiet" Sabrina said, cutting me off. "Don't make me send you to HowNotToBeAnnoying.com."

I definitely did not want to be sent there so I shut my mouth.

"Turn on the music!" Valerie screamed at the limo driver. He fiddled with the dial and turned on some hip-hop music. Valerie and Nikki started to dance in their seats.

"Are you ready to shake what your mama gave ya?" Valerie said, bumping her shoulder into Sabrina's.

"Look what I just bought!" Nikki said, pulling a sleek digital camera out of her purse. "Sabrina and Valerie, get closer together. I want to take your picture."

Valerie went over and put her arm around Sabrina.

"Get off me," Sabrina said. "I have a splitting headache. And turn that music off!"

The driver quickly turned off the dial.

Valerie and Nikki sat back in their seats. They kept looking at each other with confused, bug-eyed expressions.

We drove to the party in complete silence. For many reasons, it was very different from the first time we rode together in the beginning of the summer to the *Spinning the Wheel of Fire* premiere. Bronson wasn't here. I missed him sitting next to me and giving the behind-the-scenes lowdown of Sabrina's world as I skinny-dipped in his blue-gray eyes. The Strap Girls weren't shaking their butts and snapping their manicured fingers to the beat of pulsating electronica. And Sabrina wasn't filling up glasses to make a toast to all her friends. Instead, she lay collapsed on the backseat, tossing and turning. Her lipstick was smudged so it went above her mouth, and her face looked pale and sullen.

I prayed Sabrina would feel okay once we got to the party. I remembered how embarrassed she sounded when she told the story about drinking too many cosmic lemonades and vomiting on a government ambassador in Nigeria. I feared that tonight, if she wasn't careful, something equally or more humiliating could happen.

Chapter 16

WHEN SABRINA, VALERIE, NIKKI, and I arrived at the Saddle Ranch, we were immediately directed onto the red carpet. Sabrina pulled it together, waving at the photographers. This time, I kept up with them the whole time, smiling and strutting. It was a relief not to be carrying a dog in my purse.

A mob of people swarmed around the entrance, yelling at the bouncer and trying to get inside.

"Not on the list. Keep moving!" the bouncer said to two high-school girls who walked away dejected.

Bert stood outside next to several party planners, young fashionistas in their early twenties with walkie-talkies. Antonio's assistant, Michelle, was also outside helping check people in off the list. As Sabrina spoke with Bert, I had a quick chance to catch up with her.

"Hey, Michelle," I said.

"Hi! I've been helping Antonio prep the party since eight in the morning. It has been nutty," Michelle said.

"A little tip," I said. "Don't let in a woman named Lucy Myerstone from *Glamster* magazine. She's trouble."

"Thanks for letting me know," she said. I looked over at Sabrina. She was in the middle of a conversation with Bert.

"When do you head back to Brown?" I asked Michelle.

"In a few days," she said. "I'm packing up the car and driving back to Rhode Island with my best friend."

"That sounds so fun. I can't wait to go to college."

"When you come up for a campus tour, look me up. I'll introduce you to my friends and take you to a fun college party."

"It's a deal," I said.

"Come on, Lily! Let's go!" Valerie yelled to me as Sabrina and Nikki headed into the restaurant.

"See you later," I said to Michelle, and followed them inside.

"This way first!" Sabrina said. She was revved up, ready to attack the party like a wild animal. We ran across the sawdust floor and headed straight for the bar.

The room was packed wall to wall with guests, but everyone moved aside when they saw us with Sabrina.

The bartender came right over to us. "Four lemon-drop shots," Sabrina told him.

"Coming right up," he said.

I turned to Sabrina. "He doesn't care that we're underage?"

"Nope. All he cares about is about making *me* happy."

The bartender slid the four shot glasses across the bar. Sabrina passed them out to us. We downed them.

"Hey, if it's not too much trouble, can I have your autograph?" the bartender asked.

Sabrina grabbed a pen off the bar and started to sign a napkin.

"No," the bartender said. "I want you to autograph me on my bicep." He picked up his shirtsleeve.

"Whatever's clever," Sabrina said, shrugging her shoulders and writing her name in cursive on his muscle.

He thanked her by giving her another four lemon-drop shots.

"One more time!" she screamed, passing out the new round of shots and clinking glasses with Nikki, Valerie, and me. "Down the hatch, sisters!"

I threw my head back and swallowed the whole thing in one gulp. Then we all grabbed fresh-cut lime wedges and sucked on them.

Sabrina smiled at me with the lime still in her mouth. "Let's go say hi to my agent, Eddie. I want to thank him for taking me to the theater today," she said.

Crazy Eddie was sitting at a VIP booth by the stage, schmoozing with Antonio and Sabrina's publicist, Violetta. As the country band rocked out on banjos and fiddles, Sabrina and I swung into the booth next to them. Crazy Eddie gave Sabrina a big hug as Valerie and Nikki stood by the edge of the booth, scoping the room for cute boys.

"I forgot to thank you today for the birthday goat," Crazy Eddie said.

"You liked it?" Sabrina said.

"Loved it. What a great idea for a present—donating a goat to a Third World country."

"Thank you. These things just come to me," Sabrina said.

I looked at her. I couldn't believe she was taking credit for my genius.

"Well, you're smart, and tonight you look like a billion dollars," Eddie said, admiring Sabrina's black leather pants and halter top made of gold sequins.

"Maybe because I'm about to make you a billion dollars," Sabrina joked.

"You're my girl," Eddie said. "I'm proud of you. This part is made for you. I know you're going to deliver an award-winning performance. You're like a mix of Marilyn Monroe and Natalie Wood."

"Really?" Sabrina said. "I like to think of myself as a mix of myself and . . . myself."

Eddie burst into laughter. He had a loud, hearty laugh.

"Hi, Eddie," I said, leaning into their conversation. "Thank you so much for introducing me to Sabrina and telling me about this internship."

"Yeah, sure, no problem," Eddie said. "I heard you've been doing a good job. Keep it that way. Oh, and say hi to your dad."

I suddenly felt very guilty. I imagined my dad watching movies and eating popcorn at home, still angry with me.

"Come on. Let's do a lap," Sabrina said, grabbing my arm. We continued walking around the party. Sabrina kept stopping to say hi to any familiar faces.

"This is called working the party," she whispered in my ear. "See how I'm giving everyone their thirty seconds of attention? And I always look them in the eye when I speak to them. It makes them feel important, like they're the only one in the room."

"Who are all these people?" I asked.

"It's the cast and crew for my upcoming movie, plus any socialites lucky enough to get on the guest list."

Sabrina noticed the Strap Girls standing around the

mechanical-bull pen and ran over to them. I followed her.

"Listen, girlies, I have a dare," Sabrina said. "Tonight, we are all going to ride the bull. Doesn't it look fun?" I saw her stumble for a moment and then hold on to the side of the ring for balance.

"It looks hilarious," Nikki said, snapping a picture with her camera.

Sabrina grabbed a few drinks off a waitress's tray and handed them to us. "Once I saw a girl on one of those," Sabrina said. "And she had toilet paper hanging out of the back of her underwear. How embarrassing!"

"Once I saw a girl riding one of those and she got her period while she was on it and everyone saw," Valerie said.

"Ouch," we all said, feeling the pain.

"So who wants to go first?" Sabrina said.

"How 'bout Lily?" Valerie said, pushing me into the ring.

"It's okay. I'll go a little bit later," I told her.

"No, you go first, Lily," Sabrina said. "You're going to do great."

"Here's your next victim!" Valerie screamed to the man operating the mechanical-bull machine. Then she shoved me through the gates into the ring.

"You can do it, Lily!" Sabrina said. "You're my Wild West sister!"

The crowd stared to cheer. My adrenaline began to race.

I turned to the man operating the bull and said, "It's my first time. Any suggestions?"

"Don't fall off," he said.

I climbed on cautiously, and the man threw the switch. The bull started to buck. First slowly, then rapidly, up and down. I held on to the metal grip with one hand and waved the other in the air to balance. My knees dug in. My left hand flailed uncontrollably in the air. I expected to be terrified, but I actually started laughing like I was riding my own personal roller coaster.

"Don't fall!" Sabrina screamed.

"Don't lose your balance!" Nikki screamed.

I saw Valerie walk over to the mechanical-bull operator. "Don't be such a sissy," she told the guy. "Make it go faster! Faster!"

The bull master followed her orders and made it speed up.

"Is that all you got? Faster! Faster!" Valerie shouted at the bull master.

I held on for my life. The mechanical bull went into overdrive and within seconds, I slid clumsily down the animal's side onto the padded ground.

I jumped to my feet. My head was spinning and my legs and arms were burning. As I walked out of the ring, I slapped a bunch of people high fives.

"Forty-five seconds! Nice job," a guy said.

"Yeah, you did awesome!" another kid said.

I flashed Valerie a smile of victory. She yelled at me, "You got off lucky."

Sabrina suddenly ran into the ring, pushing past me. "My turn! My turn!" she screamed, wobbling slightly.

I could tell she was buzzed now off of those drinks. "Are you sure you're okay?" I asked her.

"I'm fine!" she said, running past me.

I watched Sabrina climb on the bull. The entire crowd in the restaurant gathered around the pit, cheering. I stood next to Nikki and hollered along with everybody else.

Sabrina screamed out, "Yeeeeehawwwww!"

She knew she had the entire party's attention, and she was amped to put on a good show.

"Faster! Faster!" she screamed to the mechanical-bull operator. "Do it like you did before."

The man controlling the bull's speed followed her orders.

"Is that all you have?" Sabrina hollered.

The guy turned it up even faster. Everyone screamed and went wild. Sabrina yelled at the crowd, "Who's your Cowgirl Willie?!"

The room cheered. Antonio and Crazy Eddie were on the sidelines hollering, "You are! You are!"

Then Sabrina took one hand off the bull and threw it in the air, waving it around like a lasso. She threw her imaginary lasso to a cute boy in the audience. He laughed and played along, pretending it was pulling his neck toward her.

The bull master made the bull go even quicker. Then I noticed Sabrina's head shook back and forth like it was going to snap. As the bull lurched forward, Sabrina suddenly flew off of it, catapulting down onto the mats. The crowd gasped. Valerie, Nikki, and I jumped over the fence into the ring.

"Owwwww!" Sabrina screamed. She was lying on the matted floor, wailing and holding her arm. "*Owwww!*"

Antonio, Michelle, Bert, and Crazy Eddie ran over to her.

"What's the matter?" Bert said. "Tell me what hurts."

"My head. My arm. My shoulder. All of it kills!" Sabrina yelled out.

"Are you okay, Sabrina? We called an ambulance," Antonio said.

"Help is on the way," Crazy Eddie said.

"Sabrina, you're turning white," Valerie said.

"I feel like I'm going to pass out," Sabrina said.

"Get some cold washcloths!" Michelle screamed.

"Someone hold her head up," Antonio said.

Bert looked at me and shook his head. "I told you to keep an eye on her. Now look what happened. This is your partly your fault."

We heard sirens, and then two paramedics rushed through the front doors, pushing a stretcher. Sabrina's eyes filled with tears, and she looked just like a little girl. The paramedics strapped her in and lifted her up onto the gurney.

Valerie, Nikki, and I ran to keep up as they wheeled her away. After they pushed the gurney into the back of the ambulance, the paramedics said only one of us could ride with Sabrina to the hospital. Val and Nikki said they would stay together and take a cab, so I jumped inside.

It was strange being inside an ambulance and looking through the back window at the cars behind us. I sat on a seat next to the side wall, my knees inches away from where Sabrina lay on the stretcher. A paramedic sat on the other side of Sabrina. He asked her about what happened.

"I'm in so much pain," Sabrina kept crying. "Help me. Make it go away."

When we got there, they put her into a bed in the emergency ward. Valerie, Nikki, and I sat around giving Sabrina Kleenexes to dry her tears. Bert and Eleanor were also there for support.

The doctor came in to examine Sabrina. "Let me take a look at you," he said, walking over to her. He asked her to try moving her arm and shoulder. "It looks like you may have dislocated your right shoulder. We're going to take you down to the X-ray room shortly and determine exactly what is wrong. Also, a nurse will be by to take a blood test. And we'll need a urine sample."

"I hate doing that," Sabrina said. "It's so humiliating."

"I understand, but we need to find out exactly what is wrong with you," the doctor said.

After a nurse took the blood test and Sabrina sheepishly disappeared into the bathroom with a plastic cup, she was wheeled away for a series of X-rays.

"Are they going to stick me into one of those claustrophobic capsules that look like a tanning bed?" Sabrina asked as they pushed her into the hallway.

"No, you'll just lie down on a metal surface," a male nurse said, pushing her down the hall and out of sight.

After the technicians ran a series of X-rays, Sabrina was wheeled back to her partitioned area in the ER. The doctor came by shortly after. He confirmed after reading the results that Sabrina had dislocated her right shoulder and sustained a mild concussion. He recommended she stay at the hospital for two nights, as he wanted to monitor her recovery.

The doctor went on to explain that the blood and urine tests showed traces of a chemical called phenylpropanolamine (PPA). He said he knew that this ingredient was found in some cough-and-cold products, but it was also in certain diet pills. The doctor warned Sabrina that there was research done that said PPA can cause loss of balance and may increase the risk of certain types of strokes or bleeding into the brain for young women.

Sabrina had trouble looking the doctor in the eye while he told her this information. Bert also got especially agitated during this conversation. He stopped the doctor on the way out.

"Do you have a recommendation for a nutritionist?" I overheard Bert whisper to the doctor. The doctor nodded and said he would provide a referral before Sabrina left the hospital.

I looked over at Sabrina, who was staring down at her lap. Her face grew very sad. I sat down on the chair next to the bed.

"How are you holding up?" I asked.

"I wish my mom was here," she said.

"I understand," I said. "Times like this, a girl needs her mom."

"But I'm still pissed about what happened between me and her," Sabrina said.

"None of that stuff in the tabloids is true, right? About you socking her in the eye or lighting the house on fire?"

Sabrina gave me an incredulous look. "I'm passionate," Sabrina said. "Not psychotic."

"I thought it was a lie. But I just wanted to make sure," I said. "Can you tell me what happened?"

Sabrina looked over to make sure Bert wasn't listening in. Then she leaned into me. "This past May, my dad called me from Japan to say he was gonna marry that Sushi Mambo waitress. That he loved her more than he ever loved my mom. I kept calling my mom's cell to tell her, and she wouldn't pick up. I left a hundred messages. She never called me back that night, even though I left her tons of voice mails telling her how badly I needed to talk to her. She didn't even come home. She slept at some producer's house. And I had to deal with it all by myself—my dad and that sushi waitress were terrorizing my head. My mom should have been there for me, but she wasn't anymore. So I decided I wanted to move out of the house and get my own place in New York. I didn't have a mom anymore. She was now only the Countess of Malibu."

"Do you want me to call her and tell her what happened to you?" I asked.

Sabrina looked at me shocked. Then she said, "Don't ask me so many questions. You figure it out." Then she tugged on my shirtsleeve and pulled me closer to her.

"Lily, I need you to do something for me."

"What is it?" I asked.

"Mercedes is all alone at the hotel room. I need someone there taking care of him while I'm in the hospital. Mercedes hates Bert and Eleanor. And I don't want those hotel clerks popping by to walk him. Mercedes doesn't know them. He knows you. Please go stay with him at the suite. He hates being alone," she said. "And make sure he gets walked three times a day."

"I'll head over right now," I said. "I have everything under control. Don't you worry about a thing."

"Thank you," she said. "You're a lifesaver." And for the first time, it sounded like she actually meant it.

It was nice to have Sabrina depending on me so much. Besides, now that there were only five days left of the internship, it was easier to take all of her orders. I could see the finish line.

I took a cab back to the hotel. I couldn't stop thinking about Sabrina and her mom. I don't know what I would do if my dad and I stopped talking. I didn't want to end up like them—becoming strangers.

I decided it was a good idea to let Sabrina's mom know that she was in the hospital. I knew that Eleanor had probably called her already, but just in case, I wanted to cover all bases. I looked through the Rolodex in my BlackBerry and pulled up her mother's phone number in Malibu. Then I called and left a message on the home machine. "This is Lily Miles, Sabrina's intern," I said. "There's been a bit of an accident. . . ."

Chapter 17

MERCEDES RAN OVER TO me when I walked inside the door of the suite. I patted him and then he curled up on the bed. The now-working television was left on and playing a show on Nickelodeon.

I picked up the phone and dialed my parents. It was one in the morning—an hour past my midnight curfew—but I needed them to know I wasn't coming home this evening. My mom picked up.

"Hello?" she said, half asleep. "What time is it? Where are you?"

"Hey, Mom. Sorry to wake you, but I wanted you to know Sabrina hurt herself so I'm crashing at the Mercer tonight. She needs me to dogsit."

"Is she all right? Are *you* okay?"

"I'm fine. Listen, it's a long story, but I need to stay in her suite. I didn't want you to worry."

My mom sighed loudly. "I'll let your father know."

"Thanks," I said. "Hey, Mom?"

"Yeah?" she said.

"Is he very angry with me?"

"He's not pleased. We'll deal with it tomorrow. Get some rest."

"Okay," I said. "Good night. Love you," I said.

"Love you, too."

When I hung up the phone, I felt bad. I could tell by my mom's tone that my dad was very upset with me. I wished he would loosen up and realize I wasn't a baby anymore.

Bing. Bing. My BlackBerry rang with a message from Sabrina.

> STRLT4EVER: Don't forget to feed Mercedes.
> And walk him tonight.

> L332203: I'll get on it right away! How are you
> feeling?

I grabbed the leash from the living-room table. Mercedes saw me and got excited. He started running around in quick little circles. I clasped the leash to his collar and took him for a walk. It felt dangerous being outside this late, so I stayed close by the lights of the hotel.

A couple walked by me, their arms around each other. It looked like they were going home after a date. It made me think of Bronson. I wondered how he was doing. He would be leaving in a week to go back to Los Angeles. I wondered if he would call to say good-bye like he said he would.

Then I started thinking about Max and Evie. I hadn't talked to Evie in a while. I owed her a phone call. I bet she was having a great summer. She probably had a boyfriend at camp and was madly in love. I couldn't wait to hear all of her stories.

I walked back into the lobby and got into the elevator.

Before the doors closed to go upstairs, my BlackBerry went off again. *Bing. Bing.*

> STRLT4EVER: Tell Mercedes about my shoulder and concussion. What's new at the suite? Anything I should know?

I decided to write back when I got upstairs outside the elevator where the reception was better. As soon as the doors opened on the fifth floor, my BlackBerry started to chime again.

> STRLT4EVER: Hello? Are you there? I just sent you a message.

I started to type back, but it went off again.

> STRLT4EVER: Lily, are you not getting my messages? You haven't answered me.

I started to type again.

> L332203: Walked dog and—

Before I had a chance to send it . . .
Bing. Bing.

> STRLT4EVER: I'm worried. Are you not getting my messages? Hello?

I wrote back as quickly as possible, plucking my fingertips on the mini keyboard.

> L332203: Walked dog. Feeding him soon. No new packages. Everything is under control.

STRLT4EVER: Phew. I am counting on you to
hold down the fort. Going to sleep now. Gnite.

When I got back into the suite, I filled Mercedes's dish
with water and poured dry dog food into his bowl. As he
ran over to lap up some water, I threw myself on the sofa. I
felt exhausted. My new lifestyle wasn't the pure glamour and
wonderment that I thought it would be before I started.

But still, there were the occasional perks and rewards. I
looked around at the suite. I couldn't believe this was all mine
for two nights. *Lily Miles, you are living large,* I told myself. I
look over at the bureau. On it was Sabrina's brown-and-white
Bendel's beauty bag with the bottle of pink bath gel. *Ooh,
how delightful,* I thought to myself. *A pink bubble bath is just what a
hardworking girl needs to unwind before bedtime.*

I went into the bathroom and drew a hot bath. I filled the
square tub up with pink bubbles and climbed inside. *So this is
what it feels like to be Sabrina Snow,* I thought. While I lay in the
bath, I noticed a new hotel razor wrapped in plastic by the
soap dish. I decided to crack it open and shave my legs with
Sabrina's high-end roses-and-vitamin E shaving cream.

Then I picked my leg up and looked at the bottom of my
feet. After running around the city all summer for Sabrina,
the bottom of my heels were now covered in patches of dry,
rough skin. I decided my feet needed a little TLC. I noticed
her green tin of Bag Balm, the cow-udder moisturizer, on
the side of the tub. I got out of the tub, put on a freshly
washed bathrobe, and massaged the balm into the soles of
my feet. It felt like I was rubbing honey and butter onto my
skin. That's when I heard a sound coming from inside the

suite—the noise of the front door opening and closing.

I froze. Sabrina didn't mention that anyone was coming by. It was such an odd hour, too. It was probably someone from Sabrina's inner sanctum, like Bert or the Strap Girls. *Oh no,* I thought to myself. *What if it's Valerie and Nikki and they catch me using Sabrina's bubble bath?*

Then I started to worry that maybe it was a burglar or an ex-convict coming to steal all of Sabrina's jewelry. I poked my head outside. I saw a flash of movement—a figure quickly crossing from the living-room area into the back bedroom.

I heard drawers being opened as if someone was going through Sabrina's things. I quietly walked through the living room and peeked through the crack in the door to the bedroom. It was Eleanor. She was opening Sabrina's drawers and packing clothes into one of Sabrina's Bottega Veneta suitcases.

"Hi," I said.

She jumped, startled. "Oh, hi, Lily," she said.

"Do you need help?" I asked.

"No. I'm grabbing a few things to take to the hospital so she feels more at home."

"Be sure to pack her new flannel pajamas with the Scottie-dog design. She really loves them," I said, grabbing the pajamas from the bureau and handing them to Eleanor.

"Fine," she said, sticking them into the bag. "I can handle the rest."

"And her cosmetics," I said, grabbing the striped Henri Bendel cosmetic bag from the bathroom and handing it to her. She took the bag from me and packed it.

"Lily, I told you already. I can handle this."

I was thrown off by the edge in her voice. It almost sounded like she was angry with me. I wondered if she blamed me like Bert did for Sabrina falling off the bull. I decided to try and lighten the tone. "How's she doing?" I asked.

"As good as can be expected. They want her to spend tonight and tomorrow night at the hospital to monitor the concussion. Then she can come home, but she'll have her arm in a sling for several weeks."

"I hope she gets better soon," I said.

"We all do," Eleanor said as she finished filling up the suitcase with clothes. "I think I have everything," she said. Then she turned to me. "But I need to ask you something before I leave."

"Sure," I said, unnerved.

"Bert told me tonight that Sabrina was taking diet pills. Do you know where she got them from?" Eleanor asked.

"Not sure," I said.

"You aren't?" she asked. "Bert seemed to think you would know."

I decided to fess up. "I heard they're sold on the down low at this bodega on Ninth Street and Third Ave."

"And you picked them up for her?" Eleanor asked.

"I had to or she would get mad," I said. "She threatened to fire me."

"So if she asked you to go out and steal somebody's purse, you would do that for her, too? Do you think people should blindly do everything their bosses tell them to?"

"I told Sabrina I was worried about her. I encouraged her not to take them."

"But you brought them to her and you didn't make her

get help when she was in trouble. So what was your part in this, Lily?" Eleanor picked up the Bottega Veneta suitcase and headed for the door. "Think about it," she said.

After the door slammed behind her, I sat down on the edge of the king-sized bed. My head hurt from Eleanor preaching to me from her holier-than-thou soapbox. Still, there was truth to what she said, and the honesty in her words made me feel terribly guilty.

I had to call Evie right away. She was the only one who could cheer me up now. It didn't matter that it was the middle of the night. I needed to talk to her immediately.

"Evie," I said when she picked up the phone.

"It's the middle of the night. Are you insane? What do you want?" Her voice sounded distant and groggy.

"Sorry to wake you. I just had the worst evening ever," I started. But then she cut me off.

"I've left you, like, five messages," she said. "Where have you been?"

"I know, I'm sorry. I have been so busy—"

"Too busy to return your best friend's phone calls? I don't buy that," Evie said.

"The last few weeks have been a whirlwind," I started to explain. "It's been one thing after the—"

"Yeah, great. I've been busy, too. The Disco Dance was last week and you missed it. The guy I like, Peter, hooked up with this new girl, Caroline. The dance sucked. I gotta go—"

"Where are you going, Evie? Don't be mad. I've been chained to this suite at the Mercer."

"Chained to a suite! You're not chained to anything! Are

you kidding me? Call me when you're done being a Hollywood social climber." Then she hung up the phone.

I was so frustrated. Maybe Evie was right. What was I becoming? Maybe this world was changing me—for the worse. I started pacing around the room, and then I saw the stack of new fan letters piling up on the coffee table. Monday I would have to start filling out the form responses again, signing the fake signatures, licking the stamps.

And then I realized something—the window was finally opening. The doctor said that Sabrina would be in the hospital for two nights. I remembered what Bronson had told me: "Don't forget to take something for yourself along the way." Now was my chance to finish what I started.

I couldn't sleep that night. I tossed and turned around the king-sized bed until the morning. At nine A.M., I picked up the hotel phone and called Taylor.

"It's Sabrina. I'm coming," I said. "Get ready for Six Flags."

"I can't believe it! I'm gonna go tell my parents," she screamed into the phone.

Next I called the number I had for Sabrina's car service. A woman at the chauffeur company picked up.

"I'm calling from Sabrina Snow's office. I need to order a car for her," I said. "And please have it here as soon as possible."

"Account number please?" the woman said.

I looked up the number in my BlackBerry. "SN5302289," I said.

"What type of car would you like?"

"Let me see . . ." I hadn't thought about it yet, but it was a good question.

"I know Miss Snow typically likes the black limo or sometimes the stretch Mini Cooper," the woman said.

"The stretch Mini Cooper will work fine," I said, playing it cool.

"Pickup outside the Mercer Hotel as usual?"

"But of course," I said.

"Confirmed," the woman said. "It will be there within the hour. Your driver's name is Milos." Then the woman hung up.

I got off the phone and started to jump up and down. Holy Moses. Holy mama. Holy sweetness. Holy everything!

I ran to the bathroom. I put on a little of Sabrina's My Mademoiselle lip gloss and drew eyeliner the way she did between the lower lid and eyelashes. I used the blow-dryer to style my hair with her citrus-shine serum.

Then I looked into Sabrina's closet, which was filled with colorful and glistening swag. There were perfectly folded designer jeans and sweaters with the tags still on them, dresses and shirts lined up, crisp, clean, and color-coordinated. And then I saw it. The exquisite red silk dress she wore the day she first interviewed me at the suite. I remembered how glamorous she looked sitting by the floor-to-ceiling window, drinking from a teacup, while two stylists polished her nails.

I tried on the dress. It was very tight, so I left the zipper halfway undone in the back. To compensate, I threw a long-sleeved Gucci T-shirt over it. Then I dug through her shoe pile and found her gold shoes. Over the dress, I put on her red-and-black checkered lumberjack coat and large sunglasses. Dressed in schlumpy-chic style, I imagined it would be easy to impersonate Sabrina as I ran from the lobby into the limo.

My plan was to fool the driver into thinking I was Sabrina so he didn't give me a hassle about using the car.

I looked in the mirror. I was amazed. *This is what I would look like if I was a starlet,* I thought.

The hotel phone rang. I answered it. "Hello, Miss Snow. It's the concierge. Your driver is out front," a man's voice said.

"Thanks!" I said, jumping off the phone. I grabbed my purse but remembered there wasn't any cash inside. Last night, I had spent the last of it on my cab ride from the hospital. I opened up Sabrina's drawer and borrowed a few twenties from the petty-cash purse. As I headed out the door, Mercedes ran over to me and started jumping up on my legs.

"Oh, no," I said to him. "I completely forgot about walking you."

I ran to the nightstand and called down to the concierge.

"Good morning. This is Jean-Paul."

"Hi. Does the hotel offer a dog-walking service?" I asked.

"Let me check," the man's voice said. He had a thick French accent. "It's my first day so bear with me." He put the phone down.

"Please, please, please," I started chanted to myself.

A minute later, Jean-Paul came back on the phone. "Yes, we do," he said.

"Awesome," I said. "I need to request a dog walker for this morning and afternoon."

"Let me just write this down. A dog walker tomorrow morning and afternoon," he said with his thick accent.

"No," I corrected him. "Today."

"Oh, today," he said. "This afternoon."

"And morning."

"All right. I have it written down. I'll take care of that," Jean-Paul said. Somehow I didn't totally believe him. His voice sounded tentative like, because it was his first day, he didn't know exactly what he was doing.

I filled up Mercedes's dish with fresh water and added more food to his bowl. Then I gave him a kiss on the head and ran out the door.

When I left the hotel, the driver was standing outside the stretch, turquoise Mini Cooper. He held the door open for me as I ducked inside. I recognized him as the chauffeur that drove us on premiere night for *Spinning the Wheel of Fire*.

As he slammed the door shut behind me, I took a deep breath. He got into the driver's seat and the car sped off.

The partition slowly lowered. "My name is Milos," he said. "Where are we going today?"

"New Jersey," I said, ducking my head down under the hat's brim. "The address is 31522 Lime Orchard Lane in Morristown" I said. I was happy. I must be fooling him dressed in schlumpy chic.

The driver typed the address into his GPS system, then he cruised along Houston Street toward the West Side Highway. When we stopped at a red light, I noticed he was staring at me in the rearview mirror.

"Why are you dressed like that?" he asked.

"What do you mean? I'm always dressed like this," I said.

"You can't fool me," he said. "Even under all those big clothes. You're not Sabrina." The driver gave me a look. "Oh, wait. I know you," he said.

"Yeah, that's 'cause I'm famous," I said. "And you've driven me before."

"You're not famous," he said. "Aren't you the girl they dumped at the premiere?"

"Maybe," I said, slowly giving in. "It's that obvious?"

"I saw you coming out of the theater. The young guy told me to pull over, but the girl with the china-doll haircut screamed at me to keep driving."

"The one who kept cracking her knuckles?"

"Yeah, that's the one." He nodded.

I knew he meant Valerie. She had orchestrated the bona fide ditch session.

I leaned closer to the partition. "Listen, I need to go to New Jersey. Sabrina is in the hospital until tomorrow. And there's something I must take care of."

"I'm at your service," he said.

"So you don't care that I'm not actually Sabrina?" I asked.

"Her office called and ordered the car. It's already charged to the account. It's up to Sabrina who actually uses it."

"Great," I said.

"She knows you're using it, right?"

"Definitely. She approved it," I said. I felt bad lying, but it was the fastest way I could get to Taylor.

"Oh, no!" Milos suddenly yelled out. "Not again."

"What's the matter?" I asked. "Is everything okay?"

"Somebody's following us," he said.

"Are you serious?" I said, staring out the back window at a maroon station wagon driving close behind us. I could see a man with thick sideburns poking his head out the passenger seat, with a telephoto lens.

"Looks like Dan Divalte," Milos said. "And a few of his guys."

"Who's Dan Divalte?" I asked.

"One of the biggest members of the paparazzi," he said.

"Can we lose them?" I said.

"I'll try my best." Milos suddenly flew off the freeway's exit. The station wagon sped behind us as we raced down the off-ramp, making a quick right onto a main street. Milos hit the gas as we raced through a yellow light, making a sudden U-turn in the opposite direction. As we flew down the street, we almost collided with a truck. Then we made a sharp turn down an alleyway and shot out onto a nearby side street.

"I think they're gone for now," Milos said.

I looked behind us and saw the wagon was no longer there. "Good work. Frightening, but good."

As we drove toward New Jersey, I started to devise my game plan. I would have to explain to Taylor why I was suddenly showing up and not Sabrina. I would just tell her that Sabrina was sick, but she didn't want to leave Taylor stranded so she called on me, her faithful intern, to make the voyage instead.

The car exited off the highway. "Only a few miles away now," Milos said.

My stomach started to ache with nerves. I felt like I could hurl. I rolled down the window and stuck my head out.

The limo raced past a gas station and a Salvation Army. It

flew past a McDonald's and a restaurant with a sign blinking in red letters, ATHENIAN DINER.

I noticed an old couple walking down the steps of the diner. They looked up with fascination as the stretch Mini Cooper drove past. We turned right on High Street, passed a reservoir, and then drove onto a more quiet residential neighborhood.

"It should be just up here in a few blocks," the driver said.

I couldn't believe I was minutes away from Taylor's house. This was crazy. We turned down Lime Orchard Lane, and the car slowed down in front of a small one-story house painted peach. There was a path that led up to the door, and on either side of the path were yellow and pink rosebushes. The number 31522 was painted on a black mailbox.

"This is it," I said, taking a few deep breaths, getting up my nerve. The driver walked around and opened my door. I got out and dumped the hat, oversized coat, and sunglasses in the car.

Chapter 18

I WALKED SLOWLY UP to the house and rang the doorbell. I heard a woman's voice inside. I could hear her feet approaching the door. Then I saw a woman peek through the
curtains from the side window. Her mouth dropped when
she saw the turquoise stretch Mini Cooper.

"She's here! She's here," the mom screamed as she opened
the front door.

"Hi!" I said as soon as the door flung open. "Are you Taylor's mom?"

She nodded her head as her husband appeared in the
hallway. He was tall and lanky with bifocal glasses and bald-
ing red hair.

"Who are you? You're not Sabrina," the father said.

"I'm her intern," I said. "She couldn't make it at the last
minute. She feels just terrible. But she sent me in her place to
take your daughter to Six Flags. After she called Taylor this
morning, she got a bad stomach virus. She wishes she could
have been here."

"That's very disappointing," the father said, sizing me up
with his eyes. "But I know from experience, those stomach
bugs can be tricky."

"She isn't in shape to go anywhere."

"Where's Taylor? Get Taylor," the mother said, chiming into the conversation. "Taylor!"

"Are you taking her to the amusement park in that limo out there?" the father asked.

"I was planning on it," he said.

"I've never seen one like that before," he said. "Mind if I check it out? Are there seat belts?"

"Yes," I said. "Feel free to look inside yourself."

The father stepped outside and walked over to Milos. I watched as Milos gave him a tour of the limo.

"She's so excited," the mom said, leading me to Taylor's room. "She's been too nervous to leave her room."

"I hope it won't be too much of a disappointment that it's only me."

"Me, too. I hope she'll take it okay," the mom said.

We were outside Taylor's door now.

"I can hear she's listening to the tapes again," the mother said. "It was great timing. Henry bought the voice recorder right around the time Sabrina first called. So we got to preserve all of Sabrina's phone conversations. Taylor loves listening to them over and over."

"What a great memento," I said.

The mom knocked on the door and then opened it.

"Honey," the mom said. "Someone's here to see you."

The door opened and there was Taylor seated cross-legged on the floor, listening to our tape-recorded phone conversations. She looked at me and then awkwardly stood up.

It was amazing to finally see her. After reading her letter and talking to her on the phone, she had almost become a character in a movie in my head.

Standing in front of her now, I was reminded that this character was real. She had a slightly big head, round face, big cheeks, pale skin, acned forehead, thick wavy hair down her back, freckles, and slightly bucked teeth. Her parents were super dorky (I feel bad saying that, but I swore to be honest at the beginning of this book), and I realized it wasn't her fault she had turned out to be the way she was. She was a victim of circumstance—a social misfit and the product of an unlucky gene pool. She was a little version of her nerdy parents. And in part, they were to blame for making her ascent into adulthood so painful and overwhelming.

Her walls were covered with images of Sabrina from *Party Weekly* and other entertainment magazines. I noticed a photo of Sabrina and Bronson holding hands outside the premiere of *Spinning the Wheel of Fire* and the infamous shot of Sabrina dancing in the sequin-studded bikini at the after-party for the Rock the House Awards. Also, there were pictures of Sabrina and her mother from the day she was honored with the star on the Hollywood Walk of Fame.

"Hi," I said. "I'm Sabrina's intern, Lily. I came to visit you."

Taylor walked over to us.

"Sabrina got sick at the last minute," I continued. "So she sent me instead. She wanted to come more than anything. She was looking so forward to finally meeting you. After your phone conversations, she feels like you guys are friends. I hope you're not too disappointed, but she sent me in her place."

Taylor swallowed hard and looked at the floor.

"Sabrina's not coming? She promised this morning she would be here."

"She got sick with a nasty stomach virus and is absolutely devastated she couldn't make it."

"Oh, gosh." Taylor glanced down at her orange socks. "Are you still going to take me to Six Flags?" she asked.

"Yes," I said. "In a limo."

Taylor froze, expressionless. And then a huge smile grew on her face—a wide grin with a hardcore overbite.

"Six Flags!" she said. "When are we going? When are we going?"

"As soon as you put your shoes on," I said.

In the meantime, her mom packed a lunch bag filled with healthy snacks—raisins, prune juice, and turkey sandwiches. Then her parents walked us out and gave Taylor hugs and kisses good-bye.

"Can I have your cell number in case of emergency?" the mom asked me. "We don't usually let Taylor go out with strangers. But you're Sabrina's intern so I feel like it's all right. Sabrina is hardly a stranger, after all. We have all her movies. She's on our television ten times a week."

"You can trust me," I said. "I'll take good care of her." I wrote my number down on a piece of paper and handed it to her.

"By the way, I checked out the limo. It looks safe," the dad said. "Found the seat belts. Top of the line."

"I knew you wouldn't be disappointed," I said.

"Oh, here," said her mom. "I cut these coupons out of the paper. Two-for-one summer special."

"Great, thanks," I said, taking them and sticking them into my pocket.

"I can't believe this car! It's out of this world!" Taylor said as she stepped inside of it.

Taylor immediately started playing with all the buttons and gizmos, raising and lowering the windows and the sunroof, turning the air-conditioner vents so they blew directly toward us, and opening the jars filled with pistachio nuts and jelly beans.

"Where are we going now?" Milos asked me.

"Please take us to Six Flags," I said. "Here," I said, passing him one of the coupons Taylor's mom had just given me. "There are driving directions printed on the back."

"Bye, Mom! Bye, Dad!" Taylor yelled out the car window. Her parents waved as we drove away.

When the car stopped at a light, Taylor looked down at my feet. "You have something on your heel," she told me.

I followed her gaze. There was a piece of toilet paper stuck to one of Sabrina's gold shoes.

"We must have missed a few pieces when we cleaned up the front yard," Taylor said.

I flicked it off and dumped it in the ashtray. I couldn't believe I was *that* girl—the one with toilet paper on her shoe. At least there weren't any hotties around watching.

"Thank you for coming to get me," Taylor said. "I wish Sabrina could have made it, though. I was looking forward to finally meeting her in person."

"I know. I'm not Sabrina. But I'm the next best thing. She didn't want to leave you hanging."

"That was very nice of her," Taylor said. "I really like your dress."

"Thanks," I said, looking down at the silk number I had borrowed from Sabrina's closet.

"I couldn't decide what to wear this morning," Taylor said. "It was between a skirt because it's a special occasion or shorts because it's hot out, so I wore a skort. See, it looks like a skirt, but if you pick up the front flap, there're really shorts underneath." She picked up the front flap to demonstrate.

"That sounds very practical," I told her. I had heard of skorts, but I never knew anyone who wore one. Skorts, in my book, belonged to the dork parade. Right up there with penny loafers with tassels, bright plaid golf shirts, and rolled-up jean shorts.

"My parents won't let me pick out my own clothes," she told me. "My mom picked out everything I have on. The skort, the penny loafers, these orange-tinted sunglasses, and my fanny pack. They didn't do that with my sister."

"You have a sister?" I asked her. "I always wanted a sister. I'm an only child."

"I am now, too. My sister died a few years ago," Taylor said, looking down at her lap. "She was playing kickball outside our house, and she got hit by a car."

"Oh my God," I said. "I'm so sorry. I had no idea."

"We were supposed to go to Six Flags that morning, but we never got to go."

There was an awkward silence. Taylor looked out the window. Maybe that's why her parents dressed her so dorkily. The more of a social misfit she stayed the more she wouldn't leave the house or go away.

Bing. Bing. I shuddered as I heard my BlackBerry go off. I was scared as I clicked on the screen to check the message. It was Sabrina, of course.

STRLT4EVER: I can't wait to get out of here. I hate hospitals! They feel haunted!

Then it went off again.

STRLT4EVER: The Dr. man said my concussion is getting better, but I have to wear a sling on my shoulder. Call every designer in town and find me a fashionable sling pronto.

"Is that Sabrina?" Taylor said.
"Yes," I said.
"Tell her I say hi and that I miss her. And to feel better," Taylor said.
"I'm typing her that right now."

L332203: I will find you the trendiest sling out there.

"Wow, do you get to text with Sabrina every day? That is the neatest," Taylor said, trying to look over my shoulder at the BlackBerry screen.

I turned it like a hand of cards so she couldn't read what I wrote. *Bing. Bing.*

STRLT4EVER: Thanks. How is everything at the suite?

L332203: Great! I have been holding down the fort.

> STRLT4EVER: Text me if anything comes up.
> Oh and the Countess of Malibu showed up at the
> hospital today. She hasn't been too annoying yet.
> She brought me tulips and tangerines. She said
> she got your message. Thanks (I guess). Taking
> a nap now.

I had to read that last text message twice. I was surprised her mom had flown to New York so quickly. I wondered if she heard my voice on her answering machine and ran to the airport to catch the red-eye. It was nice to think of them finally talking again. Hopefully, they would work through their differences, hug-hug, kiss-kiss, and make up.

I put the BlackBerry on the seat next to me and waited to see if she would write back. After a few moments, she didn't, so I felt relieved that I had satisfied her demands—for the time being, at least.

Suddenly Milos picked up speed and veered into the other lane.

"Not again," he said, looking over his shoulder.

I turned around. Out the back window, there was the same maroon station wagon with tinted windows driving behind us.

"What's the matter?" Taylor said.

"It's okay. We're just being followed."

"Followed?" Taylor said. "Who's following us?"

"The paparazzi," I said. "They recognize the car. It's Sabrina's trademark."

"Ohmigod!" Taylor said. "We're being followed! Like in the movies! Are they mafia? Are they going to kill us?" She jumped down onto the floor and covered her head. "What if they start shooting at us with machine guns?"

"It's not the mafia!" I told her. "They're just hoping for Sabrina's pictures, *not her blood.*" Then I stopped and realized, they kind of were like the mob, an underground society with a secret agenda willing to break all the rules to get what they wanted.

I hit the switch to make sure all the doors were locked. And I rolled up my window. Taylor kept peeking her head up like a gopher to check on how close the maroon station wagon was to us. "They're getting closer. Lily, please, don't let me die. Don't let me die," she started saying.

"Relax, everything's going to be okay," I said, trying to calm her down.

The maroon station wagon was riding along our side now. It veered in close to our car, forcing Milos to swerve into the next lane, almost crashing into the vehicle next to us.

As we approached the next off-ramp, Milos waited until the last second to exit off the Garden State Parkway. It was too late for the maroon station wagon to follow us, so it was forced to continue on straight.

"We're going to take the backstreets for a while," he said. Taylor and I held on to the seats as Milos made a few quick, hard turns, racing down a street and back onto the freeway.

When we got on highway I-195, we had lost the station wagon. Milos exited onto Route 537, and then we drove for a mile before we saw the first signs for Six Flags appear outside our window. Taylor banged on the glass.

"There it is!" she said. "Look at all those roller coasters!" she said.

Milos dropped us outside the main entrance. I walked up to the ticket booth and paid for our tickets using the coupon Taylor's mom gave us along with cash from Sabrina's petty-cash purse. The cashier handed us a map of the amusement park.

Taylor opened it up and stared at it. "I want to go on the rides first!" she said.

I let her take the lead as she skipped into the park. We jumped from Stuntman's Freefall, rode the Big Wheel Ferris wheel, and screamed on the Great American Scream Machine.

Then it was lunchtime. We sat down at a table in the Old Cove Country Picnic Grove. I took out the bagged lunch from my purse that Taylor's mom prepared. I went to take my BlackBerry out to make sure I didn't miss any messages, but it wasn't in there. I realized I must have left it in the limo. I had put it down on the seat after text-messaging with Sabrina, and then I got sidetracked by the paparazzi chasing our car. I debated going back for it, but Sabrina had said she was going to take a nap, and we would only be at Six Flags for a few more hours.

"Here you go," I said, pouring the contents of her mom's packed lunch on the table.

Taylor started eating the raisins first. A girl walked by eating a corn dog, and it caught Taylor's attention.

"That looks freakalious," Taylor said.

"Freakalicous?" I asked.

"That means ridiculously delicious."

"I'd get you one, but your mom probably wouldn't like it," I said.

"Corn dogs aren't healthy," Taylor said. "But I really want one."

"I don't want to get you in trouble."

"I'm twelve years old," Taylor said. "I think I'm ready to have my first corn dog." She stood up from the table. I gave her some cash. She went up to the stand to buy one, and on her way over, she threw away the rest of her brown-bagged lunch. Taylor filled up a bunch of small plastic cups with ketchup and came back to the table. She devoured the corn dog while dipping it, between bites, into the cups of sauce.

"I have been missing out," she said. "I love this." When she was done, she wanted to try a candied apple and some frozen lemonade.

I noticed Taylor had some food stuck in her teeth. "You have some brown stuff in between the top two," I told her.

"Thanks," she said. Then she pulled a hair from her head and used it as dental floss. "My dad taught me that trick," she said proudly. I could begin to see why she stood out as a little weird in school.

There was a loud noise as two punk kids started throwing meatballs at each other while they ran around the food court. One of the meatballs whizzed over our heads, landing in an old man's hair.

"Oh no," Taylor said, hiding her face when she saw them.

"What's the matter?" I asked.

"Oh no, oh no, oh no," Taylor kept saying over and over.

"Do you know those boys?" I asked.

"I want to hide."

I looked over at the boys. They had noticed Taylor now,

and they were pointing at her and laughing. I assumed these must be some kids from her middle school. Another meatball came flying our way, smashing into the side of the table.

"Help me," Taylor said. "Protect me."

"Who are those guys?" I asked, standing up from the table.

"The one in the green T-shirt is Mike and guy with the buzz cut is his best friend, Evan."

The boys were walking over to us now.

"Look who it is," Mike said. "Ostrich Girl."

His friend Evan starting making birdcalls.

"Do you have any more love letters to stick in my locker?" Mike said.

"Maybe you wrote one on that toilet paper we left on your front lawn?"

"Leave her alone," I said.

"Ooh. What are you, her best friend? Defending her?" Evan said.

"Yeah, I am her best friend," I said.

"And she interns for Sabrina Snow, so watch out," Taylor said, finally speaking up and going along with it. "She just drove all the way up here in a limo to visit me. Sabrina was gonna come, too, but she got sick."

"You're a liar," Mike said. "Sabrina Snow wouldn't waste her time with a loser like you."

"Sabrina's my good friend. I talk to her on the phone," Taylor said.

"Yeah, right." Evan started laughing his brains out.

"Like she doesn't have anything better to do than hang

out with a woodchuck," Mike said. "How much wood could a woodchuck chuck, if a woodchuck could chuck wood?" Evan said.

"I thought she was an ostrich," I said. "Get your animals straight."

"She's Ostrich Girl, but her teeth stick out like a wood-chuck's."

"Who are you to talk?" I said. "You're just two stupid, prepubescent losers."

"Look at you. Standing up for Taylor. You're so tough," Mike said, teasing me.

I didn't want to keep stooping to their level. Calling each other names seemed beneath me.

"Just go. Go away," I said flicking my wrist. "You're both annoying."

"Ouch," Evan said to me. "Okay, hot buns. We've got some rides to go on. But we'll find you both later."

"Bye, ugly," Mike said to Taylor.

As soon as they went away, Taylor leaned over on the picnic bench and grabbed her stomach.

"They're going to get me," she said. "How can I go back to school? It will just be another year of torture."

"Those boys are evil," I said. "I can't believe what you have to deal with."

I knew that she had told me about it on the phone, but witnessing the abuse in person made it more real and disturbing.

I needed to help her. "I won't let them hurt you," I said. "I'll be by your side all day."

But I knew this was just a temporary solution. She needed to stand up to them herself, or next year at school would be a whirlpool of perpetual misery.

"You have to keep facing up to them yourself," I said. "Or they won't stop picking on you. Refuse to see yourself as a wimp. Look them in the eye. And if they ever try to shove chalk down your mouth again—go ballisto on them."

"Ballisto?" Taylor asked me.

"Yeah. They're making fun of you because they think you're different. So take your weirdness to the extreme. Like this." I threw my hands up in the air and danced around like I was a spastic, wild woman. "And drool and scream out nonsense sounds like you're talking in tongues. Act like you're possessed. It will freak them out and they won't know how to react."

Taylor nodded her head, soaking in my advice. She still looked deathly afraid.

"Do you want me to take you home?" I asked.

"No," she said. "I have been dreaming of this day for way too long."

I smiled. I felt proud of her for not running home, and pulled out the Six Flags brochure.

"The Movietown Stunt Show looks fun," I said. "It says here the next one starts in five minutes. Wanna go?"

Taylor nodded her head yes. "I heard people get shot out of cannons."

We got up from the table, dumped our trays, and headed for the Movietown area. I noticed Taylor kept twitching and looking over her shoulder. I knew she couldn't get the two boys out of her head—and for good reason.

Once we arrived at the Movietown Stunt Arena, we walked inside and grabbed some seats on the back left side.

"Don't you want to sit in the center?" I asked.

"No, my parents like me to sit near the emergency exits in case something terrible happens and we need to evacuate."

"Oh, right," I said. Another strike on the board for the whacky parents.

As the stuntmen and -women jumped out of windows and swung through balls of fire, Taylor started asking me about Sabrina.

"How did she get to be the way she is?" Taylor asked.

"What do you mean?" I asked.

"So perfect. She's pretty, smart, she's an extremely talented actress, and now I see how much she really cares, too. Even about people like me."

If only she knew how little Sabrina truly cared about her. But I couldn't tell her that. "I guess some people get lucky," I said. "They are given certain opportunities that other people don't have. Or else they're born with certain talents, and those talents help them shine and rise to the top."

"I wish I was more like Sabrina," Taylor said. "Then everything would be easier. Will you give her a message from me?" Taylor said.

"Yeah," I said.

"Tell her that I think she is the kindest, nicest, coolest person in the whole world. And thank her for sending you here to fulfill her promise."

I looked up at the stage as a woman lowered herself out of a window and hurled herself into a well of water. "I'll be sure to tell her all of that."

The audience burst into applause, and the stuntmen and stuntwomen came out to bow.

After the show, we walked along Main Street to the boardwalk. I looked at my watch. It was getting kind of late. I had to drop Taylor back off at home and get back to the city soon. Milos was waiting outside in the car.

"One more ride," I told Taylor. "Your choice."

She looked over the amusement park map. Then she pointed to a picture of a waterfall. "The log ride," she said. "Can't leave here without doing the log ride."

We waited for ten minutes to get onto the log ride. When we got to the head of the line, we loaded into the log, which held two people in the front and two people in the back. Taylor and I sat in the front compartment.

"This is my favorite ride of all time," Taylor said as the log started to lurch forward.

"It's one of my favorites, too," I said.

"*I really love it also,*" a voice said from behind us.

Taylor and I turned around. There were the two bullies from her school. They were sitting in the back compartment of our log.

"What are you doing?" I asked. "You weren't waiting in line. I would have seen you."

"Maybe that's because we *cut?*" Mike said.

"Or else maybe you're both stupid," his friend said.

"Let's get out of here," Taylor said, trying to stand up, but the log was moving and the man managing the ride ordered her to sit down.

"This is gonna be a ride you will never forget," Mike

said, leaning forward and whispering in Taylor's ear.

"Just ignore them, Taylor," I said. Taylor and I sat there in silence.

"We have a list going of all of the terrible things we are going to do to you this year at school," Mike said.

"Do you hear anything?" I said to Taylor.

"Not a thing," she said back.

"First, we are going to take a picture of you and alter it so we stick your head on the body of a naked sumo wrestler and hang it all over school," Mike said.

"Then we are going to put Ex-Lax in your food when you're not looking so you won't be able to stop running to the bathroom."

"And I'm going to sneak into your house and put Nair in your shampoo so when you use it, you'll lose all your hair."

"Then we're going to push you out on the street one day when you're walking home and hope you end up like your older sister. Hit by a car."

Taylor's face turned bright red. "Don't you say that," she said. "Don't you ever say that!" She turned around in her seat and leaned over in the log.

"I'll say what I want," Mike said.

"Taylor, be careful," I said. "You're not balanced."

"No, you won't," Taylor said. "I'm sick of it. If you do any of those things to me, I'll make a banner six feet tall and hang it in the lunchroom saying that I love you just to embarrass you out of your mind."

"You wouldn't dare," Mike said. "You're too much of a pussy."

"Watch out," I said, grabbing the bottom of Taylor's legs to hold her steady. I looked up ahead. We were approaching a ten-foot drop. "Sit down," I said. "You're gonna fall over."

But she wouldn't listen to me. "I'll put notes in your locker every day with pictures of hearts, and I'll make sure everyone sees me doing it. You won't be able to get rid of me. Everywhere you go, I'll be there telling the world how much I love you."

"I'd like to see that," Mike said.

"I bet you would," Taylor said. "And if you keep teasing me and calling me animal names—I'll start acting like one whenever I see you at school. I'll pretend I'm a woodchuck. And sometimes an ostrich." Taylor squinted her eyes and then made them huge. She took her buckteeth and stuck them as far over her bottom lip as possible. I realized this was her own way of going ballisto.

A look of surprise come across both the boys' faces.

"You're a whacko," Mike said, backing up a little in his seat.

"Come on, Taylor!" I said. "Sit down. We're almost at the waterfall."

But it was too late—the log was tipping on its side, going down the drop. Taylor lost her balance and jerked around as the log landed on the bottom. I grabbed on to her so she didn't fall over, but because of the way she was leaning over, her body was caught by a tremendous splash of water. She was drenched, and her white T-shirt was soaking wet.

The two boys looked at her and broke out laughing. "Flasher!" they screamed.

Taylor looked down at her now see-through T-shirt. "Oh, no!" she said, trying to cover herself up.

"Gross! Don't make me throw up! Get a bra!" the boys yelled.

As we climbed out of the log, Taylor desperately tried to hide herself with her hands. I wish I had something to give her to cover herself up.

"Everyone look! Naked girl!" one of the boys screamed out. A lot of kids gathered around, laughing and pointing at Taylor.

Taylor stuck out her top front teeth, and flashed Mike a "woodchuck face." He shut his mouth.

Still, she looked like she was about to die from humiliation. I grabbed a towel I saw on a bench and ran it over to her, but it was too late. *Flash. Flash.* A camera was going off. I looked over and there was the photographer I saw leaning out of the maroon station wagon that was following us. I recognized the thick sideburns. It was Dan Divalte.

"Come on. Let's get out of here," I said, wrapping the towel around her. Taylor was shivering. We rushed back out the entrance and into the limo.

As soon as we got inside, I grabbed my BlackBerry and checked the messages. There were none. Thank God.

Taylor was curled up in a ball now on the seat. "I'm so embarrassed," she said. "Now I never want to show my face again at school *or* at Six Flags."

"Taylor," I said, "I know it didn't end perfectly, but you did well. You stood up to them. That's what you had to do, or they would keep hunting you down."

"It doesn't matter. They still hate me and want to hurt me."

"But they know now you won't just take it. You're gonna stand up for yourself next time, too."

It didn't matter what I said, though. She looked miserable.

"I'm so scared about school next year. I don't know what to do."

I felt terrible. I had set out trying to make Taylor's life better. Today was supposed to be perfect—it was supposed to be one of the best days of her life.

Maybe I should try to give her one of those pep talks that Sabrina gives. "Listen," I said, "you just need to believe in yourself. Understand that right now you may just be all right in some people's eyes, but you're going to make the leap from all right to awesome. And you're going to do it for yourself. Because you believe in who you are."

Taylor looked confused. "What are you talking about?" she asked.

"Listen, I came here because Sabrina and I wanted to make things better for you. But I see now, it's not in my control. I can't magically make you popular at school or protect you from terrible things. You're going to have to deal with them yourself. I won't always be here, and neither will Sabrina. But I just want you to know that you're not alone. I used to get teased, too. When I was in middle school, guys called me fat and chubby when I started going through puberty. And I think I came out all right. At least on a good day. And I guess I want you to remember that even the most popular people or famous people in the world aren't always . . ." I trailed off.

"What?" Taylor asked. "They aren't what?"

"Happy, or normal." I looked over at her sad face with her wet hair sticking up.

"I have nothing the other kids have. They get to sit at the lunch table with friends. I eat the brown bag lunch from my

mom in a bathroom stall. They get to go to the movies together and the pizza stand. Everyone in my grade has someone to go to the mall with and buy new T-shirts and skorts.
And I don't get to do any of that. I go home from school and
sit in my room, add pictures to my wall, and watch Sabrina's
movies. . . ." Taylor turned her head from me and looked out
the window. "I don't want to go home," she said. "Please take
me with you to the city. I want to see Sabrina. Can't I come
back with you? Don't make me stay here." Her nose was running. I watched as a tear ran down her cheek.

"Look," I said. "I can't take you back with me. I'm sorry.
But I want to make it up to you." Then I came up with an idea.
"Have you heard of the Rock the House Awards?" I asked.

"Yeah," Taylor said. "Everyone has."

"I get two tickets to the Rock the House Awards as my
summer bonus. I'm giving them to you. You can ask anyone
to go with you. It'll be a great way for you to make a new
friend."

"You're gonna give me two tickets to the awards?"

"It's the least I can do. I don't have them on me, but I'll be
sure to deliver them to you."

"But they're your tickets," Taylor said. "Don't you want
them?"

"Trust me," I said. "You deserve them."

Taylor wiped her nose with the back of her hand. "Are
you sure?"

"Absolutely. I won't let you say no. They're all yours."

She looked at me as if weighing her options. "Okay, thanks.
That's very nice of you," Taylor said. Then she jumped out
and ran up to her front steps. I got out of the car as Taylor's

mom opened the front door. I saw the look of concern on her face as she watched her daughter, soaking wet and wrapped in a towel, sprint past her inside the house.

Her mom came to the front door. "Is something wrong?" the mom asked me.

"She's a little upset. . . ." I explained. "We ran into some mean kids from her school."

"Oh my goodness," the mother said.

"They tormented her on the log ride."

"Is my sweetie all right?" her mom said, and ran back into the house. "Taylor? Taylor? Where are you, sweetheart?" I heard her screaming.

"I'm sorry for any trouble I may have caused," I said, calling after her.

I stood in the doorway for a moment and listened. In the distance, I thought I could make out the sound of Taylor crying. Then I heard the muffled voice of her mom saying, over and over again, "Shhh, honey, it's okay. It's okay. Everything's going to be all right."

Chapter 19

AS SOON AS WE drove off in the limo, my BlackBerry buzzed with a text message from Sabrina. The sound made me jump.

> STRLT4EVER: Where the &^%$!! are you? I'm back at the suite. The doctor let me go a day early because I recovered from the concussion and my mom can look after me.

I froze. Ohmigod. *What do I say? What do I write back?*

> L332203: I'll be there soon. Do you need anything?

Then I pressed SEND and waited for a reply. *Bring. Bring.* It vibrated and went off again. I looked at the screen.

> STRLT4EVER: Yes, I need something. YOU back HERE at the suite. Mercedes has peed all over the carpets.

Then it vibrated and jingled again.

> STRLT4EVER: It smells like crap.

I knew I shouldn't have trusted that new guy Jean-Paul at

the concierge desk. I bet he didn't have Mercedes taken out for one walk even though he promised he would!

STRLT4EVER: WHERE THE HELL ARE YOU???

I started to panic. Deep breaths. I had to answer or she would keep up the onslaught of messages.

L332203: Be back ASAP

Then she wrote her last message:

STRLT4EVER: YOU BETTER BE HERE ASAP!

I started biting my nails and eating the pistachio nuts from the limo's snack bar like a hyperactive squirrel.

"Everything okay back there?" Milos asked.

"Yeah. Great!" I said.

It seemed like it took forever, but the limo finally pulled up in front of the Mercer. I grabbed the lumberjack coat from the backseat and walked into the lobby and pressed the familiar elevator button. Got out on the fifth floor. Walked down the hall. One, two, three—approximately forty steps to knock on the suite door.

"Come in!" Sabrina said.

I turned the knob and walked inside. Sabrina sat on her bed, leaning against a bunch of pillows. Her arm was crossed in front of her, hanging in a brown sling. There was a woman with long red hair sitting next to her. A bunch of pamphlets were fanned out on the bed in front of her. One said: "The Food Pyramid."

"Oh, Lily, there you are," Sabrina said. "This is my nutritionist, Mary Belle."

"Nice to meet you," I said.

"We were just going over the five food groups," Sabrina said. "Bert hired her for me. Do you know that you should have at least seven servings of fruits and vegetables a day? And that blueberries can make you smarter?"

"I think I read that somewhere," I said. I was thrown off by Sabrina's friendliness.

I heard the front door open, and in walked another woman with sandy blonde hair. I recognized her from pictures in magazines. It was Sabrina's mother carrying a bunch of plastic bags.

"Finally, you're back. The nutritional pamphlets were making me hungry," Sabrina said.

Her mom opened up the plastic bag and pulled out a container with a grilled chicken breast salad. "Here you go," her mom said, handing it to Sabrina. "Do you want a nice plate, darling?"

"Nope. This is fine." Sabrina took a bite of her salad.

"How about a real fork and knife? I know you hate plastic."

"I'm okay, Mom. Thanks."

"Water. Flat or bubbled? I got you both," her mom said.

"The flat one's cool." Sabrina reached out her hand.

Her mom handed her the bottle of flat water.

"Here're more napkins. Do you want the salt and pepper packets?"

"Just drop them on the nightstand," Sabrina said.

"You must be Mrs. Snow," I said, breaking into their mother/daughter banter.

"Oh, whoops," Sabrina said. "Mom, this is my intern, Lily."

Her mom shook my hand. "I've heard so much about you."

"You, too," I told her.

"Thanks for leaving me that message. It meant so much," her mom said.

"Of course," I said. "No problem at all."

"Look, Mom. Could you and Mary Belle leave me alone for a few minutes?" Sabrina said. "I need some private time with my intern."

"Sure. No problem. We'll wait in the living room," her mom said. "Whatever you need. Take your time."

I watched as Mrs. Snow and Mary Belle slipped out of the bedroom. As soon as the door closed behind them, Sabrina said, "I wish she'd take it down a notch. She's such a nag sometimes."

"Who?" I asked. "Your mom?"

"Forget it." Then Sabrina quickly changed tones. "Sit!" she yelled.

I sat down quickly on a chair.

"Not you. I'm talking to Mercedes. He has been running around here taking leaks like they're going out of style."

"I'm sorry, Sabrina. I can explain."

"When I got back here from the hospital, my room looked like a urination museum."

"I asked the guy at the concierge to have someone walk him while I was out. He promised he would."

"But I asked *you* to look after him—not the concierge. And where is my designer arm sling? You told me you were getting that for me."

"I planned on it. I still am going to. I just haven't had a chance yet."

"What have you been doing exactly?" she asked. "I noticed there was money missing from my petty-cash purse. You didn't ask my permission."

"I can explain everything. I promise."

"You can?" she said. "I can't wait to hear this."

"There was an emergency I had to deal with immediately."

"You promised me you would be here taking care of things. You told me not to worry because you had everything under control. I trusted you!"

Just then the phone rang, and Sabrina answered it. "Bert, yes . . . I told you I am dealing with it. . . . I'm not going to tell you again—*I'm dealing with it!*" Sabrina slammed the receiver down.

"I'm so pissed off," she said. "My shoulder is in excruciating pain. And I can't even sleep in here tonight. They're moving me to some other suite—on a lower floor, without a view—while they steam-clean these carpets."

"Sabrina, I'm sorry—"

"I'm sick of hearing 'I'm sorry.' It's just not good enough. And why the hell are you wearing my dress and Gucci T-shirt? Are those my shoes you have on? You're really weirding me out."

I looked down at my outfit, embarrassed. "Yes, I'm wearing your clothes. But I can explain."

"I told you on day one that I hate it when people take my stuff without asking! Is that my checkered coat? And my sunglasses! Are you trying to be me or something?"

"No, no, no. Please, Sabrina. I am so sorry I let you down and I wasn't here for you. There was this girl. She's a fan of yours. She loves you. Idolizes you. She's messed up. Completely alone. All she wanted in the world was to go to Six

Flags for one day. She needed a friend. So I went. And I took her to the amusement park. You should have seen the look on her face when I picked her up today."

"You think I care about the look on her face? I see that look every day when I walk down the street. What am I supposed to be, everyone's fairy godmother, fulfilling their fantasy of a best friend? That's fake. I'm not everyone's best friend."

"It's just once I read her letter, I felt responsible. Like, what if something happened to her? What if she felt so alone one day and she did something terrible—like seriously hurt herself? I wanted her to know it would be okay. That even though it hurt so bad right now, it wouldn't stay that way forever."

"Why do you care? Who gives a shit? And how do you know that things will be okay for her? I can't believe you ducked out on your duties to play Celebrity Robin Hood. You royally messed up. I gave you an amazing opportunity."

"Sabrina, I'm sorry. I appreciate everything you've given me. I want to make it up to you. I'll do anything. I'll prove to you that you can trust me again. Please give me one more shot. The summer is almost over. There's only a week left of the internship. Let me finish it for you. Please."

Sabrina shook her head. "Bert has me meeting with some-one else this afternoon to replace you. We're gonna find a new girl to start now and work through the fall."

"Excuse me?" I said.

"He's been saying all along he thinks you're a big ditz. He thought so since the moment you walked in the door."

"A ditz? Are you kidding me?!"

"I always defended you. But not anymore," she said. "You messed up the chance of a lifetime."

"So you won't give me one last shot?" I asked.

"You left your clothes on the floor of the bathroom. Change out of my stuff and leave everything that's mine here. And I noticed you didn't close the lid back all the way on my Bag Balm. You can fix that, too."

"God, Sabrina. I'm at a loss for—"

"No more," she said, cutting me off.

I followed her orders and went into the bathroom. I saw the Bag Balm on the sink and pushed the lid all the way down. Next to it was the outfit that I had worn last night to the party at the Saddle Ranch. I changed back into it, then I walked out into the bedroom and placed Sabrina's dress, folded, on the bed. I put her shoes next to the bureau.

"I'm leaving everything here," I said.

"And the BlackBerry," Sabrina said. I took it out of my bag and handed it back to her.

"Sabrina, again," I said, "if there's anything I can do to make it up to you, I'd really like to finish up the internship properly."

She shook her head. "Too late now." Then she flicked her wrist at me. "Get out of here. I never want to see you again."

I felt absolutely humiliated. I walked to the door and let myself out of the suite for the last time.

* * *

I walked all the way back uptown—almost ninety blocks. I was stuck wearing the heels I wore to the party at Saddle Ranch. The backs of the shoes cut into my skin, and I was in terrible pain. Still, I refused to get into a cab or bus. Part of me felt like I deserved this punishment. Enduring the sting of my blistering heels was a way of atoning for my terrible sins.

I walked through Central Park, cutting through the meadow and Poet's Walk, past the Bethesda Fountain. Then I cut across the horse bridal path that ran near the reservoir.

When I got home, I ran straight to my bedroom and slammed the door shut. I crawled into bed and hid under the covers. I had royally messed up. Everything I had worked for all summer was now shattered on the floor. And the shards of broken glass were digging into my skin.

My mom knocked on the door.

"Leave me alone," I said.

She came in anyway. "What is going on?" she asked, concerned.

I filled her in on the damage.

"Lily, I don't know what to say. You really got yourself in some trouble here. Why did you do all that?"

"Mom, I'm not sure. It's like I was sucked into this alternate universe."

"I don't know what to tell you," my mom said. "I'm sorry everything snowballed the way it did. I'm glad you're telling me this, but it seems like you went too far. How did that happen?"

"I completely failed. I can't tell Daddy. He'll just die. He'll be so disappointed in me. I promised him at the beginning of the summer I would stick this internship out and follow through. He was mad at me already. And now look what happened. He's gonna think I'm a total failure." Then I looked at the internship-completion form hanging above my desk. "And I never got the form signed. I'll have nothing to send to Brown as proof of all my hours."

My mom drew circles on my back with her fingers, trying to calm me down. "I know it looks horrible now, but everything's going to be all right."

"I need some air," I said. "I'm going outside." I jumped up off my bed.

"Do you want me to go with you?"

"No." I gave her a kiss and walked out the door. "I'll be okay," I told her.

On my way out of the lobby, Damien waved at me.

"Look who's visiting today!" he said, pointing to his son, Junior, who was standing beside him.

Junior ran over to me. He was holding a bag of classic potato chips. I wondered if he noticed the sour-cream-and-onion ones gave him bad breath and decided to switch flavors.

"Hey, how's your summer going?" he asked.

"Super," I said, walking through the revolving door.

"Where are you going? Can I come with you?" he said, running after me.

"If you want," I said. I didn't have the energy to argue with him.

He followed me out of the building, and we started walking down the sidewalk to Central Park.

"I've wanted to hang out with you all summer. But you're never around."

"Yeah, I've been super busy," I said, crossing over Fifth Avenue to the park side.

"Want a chip?" He offered me the bag as we entered the park.

"Sure," I said, taking a bunch in my hand.

"My dad said he heard you've been interning for Sabrina

Snow all summer. I couldn't believe it when he told me. You must be so smart to get hired by her. How's it going? You've really made it big. You could probably do anything you wanted in this world now. "

He was giving me a splitting headache. I stopped at the Great Lawn and turned away from him, praying he would quit talking so much.

That's when I saw my father. He was walking across the Great Lawn like he used to do with my mother before she got so busy with her new company. He saw me, and our eyes locked.

"Junior, thanks for keeping me company, but I need to be alone now."

"Yeah, I understand. Well, I'm around. Let me know if you want to go to the movies sometime."

"I will," I said. "That would be nice. Just give me some time for this whirlwind to die down." I waved good-bye to him and walked toward my dad.

We met in the middle of the field.

"What are you doing here?" he asked me.

"Just walking," I said.

"Your mom told me you've been staying at Sabrina's hotel suite. Is that your fresh take at running away from home?"

"Dad, I got fired."

"What? You got fired?" he said. "In other words, you quit. That's what you're saying, right?"

"I didn't quit. I promise."

"Sure. You never follow through. I know how it goes."

"Dad, I didn't quit. I wish you would listen to me."

"Why should I? You don't listen to a word I say anymore."

Then he started lacing into me. "Who do you think you are? I don't care if you end up the president of the United States one day—you will always be my daughter. I deserve to be treated with respect. I brought you into the world, loved you and raised you and—I don't know where you get off running around with this smug look on your face like you know everything. You're leaving next year for school. You have one year left having to live with Mom and me. Then I won't be there to set boundaries for you. When you go off to college, you can come home at five in the morning every night. You can sleep wherever you want to sleep, do whatever you want to do. You'll be free to be your own boss. You can become a wild animal, if that's what you want. But until then—"

"Dad, I know I didn't follow my curfew all the time this summer. And I wasn't around as much. I was just trying to do my best. You helped me get this internship. You knew how important it was to me. And now you're throwing it back in my face."

"I'm not throwing anything in your face. All summer, you wanted to run around out of control like that Sabrina does. But you're not her. You're lucky you actually have parents who care where you are and worry about you." He shook his head and rubbed his face in his hands. "I just want to know that I did the best I could. That I raised you the right way." Then he lowered his voice. He was no longer yelling at me. He sounded softer now. "I can't believe this is your last year at home. . . ."

"Dad, I'm sorry I got so caught up in the glamour of it all. And if I was a brat. I guess I've been torn between enjoying all the excitement and following your rules."

"One more year, Lily, of following my rules," he said. "Then you'll be set loose to make up some of your own. Okay?"

"Okay," I said. "It's a deal. But can we maybe make that curfew twelve thirty?"

"Fine. But not a minute later," my dad said.

He gave me a hug, and we walked back home together. That night, we decided to have a family evening. We ordered in Mexican food and rented a movie. I told my parents they could pick out anything they wanted, as long as it wasn't a film that starred Sabrina.

When I went to bed that night, I lay there worrying over my Brown application. I decided I could still put the internship on it, but I would just have to pray that the board of admissions never called Sabrina for a recommendation.

I decided everything would come around just fine—until two days later when I woke up in the morning and saw the headline of the new issue of *Party Weekly*.

SABRINA ALMOST DROWNS GIRL!

And inside the magazine was the picture of Taylor in her wet white T-shirt at Six Flags. The article talked about how Sabrina sent her intern to take a devoted, "socially challenged" fan to Six Flags Great Adventure. And in a ride "mishap," the young fan fell out of the log and almost drowned.

"What a complete exaggeration," I told my parents. "She didn't fall out. She just got splashed."

It didn't take long before the phone started ringing. Taylor's angry parents. Eleanor. Sabrina's mom. It was too humiliating. My parents stopped picking up the phone and started letting calls go straight to the answering machine.

That is when Bert called and left a vicious message on the

machine. He said, "You should be ashamed of yourself. How dare you lie to us. Lily, I know that you called our chauffeur service and hired a limo without our approval. I will be forwarding you the bill. Also, I am contacting the police and our lawyer. I'm not afraid to file charges against you for impersonating Sabrina. This is a serious offense, and I will punish you to the greatest extent of my capabilities."

My parents sat me down to say they couldn't believe what a mess I got myself into. I explained to them that I had the best of intentions. They said they would stand behind me, but I was never to behave like this again.

I holed up in my apartment. I couldn't imagine facing the world again. I was scared of being forced to spend the next few years in a juvenile detention center.

My dad placed a few calls to some lawyer friends of his from Columbia Law School. He said if Sabrina dared to press charges, not to worry, because he would have the best lawyers in town—his friends—defending me.

That night I sat watching TV with my parents, pounding back mint chocolate chip ice cream. With a spoon in one hand and the remote in the other, I clicked through the channels until I came to *Entertainment Tonight*. The show's host was talking about Sabrina. He was saying how nice it was of Sabrina to send her intern to visit one of her lonely fans, even if it ended up in a mishap. He said that as of that evening, Olivia Carlyle and a few other big-name celebrities were planning on doing the same thing. They were going to take a day and visit a fan in need who felt lonely or lost in the world. When the host signed off, he thanked Sabrina for starting a generous trend with such a good humanitarian message.

I flicked through the channels and discovered other entertainment news programs had the same spin on things. I couldn't believe it. All the commentators were saying that Sabrina was so generous.

The next morning, there was a knock on my bedroom door. My dad woke me up.

"Lily," he said, "Sabrina is here to see you."

I sat up, shocked. "What?" I asked.

"She's in the living room. The doorman didn't ring up. She must have walked right by him."

"I can't believe she's in our living room," I said.

"Neither can I. Do you want me to make her leave?" my dad said. "Or do you want to see her?"

"I'll talk to her," I said. I was curious to hear what she had to say. I felt safe because I was on my home turf and my parents were here.

"Just be careful," my dad said. "If she presses charges, she could potentially use anything you say against you in a court of law."

"Got it," I said. I threw on some jeans and a T-shirt. Then I went out into the living room.

My mom was serving Sabrina a cup of tea. She looked like she was getting a kick out of having a celebrity in our apartment.

Sabrina struggled as she picked up the cup with her left hand. I noticed she was wearing a new sling with a Diesel logo on it over her right arm.

"I see you found what you needed," I said, motioning to her sling.

"Diesel came through. They custom-made this for me."

"It's much nicer than the plain brown one," I said. I waited to hear what she really wanted and why she made the trek to my apartment.

Sabrina smiled and looked at my parents, who were leaning against the far wall watching us. Then she turned to me. "Can we go to your room?" she said.

"Sure. This way," I said, pointing toward my room. I looked back at my dad.

"Scream if you need anything," he mouthed to me.

Sabrina sat down on the edge of my bed. The she turned to me. "Look, I wanted to apologize to you for the other day," she said.

I was stunned.

"I realize," she continued, "that even though you acted like a manipulative liar, you had the best of intentions."

I nodded. "That's true. I promise I didn't mean for things to get so out of hand."

"But it's funny, isn't it? How everyone is copying me now?" Sabrina changed her tone. "At first my publicist was madder than hell, but now Violetta's actually very pleased. I've been contacted by tons of clothing and beverage companies. They all want me to be their spokesperson. A company in Asia wants me to be in this Japanese commercial for a new diet soda. They offered to pay me three million dollars for one day of filming. All I have to do is stand there with the soda can and say, 'Oishii!' That means 'delicious' in Japanese."

"Must be quite a soda," I said. I couldn't believe it was possible on this planet to make three million dollars for saying just one word.

"Listen, Lily, I think we should try and work things out here. We're finally starting to understand each other. That's priceless. It's difficult for me to find someone I even like. I know this summer's basically over, but I want to invite you back next summer."

"Really?" I said. "You want me back?"

Then it hit me. This might be my one chance to get what I really needed. "I'm really touched," I said as I walked over to my desk. I took the internship completion form down off the wall and grabbed a pen. "Could you first please sign off on this summer? I really need this for school," I said, pushing the form in front of her.

Sabrina glanced over the document. "What is this?" she asked.

"I told you about it the day you hired me. I have to show it to my college advisor when I go back in September."

Sabrina read it over more carefully. "When did you start working for me?"

"June twenty-ninth," I said.

Sabrina picked up the pen and signed the paper. "I wrote you something nice to make you look good," she said.

A rush of euphoria raced through my veins when she handed me back the paper. Finally the empty spaces on the page were filled with writing:

INTERNSHIP COMPLETION FORM

This form is to be filled out by the Internship Advisor.

This letter certifies that <u>Lily Miles</u> completed her internship working for <u>Sabrina Snow</u> on the following dates: June 29–August 28. Please write a brief evaluation on the page below:

Lily Miles went from all right to awesome. —Sabrina Snow

I smiled. "Thanks, Sabrina. This means so much."

Sabrina took a sip of her tea. When she wasn't looking, I slipped the form safely underneath the mattress of my bed so now, if she changed her mind, she couldn't grab it from me and rip it up.

"So what's your answer?" Sabrina said. "Are you coming back next summer?"

I thought about it. This could be another brilliant chance for me to rise to the top. "Didn't you find some new girl to replace me, though?" I asked.

"I didn't like her. She was too much of a social climber. Besides, that would have only been through the fall anyway. I've already invested in you. Next summer, you could be my intern again. And you can even intern for me during college, and when you graduate, I promise that I will hook you up big-time."

"You will?" I said. "Like, with what?"

"I travel a lot. I'd want you to come with me wherever I go—Cannes, Venice, London, Tokyo, and Madrid. Whenever I stay at a hotel, I will pay for your own room plus meals. Wait till you see how fun it is abroad. The guys in Venice and Tokyo are dreamy. I want to groom you to be my manager and eventually replace Bert. He is such an old fuddy-duddy at this point. What happened with the whole Six Flags thing was absolutely brilliant. It has skyrocketed my popularity—clearly above Olivia Carlyle's. There's just one thing. . . ."

"What is it?" I asked.

"The tickets for the Rock the House Awards. I'm using my plus-one to take Antonio. And now that my mom and I are getting along better and she's in town, I promised to give her the other two tickets. That way she can take one of her Countess of Malibu friends. We're trying to find a middle ground here."

"But you already gave them to me," I said. "They were supposed to be my bonus."

"I need them back. Don't worry. I will make it up to you. I'll take you shopping at Harry Winston and make sure they hook you up with some cute diamond earrings," Sabrina said. "Oh, and I know how much you love Mercedes. I spoke to her breeder yesterday, and a batch of puppies was just born from her same bloodline. People are trying to buy them for thousands of dollars just because they're related to my dog, but I'll get you one for free—your own cockapoo puppy. And next year, I'll make sure you get into the Rock the House Awards and every other award show you want to go to."

I went into my desk drawer to get the tickets. "Do you really mean every award show?"

"Almost every single one," she said.

"Oh, wow," I said. "I don't know what to say. That sounds amazing. How can I turn that down?"

"Just give those back," Sabrina said, putting her hand out. "And close the deal."

I looked down at the tickets in my hands. "I don't know if I can," I said.

"Of course you can. Hand them over."

"But I promised them to Taylor."

"Who?"

"That girl I told you about."

"Oh God, Lily, I don't have time for more games. Hand them over."

I looked at Sabrina's face. On the one hand, what she was promising me sounded great. But I couldn't bear the thought of not giving the tickets to Taylor.

"I can't give you back the tickets," I said.

"What do you mean you can't? I need them."

"So does Taylor," I said.

"I don't think you get it. I'm not asking your permission to give them back. I'm telling you that you better give them back to me *now*. Stop playing around and hand them over."

I didn't budge.

"I said hand the tickets over to me now. The show's only a few days away."

I left my bedroom and headed toward the front door.

"Where do you think you're going?" she said, following me.

I walked by my parents' bedroom. "Hey, Mom and Dad! I'm gonna run out for a bit," I said. "I'll call you both to check in."

"All right," my dad said. "I trust you."

Sabrina followed me out to the elevators. I hit the DOWN button. "Lily, stop playing around. The least you can do is give me back my tickets. This isn't funny anymore. You should just hand them over before this gets nasty," Sabrina said.

The doors opened. Three other people were already inside the elevator. They looked shocked when they realized it was Sabrina.

She said to me in a tense whisper, "You're really being ridiculous."

The elevator went down to the lobby, and as soon as the doors opened, I headed straight out the front door.

"Hi, Damien," I said, giving my doorman a wave as I walked out. Sabrina followed after me.

"I am only going to ask one more time nicely. Give me back the tickets."

"You can ask a gazillion times," I said, "but I'm not giving them back to you." We were out on the sidewalk now. I raised my hand up to hail a cab.

Sabrina's face turned bright red. She clenched her fists. "If you don't do what I say, I will see to it you never work in this business again. No one in the entertainment industry will go near you with a ten-foot pole. I'll tell everyone what a traitor you are! That you are a liar! I'll make sure you are blacklisted from everything that I can ever think of! I will do anything I can to ruin your future!"

"Great!" I said. "I don't think you could do that. Even if you wanted to."

"Trust me! I will do anything in my power to ruin your life!"

"When will you find the time? You're too busy obsessing about yourself. Your hair. Your lunch. Your costumes. Your arm sling! If I ever become a celebrity one day, I will use my power for good instead of worrying so much about me, me, me, me, me!"

A cab pulled up and I stepped inside, quickly locking the doors behind me.

"Head for the George Washington Bridge," I told the driver.

Sabrina grabbed the handle and tried to open the door. "Where do you think you're racing off to? I'm not done with you!" she said, banging on the window. "I take back everything I promised you. Say good-bye to Harry Winston's and your own cockapoo. If you try to get into any party I'm involved with, I will make sure the bouncers turn you away at the door."

The cab was stuck at a red light. Sabrina was glaring at me through the window.

"Get out," she mouthed at me.

The red light seemed like it was taking forever to change.

I rolled the window down an inch. "If you don't leave me alone—" I told her.

"What?" Sabrina said. "What are you going to do? You're an ass-kisser. Just like Bert and Crazy Eddie!"

I was left with no choice now. There was no way I was going to be grouped with them. I was not an ass-kisser. Well, not anymore. And I was done not fighting for myself, like Taylor.

"You are a miserable, selfish person," I said. "That's why Bronson left you. And that's why I couldn't stand working for you half the time. You're trapped in your own make-believe bubble. And one day, you're not gonna be a starlet anymore. You won't even make it to be a star. You're gonna wake up one day as a has-been, and you'll be completely alone. Just you and a pile of old swag."

The light turned green and my cab raced off. Sabrina shouted after me. I couldn't hear her anymore; I could only see the shape of her mouth as it moved. When I looked back the last time, she was standing angrily on the corner looking like she wanted to slam a public trash can across the street.

Then I got a little sad because I realized I had made my first enemy in this world. Most kids my age had an enemy or rival in their high-school class. Mine was a national phenomenon.

Driving along 86th Street, I was happy to be away from her. I felt a sudden rush of freedom. I asked the cab driver to pull over at an ATM machine and I took out a wad of cash—a chunk of the stipend money I had saved up working for Sabrina this summer.

Then the cab driver drove over the George Washington Bridge. On the ride, I started thinking about a new title for my college essay. Something different from "A Summer of Enlightenment" or "Uncensored: Forty Days with a Starlet— Sweat, Tears and Charm." Now it was just thirty-five days, anyway. In the essay, I would just tell my life the way it was. Expose all of me, with its imperfections and flaws. I would tell the honest-to-God truth about the way everything happened during my summer with Sabrina Snow. I would admit the mistakes that I made and how much I learned from them. That way even if the admissions people did call Sabrina, they would know my side of the story.

I took the cab until it stopped outside Taylor's house, then I ran up to the front door and rang the doorbell.

Taylor's mom answered it. "What do you want?" she said.

"Hi," I said. "I wanted to drop these off for Taylor," I said, showing her the tickets.

"What on earth are those?" she said.

"They're for an awards show. Is she here?"

"She's busy."

"Can I just see her for just a minute?"

"No. She's getting ready and then we're running out the door. I'll take the tickets."

"I'd really like to give them to her in person. Can I do that quickly?" I said.

Before the mom could answer, Taylor came around the corner and over to the door. I was surprised when I saw her. She looked a little different. She was wearing a pair of boot-cut jeans and a baseball T-shirt.

"Oh, hi," Taylor said, surprised. "Mom, can I have some privacy?"

"Are you sure you'll be okay, sweetie?"

"I'll be fine," Taylor said.

"All right, but hurry."

Taylor waited till her mom walked away.

"Do you like my new outfit?" Taylor asked.

"Yeah, I noticed," I said. "You look great."

"I convinced my parents to take me shopping and let me pick out my own clothes."

"Wow," I said. "I'm impressed." And I meant it. I was proud of Taylor for telling her parents exactly what she needed. "Look, I wanted to make sure you got these," I said, holding out the two tickets to the Rock the House Awards.

"Are you sure?" she said.

"One hundred percent," I said.

Taylor took them from me. "Thank you," she said.

"Do you know who you're going to take?"

"I want to ask Teddy, the plumber's son," she said.

"What a great idea! I'm sure he's gonna be completely psyched. Oh, and here," I said, handing her a piece of paper. "I gave back my BlackBerry, so here's my home number. I just want you to have it."

"I'll keep it somewhere safe," Taylor said. "Like up on my wall of photos."

I said good-bye and headed back into the cab. Next, I took the car all the way to the old familiar welcome circle at Ace Soccer Academy.

"How much do I owe you?" I asked the cab driver.

He read the meter and then added an extra fifty bucks for tip and toll. "Four hundred and twelve dollars," he said.

"Wow," I said. I took out the wad of money I had made while working for Sabrina this summer.

I realized this was probably the most expensive cab ride I would ever take. I could have spent the money on clothes, or new makeup, or on lots of spray-tanning sessions. But this was exactly where I wanted to be.

I heard the chime being rung. I looked over by the cafeteria, and there was the counselor, Mr. Pit Stains, banging the gong. He had noticed the cab pull up and was staring at me now. When he finished hitting the gong, he walked over to me.

"Hi!" I said. "I know you don't usually allow visitors to just show up, but I went here for the last three years and there are some friends that I really need to see."

"I remember you," he said, wiping sweat off his brow.

"You do?" I said.

"You and your friends are always running past me in the cafeteria to grab grilled-cheese sandwiches. Go check with the administration office."

I ran to the administration office next to the lunchroom and asked the guy at the front desk if I could please see the owner of the camp, Mrs. Wishner. He told me I could go inside the office and speak with her. Mrs. Wishner's eyes lit up when she saw me. "If it isn't one of my favorite campers," she said. "We've missed you this summer. What are you doing here?"

I explained to Mrs. Wishner that I spent the summer doing an internship for college, and although I had many memorable experiences, I severely missed camp. I asked her if I could please spend the day visiting my friends.

"You know that non-campers aren't allowed to spend the day," Mrs. Wishner said. "I'll make an exception since you were a camper here for so many years. But your parents must pick you up before dinner."

"It's a deal," I told her.

I ran out of the office and toward the soccer fields. In the distance, I saw a pickup game in progress. I ran over and could make out Evie playing defense. She blocked an opponent who was dribbling a ball toward the goalposts. The timer ran out and buzzed. The teammates slapped hands, and that's when she looked up and saw me.

"Lily?! What on earth are you doing here?" She ran over to me.

"I had to visit once," I said. "I couldn't royally suck all summer, could I?"

"It was becoming a possibility. I can't believe you called me at three in the morning."

"I needed to talk to you. You're my best friend. The only person I can call at that hour and the only one I can tell absolutely anything to."

"And you didn't return, like, a dozen of my phone calls. Do you remember that quiz you gave me before I left for camp?"

"Of course. Fifty questions," I said.

"Question number five. Multiple choice. If you won the lotto and could take one person on a yacht through the Caribbean for a week, who would you take: A. Bono from U2; B. Any celebrity of your choice; or C. Your incredibly cool best friend—who would you pick?"

"No-brainer. Letter C," I said.

"Yeah, man. And don't you forget it."

Evie and I went to the lunchroom, and we sat at a table with the crew—Liv, Wendy, Melanie, and Sandy.

"Come with me," Evie said, grabbing my arm and leading me across the room.

"Hey, Max. I have a surprise for you," she said, and as he turned around from the chocolate-milk dispenser, he saw me. I think I saw happiness in his eyes.

"What are you doing here?" he asked. "I mean, in a good way! I thought you became Miss Hollywood. I can't believe you're actually here. "

"Me either," I said.

I told him a little about my summer, and we decided to hang out that afternoon on Bryant Hill with some of his buddies, Evie, and the rest of our friends.

Luke stole the doughnuts from the cafeteria, Liv brought her mini stereo, and we hung out on top of Bryant Hill until the sun began to set. I had called my parents earlier, and they had agreed to pick me up at seven o'clock to take me home.

"I didn't do that much tie-dying this summer," Max said. We sat on the hill next to each other.

"You didn't?" I said. "Why not? I thought that was the plan."

"Yeah, instead I spent a lot of time perfecting bouncing a soccer ball on my head." He jumped up, grabbed a soccer ball, and head-bounced it ten times in a row until he let it fall back into his hands.

"Very impressive," I said, laughing.

We lay back on the hill, our backs blending into the grass.

"You guys better get up! We're having a dance party," Evie said.

"Dance party!" Everyone started screaming and dancing all over the hill.

Then Evie thought it would be funny if we had a rolling-down-the-hill contest, so a bunch of us lined up and rolled down to the bottom. Some of us practically rolled into each other, and when I got to the bottom, I lay on my back, out of breath. Max rolled down the hill and ended up beside me.

"Max," I said. He was lying on his back next to me now. "I have a secret to tell you," I said.

"You do?" he said.

I nodded. "But you have to come closer."

He moved closer so his head was next to mine.

"A little closer," I said.

He turned his head so our faces were almost touching.

"My secret is . . . I think we should hang out," I said. "After the summer, when you get back home." I decided I was sick of being scared of saying what I wanted.

He looked at me and squinted his eyes like he was thinking very hard. Then he said, "Um, no, I don't think so."

"Oh, really?"

"I think we should start hanging out right now."

He reached his hand down next to mine. His pinkie touched my pinkie. It felt great lying there with him and looking into his eyes. I smiled and turned away. I looked up at the impending night. The stars were starting to come out, and I could see their faint glow peeking through the darkening blue sky. I realized it was the first time all summer I took the time to look up above me. In the past two months, there had been a flurry of celestial activity—there were glow-in-the-dark stars on my ceiling, yellow electric ones on the inside roof of the stretch Mini Cooper, glittering golden star fireworks on the Fourth of July, and even a hot-blooded starlet. But here, for the first clear time this summer, it was nice to see the natural ones—beautiful and promising, shining brightly in the sky.

Epilogue

THERE'RE A FEW MORE things you need to know before I sign off and close this chapter of my life with all its spills and thrills, stammer and glamour. I spent the fall pulling a bunch of all-nighters working on my college applications. My mom offered to hire a college essay–writing coach for me, but I said, "No way." I wanted the essay to come straight from me and contain my pure, untainted voice about everything that happened. I decided to call the essay "Girl Meets Hollywood," and in it, I told it like it was. I didn't try to pretend like I was perfect, and I didn't hide my mistakes. I have to admit that I pushed myself extra hard. I heard Sabrina's voice in my head, telling me to go the extra mile. Even when I knew the essay was solid, I kept going and knocked myself out until I felt like it was excellent.

The kids at school were blown away when they heard how I spent my summer. The fact that I interned for Sabrina Snow traveled through the New York Private-School Gossip Circuit at lightning speed. I mean, at Wendy Goldlocks's back-to-school house party, there was practically a line of kids out the door dying to ask me questions about Sabrina. Their jaws dropped and their eyes turned dreamy and frosty when I dropped a few juicy details.

Bronson called me in September to say hello from Los Angeles. He told me that he and Sabrina weren't talking anymore. But he heard that she had started dating the son of a billionaire media mogul. Bronson and I stayed in touch over e-mail after that. And this time, it truly was just as friends. I still plan on visiting him one day. As soon as I get a chance to make it out to California.

Evie and I vowed to have all sorts of wonderful adventures together for our last year of high school. We made a lot more great quizzes, and some of them had saucy questions about Max—who I started dating. He would come in from Scarsdale on the train to see me on the weekends. The best part was when we went for Chinese food on one of our first dates. Over wonton soup and mu shu chicken, we played the game of Truth we used to play at soccer camp. When it was my turn to go, I admitted to him that I had drawn a naked picture of him and that I had sold it to Sabrina for a hundred bucks. "You did not!" he said. "But I *did*," I said. And then he leaned across the table and kissed me. The kiss tasted like plum sauce and mu shu chicken, but I didn't care. Because it was a real kiss. My first real kiss. And it was divine.

I sent my application off to Brown in November. I applied early decision and got a thin envelope back in February saying that I was put on the wait list. I was devastated. Two months later, though—April 9 at 3:47 P.M.—to be exact, I opened the mailbox and there was a thick envelope with Brown's name on it. I tore it open and burst into tears. "Dear Lily Miles, we are pleased to inform you that you have been accepted . . ." I sobbed with happiness in the mailroom of my apartment building, and as some woman came in to get her mail, she looked at me like I was a nutcase. I ran upstairs to tell my parents, and when they saw me hysterically crying, their faces grew extremely serious. "What's the matter, Lily? Are you okay?" they said. And that's when I screamed at the top of my lungs, "I got in! I got in! I got in!"

Still, I wondered some days about Sabrina. Of course, I read about her in the magazines. I saw the same countless glossy pictures that the rest of the world saw. And I stayed up on the headlines, bouncing them around in my head, debating if they were true or false.

Sometimes I even found myself missing her. Our lives had only overlapped for a few months, but during that time I had moved inside her private world, glimpsing parts of her that most people didn't get to see. And for that, I was grateful. Somehow stepping into her life, I learned more about my own.

THANKS TO EVERYONE at Viking Children's Books, especially Regina Hayes, for her vision and grace, and Joy Peskin, my very talented editor, for her invaluable insights and unerring sense of how to layer the characters and bring the story into greater focus. In addition, much appreciation to Linda McCarthy and Nancy Brennan for their vivid and innovative design, Lisa Grue for her striking and captivating artwork, and Nico Medina for his thorough and skillful copyediting.

I would like to express gratitude to Elaine Koster for her wisdom and responsiveness and to my agent, Stephanie Lehmann, for her development and belief in the project from the first day it landed on her desk.

Thanks to L.A. photographer Sean Smith, for sharing with me how much joy and pain can be found in a single bag of fan mail, Guy Oseary for motivating me to go wholeheartedly after my dreams, and the marvelous Barbara Andreadis for believing in me since I was twelve years old.

Thanks to my mom for reading the most wonderful books to me when I was a little kid and sparking my imagination. And to my dad for instilling in me a profound dedication to the art and beauty of storytelling. Also my older brother, David, for his honesty, off-the-wall sense of humor, and for toughening me up. Much gratitude to Steve Bello for his advice and encouragement and to my great friends in L.A. and N.Y.C.—only they know how much they mean to me.